Phoenix IRISH SHORT STORIES 1998

edited by David Marcus

PHŒNIX

A Phoenix Paperback
First published in Great Britain by Phoenix House in 1998
This paperback edition published in 1998 by Phoenix,
a division of Orion Books Ltd,
Orion House, 5 Upper St Martin's Lane,
London WC2H 9EA

A CIP catalogue record for this book
is available from the British Library.

ISBN 0 75380 462 X

Typeset at The Spartan Press Ltd,
Lymington, Hants
Printed and bound in Great Britain by
Clays Ltd, St Ives plc

ACKNOWLEDGEMENTS

None of the stories in the following pages has previously appeared in print.

'Where Do We Go from Here?', Copyright © Gerard Beirne, 1998; 'Counting the Days', Copyright © Emma Donoghue, 1998; 'Candid Photography', Copyright © Ned Lenihan, 1998; 'Simply a Leaf', Copyright © Marie MacSweeney, 1998; 'The Outfielder, the Indian-Giver', Copyright © Blánaid McKinney, 1998; 'Location, Location, Location', Copyright © Michael Mee, 1998; 'The Makers', Copyright © Éilís Ní Dhuibhne, 1998; 'Cultural Exchanges', Copyright © Gillman Noonan, 1998; 'Emotionally Involved', Copyright © Katherine O'Donnell, 1998; 'Candle Gazing', Copyright © Frank O'Donovan, 1998; 'A Slow-Motion Life', Copyright © Kaite O'Reilly, 1998; 'Coronach', Copyright © Seán Ruane, 1998; 'Thirst', Copyright © Mary Russell, 1998; 'Inside Out', Copyright © Desmond Traynor, 1998; 'In Xanadu', Copyright © William Wall, 1998; 'The Time of Poplars', Copyright © Máiríde Woods, 1998.

CONTENTS

Introduction by David Marcus

INTRODUCTION

The Irish short story has always charted the course of the bloodstream in the veins of Irish history, especially Irish social history. The anthologist – particularly in the general, rather than thematic field of the genre – has a choice of two distinct methodologies. He or she may compile a collection intended to reflect, in the main, the country's social state as seen at the time. That's the special agenda anthology, in which the stories have to satisfy certain non-literary criteria apart from reaching an acceptable literary standard. The other methodology is the strictly literary one that serves only the short story and its practitioners, i.e. the presentation of an anthology of what are, in the editor's estimation, the best unpublished stories available at the particular moment of choice, irrespective of theme or trend. The latter is the *raison d'être* of this annual Phoenix series.

The adoption of this course, however, faces the anthologist with a tricky problem: balance. If the best stories to hand during the twelve months the anthology is being prepared happen to include a comparatively high proportion involving, say, the more traditional aspects of Catholicism and its practice, will the collection be accused of reflecting an Ireland of the past? There are, also, themes or plots that run the risk of being stigmatised, and consequently deplored, as 'hardy annuals'. Life, however, is made up of hardy annuals, and the short story cannot avoid or ignore such material; what is important about it is not so much the 'what', as the 'how' of the writer's voice, vision, insight, interpretation. It so happened that, of the many stories I had to choose from for this 1998 anthology, almost half the short list of those I deemed best were concerned, to a greater or lesser degree, with two ever-recurring themes, sex and death. In such a situation, what price balance?

In her Introduction to *The Oxford Book of Travel Stories*, Patricia Craig, the distinguished, Belfast-born editor, declared that the only way to compile an anthology is 'to follow one's nose'. I have taken that advice, endeavouring only to break up, as far as possible, the sequence of similar-theme stories so as to provide the reader with some variety. (Though what reader of short story collections reads right through from first page to last without his or her own arrangement of pauses between contributions?) As to reviewers who now and again may object to what they see as an out-of-date representation of the state of the nation, I would emphasise that my sole concern is to reflect the excellence of the contemporary Irish short story.

One other point: in my Introduction to last year's collection I deplored the absence of a platform for stories of longer than usual length. There are two such stories in these pages.

DAVID MARCUS

GILLMAN NOONAN

Cultural Exchanges

Bill Duggan had expected the prospect of death to change his perception of things. Rather like John Wayne when he got the news, saying every leaf was precious, or some such. Instead he sat outside his cottage watching the tides, and his eye, following a gull or a car, signalled its usual dumb acceptance of the scene, nothing certainly for the brain to get excited about. Neighbours still chatted, his wife smiled from the old photos (shouldn't she feel nearer now?), tourists and cats annoyed at night, potholes deepened, vibrations from the Club five doors down infuriated, prayers still pattered out as idly as chatter (shouldn't they have a greater sense of urgency?), and cancers gnawed away like mice one always knew were there behind the walls.

For a while he thought that the only change was that in the time remaining he would be desperately honest about everything, not least about time itself. He would cut away all rhetoric about life as calmly as he would the shrivelled rind of cheese. He read about a supernova and the eight million years it took for the light to reach us, which was yesterday, imagine, *yesterday* after all that time. He thought: here am I going tomorrow, maybe *tomorrow*, on my journey out there where that light has come from. Just imagine . . . and he cut it off with the rind and chucked it in the bin.

Curiously, if any new perception came to him, it was that his body had less substance, as if indeed the brain had logged the fact that there was a wastage and couldn't bear not to signal this. It was quite a subtle message because it found no words, remained a sensation rather than a feeling, a nerve of truth quite palpable but no more than air on the skin. Walking out the coast road, still sturdy, raising his stick in salute, he thought it might have to do with the light (was this a perception?) in which his body felt like a net that passed through things, snaring the odd detail that looked in no way precious but which in his crusty old health he might well have simply ignored.

This at least was his feeling later when he came to think about his encounter with the young couple sitting on the wall. Would he, normally, have just passed by with a smile? But he hesitated, the net of his flesh quivered in the breeze, and two bronzed insects from another land stuck in it. A battered old Beetle with outlandish cartoons painted all over it was drawn up on the grassy verge. He had seen it before, racing up and down, often on the beach, and had noted its white German plates. How could any young modern German couple have driven such a thing all the way to Ireland? Perhaps it was this thought more than any other that caused him to stop beside them.

'Did you paint it yourselves?'

The girl laughed, a pleasant ripply sound, throwing her head back. What were they, nineteen? twenty? He looked at her thighs and thought of the colour of country butter. The boy jumped off the wall, stretched and sat into the car.

'A friend helped us,' she said. 'He's an artist.' Unexpectedly she offered him her hand. 'I'm Edith. That's Kurt. What's yours?'

'Bill.'

Suddenly music blasted out of the car, causing him to jump. The door slammed and the thing jerked forward with a great racket, its silencer gone. An extraordinary manoeuvre ensued. Kurt spun the car across the road and slammed into the ditch on the other side with its deep growth of blackberry bushes. It reversed and drove in again as if determined to forge a way through into the field beyond. A sod of grass trailing a long bramble came away on the bumper. It was like part of the ditch's entrails coming loose from the attack. Then, as if it had exhausted its madness, it turned neatly around and slid on to the verge across from where it had been. The youth got out and strolled smiling across to them.

'Neat turn,' the old man said. 'What do you do in the city? Drive through shop windows?'

They laughed, Kurt leaning on the girl's knees and lowering his head on to her lap. When he straightened up, Bill saw a slight cast in one eye that was like a flaw in the long angelic face.

'We are hoping it will break down,' Edith said.

'Hoping?'

'Yes, finished, *kaputt*. Too bad to drive home. Its name is Aristotle.'

'Then we are flown home for free,' Kurt added. 'By our motoring organisation, like your AA.'

Bill took a few moments to take this in. They watched his face as if reading it for a sign of disapproval. For an instant it seemed to him that he had their faces completely in his power and that any expression he assumed would determine theirs. He smiled and they relaxed at once, accepting his connivance in their world.

'You mean, you drove this car all the way from Germany with the express purpose of wrecking it here and getting a free ride home on a plane?'

'Kurt has wrecked many cars,' said Edith.

'I've no doubt,' said Bill, sending the youth's head down again on to his girl's lap. To see if he could worry them (after all, he might be a retired policeman), Bill put on his schoolmaster's voice with its edge of sarcasm. 'Forgive me for suggesting it, but isn't there a moral dimension to this?'

'Ah, a moral dimension,' said Kurt. 'I like that.' He looked at the sky for a moment as if for inspiration. 'I would say it is not as much moral as a dimension of probability. You see, the probability of a breakdown is very high.'

'I can appreciate that,' said Bill, looking at the sorry object.

'Then you have a machine that won't work. So it is one

machine less in the world. That is also a moral dimension, is it not? This old Beetle is going to be a total wreck some time soon. So we have a dimension of timing. We plan the timing of the probability. That is a moral dimension.'

'A kind of mechanical euthanasia?'

This they loved, laughing and embracing each other. Bill had an image of two young golden snakes twisting around each other.

'Of course,' he said, darkening his tone further, 'you think Ireland is a good burial ground for German wrecks? Is there no moral dimension in that? What would you say if Irish tourists dumped their wrecks on you?'

This truly seemed to shock them. Edith put both hands to her cheeks and Kurt vehemently shook his head, looking down at his toes.

'No, no!' she said. 'We're giving it to a farmer. For his chickens.'

'Chickens?'

'Yes, he has already an old Beetle with chickens. Aristotle will be another chicken house.'

'He would like the engine, too,' said Kurt. 'But I am not sure if I can save it while destroying the car.'

'We must have the paper from the garage saying it is no good any more.'

She jumped off the wall and turned to him with a smile, shading her eyes against the sun as if to see him more clearly. Then she surprised him by stretching up and kissing him lightly on the cheek. Kurt grinned as if he knew it was all an act.

In a moment they were roaring off in a cloud of fumes and dust.

In the next few days Duggan found himself drawn into the world of the two young people, but on their terms. He saw them as two cubs in the ring showing off their tricks, occasionally signalling to him for a response but hardly caring what it was, content that at least they had him for an audience. This was his strongest feeling: that of all the people they had met, he was the one who showed real interest. It was a different feeling from becoming involved in the teenage antics of his own grandchildren. That had the feel of an organic stream, however much he floundered in it. These two with their crazy car were different in kind, quite alien to him yet engaging him by an idea which now, as he watched them speeding along the wave line, sending up a light spray that hung like crystals in the air, lived in its own arrogance, family blood no more to it than salt water. Perhaps this too was a lure to his classical mind, the idea of sacrificial matter, in this case not wine spilt on the ground but an old wreck driven into it. To which god?

He sought them out where their small brown tent followed the line of the dunes so that one came to it each time in surprise, expecting it to be farther on. Other young people, Irish and foreign, were camping wild. He began to feel like the wise old man who came to call. Perhaps they were on their best behaviour when he was there, for another idea had come to him, the connection between anarchy and fun.

'Are you anarchists?' he said, drinking their smoky tea.

'Yes!' they cried, delighted with all his questions.

'I suppose it's only possible when you're young.'

'Of course!'

But gradually he began to winkle out their differences, tracing tensions that ran like fault lines through this wild and free terrain of their lives. At times they showed up in the mocking tones they flung at each other.

'Of course,' Kurt said once, '*she's* a revolutionary. She brought down the Berlin Wall by herself.'

'You did?'

'Of course I did!'

'She's an artist too. Even the table they sat around in Leipzig to plan their marches they made into an art object. A revolutionary table. They put it on show.'

'I was thirteen then.'

'Kurt doesn't seem very impressed.'

'He's a *Wessi* rich boy. His father is rich.'

'She's an *Ossi* revolutionary. Ha-ha!'

'His father makes underwear. Ha-ha!'

After this exchange Kurt appeared genuinely upset, as though her jibe had struck home more truly than his. He took it out on the car, juddering it around over the bumps and hollows of the dunes, finally with a hot burning roar cutting through the loose sand and on to the strand again, horn blaring as he circled a farmer piking seaweed into his trailer. Was this the farmer with the chickens?

Duggan delved deeper, inviting them for beer to his home, his mind tacking into political areas but careful to keep it playing its cheerful-old-man act. He was back again in the classroom, choosing from his vast array of mental implements built up over the years, ranging from sharp-edged irony to righteous indignation, the ham's delight. They sat on his back porch drinking from cans, Kurt's chair tilted back against the wall, a faint pulse in his neck that Duggan saw as the real pulse of continental youth beating before his eyes, undefined in the broad diagnoses of the spin doctors.

'Really?' he said in mock surprise. 'She's that bad?'

'Really,' Kurt said. 'Under her skin she's a puritan.'

'All *Wessies* think they're playboys,' Edith retorted.

'It's easy, I suppose, with rich daddies. Not so many in the East, are there?'

'It's not money that's the difference,' said Kurt. 'It's how you think, attitudes.'

'Edith's attitude is puritanical?'

'The way she goes on about my father.'

'That upsets you?' Duggan's voice sharpened in dismay. 'You think it's envy?'

'Envy?'

'He means,' said Edith, 'do I wish your father was mine. Ha-ha!'

'It's different,' said Kurt. 'It's not her wanting money but something it's hard for her to say, that *no one* should really own

it. That's her upbringing. They were against the state and all
that, but they never learnt to have things. We should still be in
some bare room waiting for a man to come and give us
something, but not from his pocket like my father's pocket but
from something that's like . . . like official, with a stamp on it,
you know?'

'You mean,' said Duggan, 'she's quite happy to take money
from the insurance company over the car because it's not
actually coming from any one person's pocket?'

'Yes, but she hates me to ask my father for money.'

'Ringing up *Vati* for another hundred marks!' Edith sneered
but now there was a tremor in her voice. 'Maybe I *am* a puritan.
A mixture of Luther and communism. Why should we not be
twisted up like that? But we admit it. We're not arrogant.'

'East meets west!' Duggan exclaimed. 'I like it!'

Edith's tone took on an incisive edge that cut deeper, causing
Kurt to sit up straight as if he felt threatened. Stumblingly, she
wandered down crooked alleyways where Duggan felt the
nearness of his own country's past, as when at one point she
said she felt 'stuck in history' in a way that Kurt was not. If she
did envy anything, she went on, it was how rooted Kurt and his
friends seemed to be in this *un*rooted West. They were quite at
home in an aimless kind of culture, whereas she tended to see
things all the time in historical terms. So, yes, maybe that was a
puritanical thing too, everything passing through the 'dark
mind', aware of every step, not able really to jump around and
not care.

'In Ireland,' Duggan said, 'instead of communism we had
dogma.'

Still, it was as if they had confessed too much, for in the days
that followed they seemed to avoid Duggan's company. He
thought he might have wounded them by making them too
aware of their differences, even bringing them closer in forgiveness. Possibly they had come to see him for what he was, an old
pedagogue amusing himself by using them as a sounding board

for ideas. He had the impression that they waited for him to appear on the scene before driving off, waving and with the horn blaring in mock salute. No more cups of smoky tea. He became again a mere observer, a voyeur even, as when once on the wide deserted beach he watched them abandon the car in the shallows, throw off their clothes and dive into the waves. Edith's voice came to him shrill as a bird's. For a moment he was tempted to stroll down to the water's edge and simply greet them, deflating their bravado with its suggestion that he might be shocked at the sight of young naked flesh. But as if to cut off that approach, too, she suddenly lay on the sand and stuck her legs straight up and wide for Kurt to lie between, while Duggan still watched, as they knew he would, for like two racy birds from abroad sporting on his strand they were too good an act to miss.

Then they were gone, and like a low mist seeping back in from the sea his mind turned in on itself again, fed on its stoic morsels, its prayers that echoed cold and hollow in the empty church. He wrote letters to his children and filled them with trivia about local events, his world that had lasted for years and would go on for ever.

In Flavin's pub, sipping a pint, he threw Kurt and Edith into the conversation, but carelessly, disowning them, no more to him now than a raffle ticket at the fête to be thrown to the ground and swept away with the other discards of a summer's day. Against doctor's orders, he puffed defiantly on his favourite old pipe. What did it matter now to his poor lungs?

'Aristotle,' he said, sententiously, to his friend Harvey, a retired solicitor who savoured a turn of phrase as if it were a sweet to be sucked in the mouth, 'argues that if you give a sick friend a liquid that turns out to be poisonous, you can't really be blamed. So can these two young Germans really be blamed if, in trying to turn their car into a philosophical refuge for chickens, they kill half the people of the parish?'

'Certainly not,' Harvey agreed, sipping his whiskey. 'The Aristotelian intention was good.'

'There are so few decent cars with chickens nowadays.'

'It's become something of a literary fossil, I would have thought.'

'Good to see it being revived.'

'Quite.'

But he paid for the smoke with fits of coughing that left him weak and bathed in sweat. Taking pills, his sleep was disturbed. The couple returned in dreams in which they watched him as in a prism, each present in the other, the young sensing the withered heart that lay in store, the old grasping, more passionately than they, the notion of love. In a protean dream in which they changed shape, he swam with them, peeling off the layers of moral family life in which he had wrapped his soul. He lay down on her and she yelled, 'Come on! Screw me, old man!', but she turned to bones, and he recoiled. He sat in the car, watching them make love, and then he realised he *was* the car and felt a great urge to roll over them and crush them because then he would triumph, as matter always did.

In a waking reverie, matter loomed up over him like an evil demon in a play, scattering all thought of tenderness, chewing up his letters to his children and spitting out the pieces. It was as if his mind in its awareness of death was impelling him to discover, not the preciousness of the leaf, but its deception, or as if some spirit was leading him out into the night not to pity the souls of the damned, but to accept, without glib recourse to redemption, the darkness itself. He drifted, an ominous light sweeping the dark space for a clue, and briefly a vision of history opened to him that was an endless avenue of sorrow, streams of pale humanity passing him by, carts piled high with their precious belongings. And the demon's only query was where to lay the bones, park the wreck.

He sat on his back porch and let it wash over him, a depression that matched the weather, the grey shroud that enveloped the land and sent the young people back into their tents and caravans to play at cards and Scrabble. Nature toyed with them, rent the shroud, poured down sun like liquid honey that had them swooping on it like bees. Then, in the afternoon, the wind shifted again to the north-west, and the warmth in the air sped off as quickly as the midges. People reacted by creating shapes of life. They became artists of time and place, shaping the preceding hours of sun and movement into happenings that often in a matter of seconds took on firm outlines in the telling, quite definite colours in the mind, even the bedlam of words taking on a unique cadence for that day beyond the meaning of anything said.

Thus he mused with a feeling of goading himself to be dismissive of all life, every shout of play from the beach. So it was like a release from hell when, with a roar that had him sitting bolt upright in his chair, a dirty dented old VW rattled past his gate, horn blowing, hands waving, a sound so brash he followed it all through the town and out the other end until its resonance, even when it was miles away, still hung in the air. They were back, but he was banished even further from any intimacy. When he strolled among the tents again, sporting a panama which he had bought from Molly Hogan's corner shop, it was to find himself accepted and ignored by the company.

Interest focused on a ramp that Kurt and his friends had built to send the car flying over a hollow in the dunes, to land with a crash on the firmer sand beyond. Kurt and his mates took turns in performing the stunt, once urging Edith to have a go, but she vehemently shook her head, while shouting others on. Her face was tense, the brown skin stiffening into a mask which she had occasionally to readjust with her fingers, running them quickly over her mouth and eyes to make them smile again. Duggan tried to move closer to her, but she seemed to be watching him from the corner of her eye, and moved away, once crawling into the tent and zipping it closed with a sharp angry sound. The young guys tired of their game, but for a while Duggan had sensed a note of savagery in it, as if a pack instinct had come alive and the car were an animal to be goaded and shaken to death. And indeed poor Aristotle sat on the beach after his ordeal, looking punchdrunk, his dirty sand-spattered eyes wondering what he had done to deserve this. A front wing was bent and gave him the look of curling his mouth in disdain. As Duggan moved away, he wondered if after all he shouldn't have a word in Sergeant Boyle's ear before someone got hurt. It was time the disciplinarian in him reasserted itself. Wasn't that still his true nature, after all?

In the early hours an idea came to him that sent him down into the kitchen to put on the kettle. He even lit up a pipe, and though again he paid the price, it seemed worth it. In the morning he strolled up as usual among the tents, but although the Germans' tent was still there, the car was gone. He waited for its sound all day, amazed that they were still able to take it out on the road, admiring almost of their effrontery, as though in the end they had shown themselves masters of this chunk of matter. For a moment they lived up to the stereotype of their race, as efficient in the fashioning of matter as in its exact destruction. Was the image a country acquired as much a breeding ground for the attitudes of its people as they were in creating it? When did the national egg become the headless chicken?

He sat on his porch and followed the drift of his musings in the clouds. His senses had come alive again, as if his more positive thought had unclogged them. Now he heard all the sounds of the place, and opened his heart to them. His prayers sounded fuller and more natural, having clawed their way back up from the ditch of despair into which they had slithered. And anyway, he had been making too much of a youthful adventure. Might they not even now have pocketed the paper from the garage, and was Aristotle being towed to the farmer's yard to open his dented doors to generations of fowl?

It was growing dark when he heard the tractor-like roar of the car entering the town. It stopped not far from his door, and he shook the cat from his knees and hurried out. He saw Kurt alone, striding down the pavement and disappearing under the coloured bulbs and canopy of the Club. Duggan decided to go for his pint, but the thought of Harvey sitting in his corner polishing his glasses, as he polished words, was tiresome. With hardly a conscious thought, he entered under the imitation nitespot gantry of the Club that had been the cause of so much protest in the town.

Bobby Hayes, a fag stuck in his wizened face, was taking the money, and his astonishment was evident. Duggan had a memory of entering Bobby's house to enquire of his parents why the young scut was as lazy as sin and half the time not even at school.

'Evening, Mr Duggan.'

'Evening, Bobby.'

'Are you looking for someone, sir?'

'Yes, but I think I'll have a drink as well.'

'Right, Mr Duggan, straight through.'

'Isn't there a cover charge?'

'Yes, sir, but you don't . . .'

'Of course I do, Bobby. Why should I not pay it?'

'Certainly, Mr Duggan. Two pounds.'

'Big house tonight?'

Like a fool Duggan waited for his ticket, as in the old days at the cinema, but when Bobby just stood there as if expecting a clip in the ear, he turned and entered the arena through the combination of thick insulated doors that the owners, quite ineffectually, had been obliged to install. The vibration that so tormented the neighbours was a physical law of conduction that no doors would shut off. A long marble-topped bar ran the length of the dance floor. On its other side, tables with il-luminated numbers had been set out on a tiered area, the highest lost behind a veil of smoke punctuated by flashing lights. Weaving in its dug-out like a snake's head transfixed by the strobes and movement was the shaved skull of the DJ.

Duggan with a slightly tottery gait gained the bar. He caught the amazement in the barman's look, another of his bright disasters from school. Clearly, in his former pupil's eyes, Duggan was blind drunk.

'Evening, Jimmy.'

'Evening, Mr Duggan.'

'A pint of beer, please.'

A red telephone jangled at his elbow. Caught up in the madness of it all, Duggan lifted the receiver and held it to his ear.

'Hello, ducky!' screeched a high manic voice.

Duggan replaced the thing and took a sip of beer. Perhaps he had already died and this was the confused antechamber to the other side. Possibly you were even given a glimpse of hell on the way. The DJ with his snake's head was really the angel of the bottomless pit, and the roaring in his ears, was that the noise of the locusts' wings? This was noise such as he had never experienced, a dimension beyond noise to which not the ear but the entire self had to yield as to an enormous wave or be battered to death, an avalanche of sound bearing down but never quite overpowering, as if magically one were skiing an inch before its deadly smothering fingers.

He felt the gentle tug of human fingers and moved as in a daze away from the bar closer to where the dancers twisted in the shooting beams of light. Edith was looking up at him, smiling, an unreal sparkle in her eyes. He stood on the same spot swaying with her. She put her arms around his waist and now he could see Jimmy's eyes popping out of their sockets. Another minute and he would be calling Duggan's neighbour Mrs O'Toole to get him home.

'I want to buy Aristotle,' he said to Edith in a quiet interlude. 'I will give you both enough for your plane ticket home.'

'Why do you want Aristotle?'

'Can you get student flights?'

'Yes, I suppose so. But why, Bill?'

'I'm afraid someone will get hurt.'

'No! We are careful.'

'Where's Kurt? Is he not with you?'

'He's with someone else.'

'You've split up?'

'He's with a boy now.' She laughed, stepping away from him,

her head tilting to see how he was taking it. 'A pretty Irish boy.'

A thunderbolt struck the air as the music started up again. To Duggan it seemed that Edith was whipped away up into it like a kite, leaving him as bewildered as a blind man unexpectedly losing the arm of his companion. On his return home, he felt foolish, transparent, all natural substance having been sucked out of him by noise and frenzied light. The cat settled down again on his lap as if the master had just stepped out for a moment, and that's how Duggan thought of it, stepping out of his own reality into a world as wild as any meteroic vision of the after-life. Thus would he pass out of life under a gantry a few breaths distant, as the Club was a mere few steps away from the familiar.

In bed he read for a while and nodded off, the cat curled beside him. He awoke when the window shook in a sudden squall. Rising, he removed the wooden prop and slipped across the catch. A figure moved under the street lamp below. He hesitated. Wasn't once enough to make a fool of himself? But then he took his dressing gown from its hook and went downstairs.

She came in with him wordlessly, shivering. He sat her down at the kitchen table and switched on the electric fire. Her skin had a yellowish pallor, and her words were slurred. But the eyes were unclouded, feverish in their dry sockets. She said there had been an accident and Kurt was in hospital but not too badly injured. The boy he had been with was thrown clear and walked away. Aristotle was finally dead 'like a real beetle with its legs in the air'.

'Poor Aristotle. We really made him suffer, you know.'

'Did you not want to go back to the tent?'

'We packed it in the car. I couldn't get it.'

'Why didn't you knock?'

'I was waiting for breakfast time.'

He gave her tea and watched the shivers course through her body like electric shocks. She looked exhausted, a refugee from somewhere, but Duggan felt no pity, rather a certain hostility;

as in a father waiting all night for a rebellious child to return, worry gave way to anger. It was all so tiresome now and what had it got to do with him? She was probably on drugs. The boy was a deviant quite outside his understanding.

The bed was made up in his daughter's room. He threw a pair of his own pyjamas on it, told Edith to get some rest and, muttering to himself as if to keep up the act, put out the cat. He dozed as the wind, like a kitten trying to reach the tassel of his blind, knocked it faintly against the glass. He worked its tap-tap into a dream and awoke, as dawn came, racked by a cough that never ended. He whooped like a child struggling for breath and felt a glass held to his lips. He lay back and slowly his breathing calmed.

'Are you okay, Bill?'

'Fine.' He fumbled for his inhaler on the bedside table and took a snort. 'I'm just a little short of breath at times, that's all.'

'I had an aunt like that. She lived in Dresden.'

She lay beside him on the bed, holding his forearm lightly, tilting it as one would a lever, an extension of his body that he allowed her to have like a toy to move about. She moved it absently, a remote control guiding her memories, to which he listened without comment, waiting for her to find the words. She talked about her father, who had been a Party official and was now unemployed. All day thin and gaunt he paced the flat, a ghost of his former self. Her mother worked in an abattoir, and sometimes she visited her there, watching the hunks of meat passing by on hooks. That's what they were like now, a vast abattoir in which people's lives came by like auras on hooks to be X-rayed in the hope that some organs were still sound and could be grafted onto the living organisms brought in from the West. But it was different from the West, where you were always talking about what was there. She was only learning to say what was not there.

'You can't lie about what is not there, can you, Bill?'

Her words tottered, fell, picked themselves up, held out their arms like pleading things, stripped themselves naked in their efforts to say: this is me, my thought, my past. He understood, even when expression failed her, yet he said nothing. She fell silent, and he waited for her to begin again, but she had fallen asleep, her fingers slowly relinquishing their grip on his arm.

They found Kurt all stitched up, but his memory had gone. He smiled up at them as if wondering who they were. When Edith told him every detail of what they had been doing, he nodded as one whose head was totally hollow, grateful for anything poured into it.

Edith posted Duggan a letter some days later when they flew out from Shannon. In it she thanked him for his help and hoped that they would all meet again. But Duggan's feeling, watching them go, had been of two people who hardly knew each other, then or ever. If both had lost their memory, they might have a chance.

Nothing happened for weeks and then a lot seemed to happen quickly. Duggan wrote to his children, telling them he was going to die. They came in waves, teenage grandchildren roaming the land and causing worry, but under strict orders to be quiet in the house. He saw himself reflected in their young eyes as a kind of life specimen, and it unnerved him. Like a demented old Lear he urged them to ignore their parents and make as much noise as they wished.

Later, when he was alone with his eldest daughter who was caring for him, Sergeant Boyle called in for a chat. The garage had condemned Aristotle as a write-off, but the farmer still came to claim him, presenting the papers Kurt had sent on. He even managed to drive the car back to the farmyard, where he stripped it down, selling the engine and tyres at a good price. He parked the shell, as Kurt had wished, in a corner of the yard 'to which his hens may or may not be attracted. You can never tell with hens, can you?'

For an instant at the gate, hand raised in valediction, the Sergeant appeared to Duggan the very personification of earthly permanence.

KAITE O'REILLY

A Slow-Motion Life

If I think of him at all, one image prevails: compact, moist soil sliced neatly on a spade when footing turf.

I would cross the bog as a teenager, going to dances. A wrong step would leave me thigh-deep in history, my toe tapping a Neanderthal skull. Not just ancients are hidden in there. People have gone missing, returning from wakes or house parties. It's a notorious shortcut. Perhaps that's why my father always kept the light on the nights I went out. I would hear its discreet 'click' as I climbed the stairs.

The more interesting boys at the dances wore ripped T-shirts or old men's suits from charity shops. We would slam-dance violently to the one daring record and foot-tap moodily to the others we felt were square. Afterwards, sharing cigarettes in the graveyard, the boys would jockey between them as to who would take me home. It was not that I was unnaturally popular, merely generous with my favours.

We have a local saying: if you lose your virginity one night, someone will find it and return it to your mother by morning. Mine had been returned so many times my family thought it a miraculous healing. I laughed at first, 'Blessed Bernadette, Patron Saint of the Hymen', although my father got drunk afterwards and my mother cried downstairs.

Many lean hungry boys furrowed their way into me. Like moles, they sought me blindly as they tunnelled in the dark. Some cried. Them I was most gentle with, guiding their smooth tapered bodies, my fingers thrumming on their razor-shell ribs.

Later, in London, it was men maudlin for a piece of home,

asking me to speak gently to them as they put their face against my cheek. Others would ask for dirty words, slapping my arse as if I was a cow. It was not my profession then, merely a pastime. A voluntary hobby which brought nothing but tears.

I first met Michael at a dance for the overseas missions when I was fifteen. I had misjudged when pogoing and split my lip on his chin. He gave me a sip of his red lemonade to rinse out the blood. It stung. He had it spiked, the flask of poteen snug in his inside pocket. The suit had been his grandfather's, a wizened wee man who once claimed to have survived the Famine. 'He couldn't count, bless him. He never went to school,' my mother said. Father was less charitable. 'Ignorant gobshite,' he said.

Michael's family were known to us, but he was uncharted territory. Born and reared in England, he had come to Ireland alone in the summer and never gone back. There was some mystery there, beyond our understanding. Our course was usually the reverse: escape or being sent to England as penance for some hushed-up crime. Why choose to be in the bog when the bright lights of London had been yours? Michael would purse his mouth and shrug non-committally. The other boys would spit and stare at their shoes and I despised having given myself to such unchoice sods.

He would never take me, although I asked him, more than twice. Instead, we would go tripping in the bog, laughing inanely as we swallowed the wizened mushrooms he kept under his aunt's towels in the hot press. 'But what if she finds them?' I asked. 'Wouldn't she flay you alive?' 'She wouldn't know what they were.' He looked at me intently. 'If I hadn't told you, would you?'

There was a sophistication in his airs which made me feel backward and unworldly. Yet he seemed to enjoy my inno-cence as if it were one big joke.

'The worst disease is cynicism. You guard against it, Bernie.' I nodded, although it pained me. At sixteen a dose of cynicism would be as cool as the clap. At one time, having an STD was tantamount to holding an ambition. None of us promiscuous girls achieved it, although we tried hard.

Eventually, as in all things, we drifted. I headed for London, he careered along some unknown path in the bog. I got news of him intermittently – a prank with a wax limb at Knock, the whisper that Michael O'Shaughnessy took drugs before Mass. As years passed the stories grew more alarming – a suicide attempt – him preventing a brawl by swallowing lighter fuel and threatening to blow himself up. It seemed he was losing control, and when he skipped country to avoid trouble with the gardai, everyone was relieved. Our town is extremely conservative. It is the one place in Ireland which would be mortified if the statue of Our Lady dared to weep.

Meanwhile, my time in England had been far from fruitful. Various unskilled jobs had landed me as receptionist in a women's clinic. I enjoyed it for a while, smiling brightly over my clipboard until all the spent faces in girls sent over from home got me down. When I resigned, they presumed it was on moral grounds. There had been a spate of fire bombs against clinics in Dublin which were known to give advice on abortion. They looked at me warily as I left – like I was part of an active cell of Pro-Lifers infiltrating clinics favoured by the Irish in London. As I parted, I warned them not to touch the kettle. A cruel joke and not funny, but there are only so many labels I can carry.

The times after that were lean. I finally succumbed to escort work – nutritious meals, strictly one kiss afterwards. Strangely, I got a lot of work. It was as largely due to my cutting words as to what the receptionist called 'my big-boned beauty'. Some men prefer calf-bearing hips and a date who towers over them. The chiding tongue was extra and any special services purely at my own discretion. If I enjoyed it, I wouldn't ask them to pay. I was still doing casual sex as religiously as my mother attended church – at least three times a week – so whether it was part of work or in my own time, it was immaterial. I think it would have delighted my parents had they known. A confirmation of their prophecies: Bernadette will go the way of the Devil.

When I heard from Michael in Turkey, I was working as Personal Assistant to a businessman from Dubai. He had taken me on exclusively for the length of his stay, dressing me in shantung silk and calling me his bawdy Schéhérezade. I was enjoying the fantasy as much as he was, especially as my duties required nothing more taxing than to spin a good yarn. When I read the postcard, forwarded from three addresses, I knew I had to go. Hamod paid for my ticket and gave me a generous amount for raki. I left Britain as the cruel summer began and haven't slept voluntarily with another man since.

In south-east Turkey there is a lake called Van – dead sea. A stagnant bottle-green colour, full of mineral salts and sulphates, it is left to stew in its own foul liquid. Nothing lives there but the Van cats, which swim in it. It moves as death, in wrinkles and billows rather than waves. Just like my life.

I sit on a balcony looking at Michael's card, the sound of dice being thrown, plastic on wood, as men play backgammon in the courtyard below. Across, a Mexican woman drinks tequilla from the bottle. Inside, a child's fierce cry of anger against the omnipotence of its elders. The evening sun is pale, wan as a convalescent's smile. A pair of men's working trousers flail against the gentle breeze, like Harold Lloyd in the silent pictures, fighting against an imaginary wind.

I cram my head full of snapshots to keep it busy. Unoccupied, it is prone to wander backwards to a grandfather's weddding suit berserking, confettied with bog cotton. I have been having vivid, violent dreams which resurface in the day like an LSD flashback. Michael tearing the teeth from his head with pliers. Michael chained to a rock as carrion birds pluck at the soft tissues of his underbelly. A Promethean haunting. 'Turn over on your face so they can't get your eyes,' I try to scream, but I'm voiceless, suspended in a sac like the ewe's foetus they dragged from the bog.

By the time I reached Ankara, Michael had gone. His

flatmate, a wealthy Turk in a Hard Rock Café T-shirt, thought he had headed for the coast. As he spoke, he wound his middle finger like a worm into my palm. I rebuked him, saying I was Michael's married sister come over with bad news. To apologise, he offered to take me to my brother. As he packed I put my Claddagh ring on to the third finger.

They had met through work, Bilal hiring Michael to write copy for his export business. 'Your brother is mad. He has heart sickness in his head.' We drove hard hours along a winding road sandwiched by fields of sunflowers, their blooms shriekingly alive. Women squatted on the side of the road, dressed in clashing floral fabrics, their heads swathed in white scarves. We stopped to buy sunflower seeds and drove on, splitting the capsules with our teeth and spitting the husks out the window. They ricocheted along the panels of the car.

Near the coast we stopped at a crowded wayside *pension*, full of locals and mosquitoes. We were given lamb cut fresh from the bone. Outside, four sheep lay tethered in the shade of a tree. 'Nearly *Korban byrhan*,' Bilal explained, nodding to the sheep and drawing a line across his throat with a guttural sound. In the centre was a crescent foundry where a half-naked man pulled out flat loaves from the oven. We ate the bread – still hot and slightly blackened – with our fingers, Bilal offering to read my fortune in the bottom of the coffee cup. Black sludge highly sugared clung to the sides. He looked closely, sucked his teeth, glanced at me and whistled.

A disabled child drew beside us in a wooden cart, stumps of his limbs wrapped in dirty cloth. He pulled at Bilal's necklace, turquoise stone against the evil eye, and chattered like a magpie as it was hung around his neck. Bilal kissed the child tenderly, crushing his head in a rough embrace. The boy wriggled and laughed, propelling the cart with muscular arms out after us. His mother bowed and murmured as Bilal folded money into her hand. Her job was to clean the *bayan* – women's toilets – and she crouched outside, tearing newspaper into squares. She blessed him and he received her benediction, bowing before her in the dust. Then he turned and became the playboy again by putting his Raybans on.

The last time I saw Michael was when I was twenty, shaven-headed and highly pierced. He was amused at my wearing so much metal on the face, so he pinned a cork to his ear as an Irish salute. My flatmates were horrified, wanting to take him to casualty. 'But the needle wasn't sterilised!' one had shouted. 'He'll get lock-jaw.' My hopes of seducing him were ruined by his retaliation of talking non-stop all night. When we all faded, slumped on the floor, he was still talking. I presumed he'd been on whizz at the time, but now I'm not so sure.

When I was a child playing in the bog, one of our favourite games was the Tortures of the Great Martyrs. In turns we would employ our most sadistic energies on each other – plucking out eyelashes – giving stupendous Chinese burns. Flogging was done with skipping ropes, inverted crucifixion by standing on our heads until our faces burnt.

I had confided this once to Michael, who asked me what was the pain I most feared. I forget my answer – something to do with boiling wax or being buried alive. It was personal, some bodily harm inflicted on myself. I know now there is a more exquisite torture. It is to be ineffectual and voyeuristic, seeing someone you love embalmed. Atheistic, it is to watch your former god become mortal, drinking himself to death.

I found Michael much changed. Had he not hailed me, I would have walked right past him in the café. We surveyed each other openly, seeing the traces of past time engraved on our faces. I have the beginnings of crow's feet perching at the corners of my eyes and the twin hillocks of a frown from squinting too much. He, if anything, has fared better. Deeply tanned and smiling, but too thin, his skin taut leather over fine bones.

We went to a bar to drink raki, then to another to sample Efes beer. At five in the morning we were on to Izmir rosé, our thirst apparently quenching the bar's other supplies. Although I protested hunger and alcohol overdose, he affirmed this would be the pattern of our days. I was *bennin genin arkadas* – his good friend – but all we were going to do was get *leyla* – drunk.

Naively I had once thought admission to a drink problem was step one of the cure. Alcoholics are rumoured to hide their habit, denying a drop had passed their lips all day. Bottles would be hidden in the laundry, innocuous glasses of clear spirit would play hide-and-seek amongst the condiments in the cupboard. Michael wore his addiction like a flag and said 'Good' when I spoke of cirrhosis of the liver. Then he smiled bitterly and rolled another joint.

I'm still unsure what kind of penance I thought I was paying by staying with him during those sleepless nights and irritable, lethargic days. We seemed to move in a different gravity, our limbs weightless but too heavy to put to any use. Ashtrays spilled their wreckage on the carpet, plates stood where they had been put down. When we ran out of clean glasses we drank from the bottle rather than rinse one under the tap. And all the time the beat and wrinkle of the Dead Sea immersed us; a slow-motion life.

My mother has a saying: what comes around goes around. Her lips would smack with satisfaction on the closing consonant, as deeply rooted in that belief as in the blood of Christ. I have often wondered what sin I have committed to deserve such punishment. Like Michael, I do not believe in divine retribution, so our pain is self-induced.

In my childhood game, the iniquities were executed to gain denial of belief. We would beat each other with hawthorn in order to renege. 'Repent! Deny your faith!' Images of saints' faces, eyes raised in an ecstasy of mutilation, mingled with Michael's in my disturbed dreams. In others, it was my own features which smiled beatifically as nails were driven through my hands. One morning I found them bleeding, weeping pus from a moist opening on my palms. I thought I was displaying stigmata until I remembered Michael had done it, clawing the hands which held him down during one of his crazed dreams.

I know now I was being a martyr, sacrificing myself so that

the infidel would not be proved right. Michael was stewing in self-loathing. He turned on me his most obnoxious stare, but yet I would not renege my belief in his goodness. I believed I was his last chance for redemption, the chemotherapy to his cynical disease. If I failed him and turned away as others had in disgust, his theories would be proven and there would be no hope of salvation. There is nothing worse than a Catholic upbringing. Even when you think you are beyond it, its jaws bite.

As a remedy to our listlessness, Bilal offered to take us camel wrestling in Selcuk, driving contemptuous of other traffic in his German registration plated BMW. His cousin, a *Gastarbeiter* in Hamburg, had driven it back one holiday, then 'lost' it along the Aegean coast. These guest workers were immediately recognisable for their frizzy perms and European casual clothing. They stood out as the American-Irish discovering their roots in Mayo. Familiar, but too strange, a warp in the traditional pattern.

Whole families journeyed on 50 cc mopeds. The son on the petrol tank, father driving, daughter behind, mother nursing a child on the luggage rack. Bilal clipped one as he lazily manoeuvred, leaving them sprawling on the asphalt. He shrugged. 'It doesn't matter.' 'Life is cheap,' Michael said. Then they tugged their ears and tapped with their knuckle on the polished wooden dashboard – pray God it never happens – and laughed.

We didn't need to get to Selcuk before I realised I was the camel to be wrestled. Bilal and Michael had been arguing in Turkish, or so I thought, until the car pulled over to a clearing and I knew they had been bartering. The colours were all of parchment – ochre, sand, bleached gold – the soil so dry it loses all colour. I focused on that as Bilal took his time.

'I'm sorry, but that's how it is.' Michael had avoided my eyes. 'And it's not like you're losing anything,' he said, stumbling against the car door as I sat cross-armed, cross-legged, in its shade. 'He's going to sack me otherwise and you never know, you might enjoy it.' Then he turned his back and drank the raki Bilal had stowed in the trunk.

It is not rape if you have been given permission from a male custodian of the woman of your choice. With no relative to ask, the woman's decision is binding. I had named Michael as my elder brother, so to Bilal there was no crime.

I lay and watched the crucifix of scavenging birds circle above me, dropping down in concentric thermals, hearing Michael dry-retch. Like the virgin martyrs before me, I endured the last trial without a word of pleasure. And still I would not renege.

They call me Little Sister of the Bog now and teenagers wave to me as they cross my path, heading for raves. Although initially suspicious when I returned, my parents soon accepted me, helping me kit out my caravan with bits from my old bedroom.

Sometimes my mother comes to pick at bog cotton and talk disloyally of my father. It doesn't ruffle me. I am serene, my lighthouse keeping all safe from the treachery of the bog. No one has gone missing since I took up my mission, bar one. He is buried deep and embalmed, his leathering skin wrapped closely in sulphate billows. On still nights I think I can hear its death knell tide. But like the bog, we keep our secrets.

MÁIRÍDE WOODS

The Time of Poplars

They were building the new hospital as he lay dying. Every morning he must have awoken to screeches and clangs, and could only lie there, unable to rant and rave about the barbarism of the modern world. It wasn't a very peaceful death-bed for someone who loved Brahms.

I think of it now as a brown time – a time between. We could go neither back nor forward, cooped up in that little panelled room off the main ward, more together than we had been for years. Between the bed and the arched window, Mum, Eamonn and Cait – and me at weekends. Joe, Cait's terminally obliging husband, sat in the corridor. He was a constant reminder that no one was waiting for me.

Sure isn't it great to be young and fancy-free, the Sunday relatives would say. They told stories of a father very different from the austere man we knew – a young lad working summers on the building sites in London, or poaching the rivers near Skibbereen. Before, they had seldom visited, but on these hospital Sundays they crowded the room. 'What a load of gobshites!' Eamonn would mutter and I would look apprehensively at the bed.

'There was a row of poplars there when he had his first attack. He used to quote some old poem about them,' my mother said wistfully, but I couldn't help her. Dad's way of reciting was pretty squirm-making.

On Fridays when I'd get off the bus and walk the few hundred yards to the house, I'd pretend that nothing had changed, that I'd find them all watching the news. But Dad's armchair was empty, and Mum, Eamonn and I ate squashed against each other in the kitchen. The dining-room that had been Dad's den – with his fishing rods, his records and his reviews – was now painfully tidy. More than ever Mum and Eamonn formed a twosome. She let him drive the car; he stood over her until she ate.

In our family we all had set personae: Dad was serious and decided; Mum cheerful and quick; Cait wild and artistic; Eamonn caring and practical. I was supposed to be clever and reliable. Except that I wasn't any more. On my father's prompting, I had taken science at university. Dad was a national teacher who believed he had missed out on Real Education. It broke his heart when Cait left school at sixteen. Before being wild and artistic, she too had been clever. The two of us had been Dad's silver and gold princesses. Now she was doing Art part-time at the Tech and leaving her baby at the crèche. We didn't mention this bit to my father; he had strong views on motherhood. He hadn't approved of Cait marrying Joe, though everyone else had been relieved. Joe was normal, whereas some of her other men had been pretty disturbing. Dad and Cait used to fight all the time, but during those long days she was the best visitor he had. She rattled on about places and people as if he could reply. And concealment didn't cost her a thought.

But it killed me. More and more I felt a fraud. Science was a disaster and I fell for a creep who broke my heart, and borrowed my money. By second year I was skipping lectures. I thought longingly of the life of a country schoolteacher – with a twinset, a Renault 4 and everything settled.

But how could I tell Dad this? Physics was the thing of the future, he said. He had planned my whole career, first-class honours degree, post-graduate work in the States, the groves of academe. I was to make up for Cait – and for Eamonn, who was dyslexic. There was a lot of making up to be done.

Mum had stayed vague about education, which she left to the resident expert. 'Whatever makes you happy, darling,' she would say when I mentioned my doubts. We both knew my father was unlikely to issue any more edicts, but that made change all the harder. I started reading the first-year English course, but I couldn't come to a decision. Not yet.

Not until after he died, I remember thinking one Saturday as I watched the scaffolding opposite. On the first floor of the new building a lithe red-haired man was winding up a pulley. As he swung the bucket, he waved. I had a moment of uncertainty. I was still a teacher's daughter, apart from the rabble. What had Dad said about girls who ran after men? But Red-head looked oddly familiar and I returned his wave. Discreetly. Over at the bed, Cait was trying to convince my father that her baby had a Devlin nose, but he didn't flicker an eyelid. One of his last coherent remarks had been that Cait's child had a foreign look. She came over to the window with Jack in her arms and gave the builders a big wave. She'd had fellows running after her since she was thirteen. I looked at her vivid open face under the frizzy red curls. Beside Cait I felt mousy and dull. When she had visited me in Dublin I'd been shocked at the places she found. She made a point of teasing me about the flesh-pots – knowing well I'd never venture near them on my own.

Imperceptibly we had moved away from the man in the bed. Because we were young. Because although we loved him, we couldn't deal with his views – on everything from the one true political party to the decline of the West. They stood in the way of conversation like a giant mahogany table that blocks a whole room. And so your mind would veer away towards mountains and stray people you might have seen days ago. Like the red-haired builder. Yet at college I kept seeing the bed and the nurses and the blue plush chair that Eamonn and I had fought over the first week, when none of it was serious.

'I'll put on one of his string quartets,' I said. Though we both hated that eerie sort of music, it seemed about the only thing we could do for him. Cait took Dad's hand in both of hers. It was no longer the decisive managing hand of my childhood. The skin had paled, leaving it a sort of blotchy white – like unwashed sheets. Cait's hands were tanned and shapely, and her nails which had been so colourful were now cut short: 'Babies eat into your nail-varnishing time,' she'd say.

And it was she who sent me out those late Saturday afternoons while we waited for Mum. 'You don't want to get gloomy,' she'd say, winking to remind me not to mention Mum's little job in front of Dad. In case he was still compos, as Eamonn put it. Dad wouldn't like Mum working in a shop. But she needed money of her own and time away from the hospital. She was only forty-nine. What was funny was the way she thought I would disapprove. As if she already cast me in Dad's role. Maybe Cait was right and I was gloomy.

Those Saturdays I walked aimlessly round Balcarr. The town I knew so well. The town my father always spoke disparagingly of, though he was the one who had brought us to the Carr's old tower house and carried us across the millrace when the river was in spate. In the days of being silver and gold princesses. He used to take us to buy goldfish in Robb's garage and Christmas presents in Woolworth's. There was my old secondary school with its massed prefabs, and that dubious café where Cait had got her taste for flesh-pots. Here was the restaurant where he had got food-poisoning his first year teaching. His presence was stronger on these pavements than in the hospital. When had it all changed? One evening when I was trying to work that out I met the red-haired builder. The one who had waved to me.

He walked to the millrace with me that first day and we laughed a lot. I wasn't going to tell him about my father. I was sick of death and disinfectant and the hushed tones people use when they're not quite sure what to say to you. But of course he knew. In Balcarr everyone knew about you. What's more, he thought I remembered him because before being a red-haired hunk he'd been a kid at my father's school. For a year he had sat across the aisle from me. He got me interested in frog-spawn and we walked up to Fonsy's pond a few times. When the class caught on, they made a circle round us and clapped hands until he kissed me. It was the sort of silly ritual kids go in for in sixth class, and it didn't mean a thing – except that I was the master's daughter. Francis got the cane afterwards, but I couldn't recall the details. He had gone on to the Tech and somewhere in those years he had changed from the slight boy with the freckles whom I could picture wading into Fonsy's pond. FRANCIS LOVES MAURA had been cut into the side of my desk. How could I have forgotten?

'Of course I knew you,' I remember saying with my usual honesty. 'What are you doing now?'

'Plumbing,' he said. 'I'm a glug-glug man. It was that pond did it.'

Dad would have been disappointed, I thought. He wanted all his pupils to go to college. It was chastening to realise how much of his snobbery I'd inherited.

But it didn't stop me taking up with Francis. Provisionally. Shamefacedly. To take my mind off things. The first Saturday when he showed me over the new hospital building, he told me he was spoken for. His girl was in England – saving for the wedding. 'She's a terrific worker,' he said. I looked out the plaster-flecked window to my father's room, where there were two upright shadows against the closed blinds. Mum and Eamonn. Keeping watch. It doesn't matter, I said, nothing matters, everything is temporary for me now. And Francis's hand had fastened over mine like a pipe. It wasn't unpleasant, but it seemed very faraway. I should be up in that brown room, I remember thinking.

Instead I was in this looking-glass hospital with Francis, who was in his first job since coming out of his time. He hadn't put a foot wrong, and he had played for the county. His proud smile made me remember my father again. What if he was dead and I didn't know?

But I was fed up with death. When Francis asked me to supper, I turned away from the ward where the nurses would have been changing the urine bottle and setting up a new glucose drip. The mechanics of survival saddened me. What were we all underneath but an arrangement of tubes and pipes? Francis was in the right business.

In the café – noisy and cheerful with music, green lights and a truly dreadful décor – I understood why Cait had got tired being a princess. Francis's red curls were slicked down, he was wearing a check shirt and he sang along with Johnny Cash, who, he said, was the best. I found myself sharing his enjoyment. The place was full of couples who looked at each other with sidelong smiles – and I too was a ship who would pass in the night. You have to enjoy life, Francis told me. Do what you can and don't worry about the rest. Come on, I've got my brother's Volkswagen outside. My father would have been scathing about such a philosophy.

Afterwards, under the trees behind the bus-station – poplars, they were – where generations of townspeople had gone to court, everything seemed dream-like. I did what seemed expected, trying to bury pictures of the motionless body on the bed, in the sweaty, Guinnessy smell of the here and now. When I looked at Francis's bare torso I sometimes thought of the assemblage of tubes and organs within. More often though I just let my fingers run along his rib-cage, his shoulder blades. The hair on his chest was hardly red at all.

When Francis told me how I'd fainted the day my father took the cane to him, I wondered how I could have forgotten something so significant, the sort of thing that seemed more a part of Cait's life than of mine. And as I looked out the car window at the bare poplars, I wondered if at this moment I wasn't missing something of significance.

Afterwards I thought probably I had. I wasn't able to sit out the hours of drills and thumps with my father when his voice had fallen silent; I wasn't able to tell him the truth about me and my unprincesslike ambitions; I wasn't able to act the lie that would have been in a way an act of love. I was absent even when I was there and I wasn't there the day he died. I was back in college, going to the wrong lectures, worming my way into a life which included advertising, an adopted country and lots of things my father would have hated more than Francis – who didn't last long after the funeral.

*

Sometimes I dream that my father comes to my flat in the old part of Lyon, and I start to explain about my job and my partner and my child – and computers and remote controls – and he sits there in a leather armchair and smiles the way he used to when I came home from college on Friday evenings. But mostly I don't dream of him at all. The saddest thing is that the gap where he would have been in my life has closed completely and even dream tentacles don't reach him. In the summer when I come back to Balcarr, I marvel at Cait's paintings and the peacefulness of her life, and I drive around in one of Eamonn's cars. Sometimes I see Francis with his string of red-haired children and I wave but don't stop. I'm the one who'd be embarrassed, for in my mind lovemaking and death are still mixed up with the sounds of building and bare poplars.

Thirst

The sand beneath her feet was simmering – a sea of small glass bubbles ready to burst. When they did, blood leaked out of them, splattering her feet and spreading across the now-still particles like a scarlet map . . .

Sten sat up wide-eyed, wakened by the sudden bang: the wooden shutter had slipped its catch and was beating violently against the wall. Outside, a sandstorm had been raging all night and the concrete floor was filmed with red dust. As she got up from the mattress to close the shutter, she felt the inside of her thighs sticky with sweat.

There was no sound from the inner courtyard. Perhaps they were all still asleep. No one seemed in a hurry to move. Last night, they'd said – Maybe. Maybe tonight, maybe not. Maybe when the sandstorm blows itself out or when the moon goes down. Or when Shadeed arrives.

But nothing had happened. Well, then maybe tomorrow, they'd said. Inshallah.

When in doubt, lay it on Allah, she thought.

'Exactly,' Shadeed had said. 'Allah is the only one who knows. We live in the palm of his hand.'

'I don't,' said Sten, and he had given her a dry, polite smile.

She slept again, waking to the sound of footsteps on the gravel of the inner courtyard. The old man in charge of the guest house came in, carrying a tray.

'Come,' he said.

On the brass tray was a glass of coffee and a plate with three yellow figs.

'Come,' the old man said again, encouraging her with a movement of his hand. The coffee was strong and thumped her in the stomach. Sometimes when they brought her a drink she sipped it slowly, relishing each drop as it slid down her dry throat. Other times, forgetting, she gulped it and was dismayed to find the glass empty without her even having thought about the quenching properties of its contents.

The figs rested on her tongue, soft and strange as tiny, dormant animals, until she bit them and their juices spread inside her mouth.

'Do you know anything yet?' she asked, and the old man shook his head as she knew he would.

'Maybe Shadeed will know,' he said. 'I think he's coming back tonight.'

'Inshallah,' Sten said to herself, but the old man nodded and beamed at her in delight.

'Inshallah,' he said and patted her shoulder.

Inshallah. It was the answer to every question – right from the start. Has the plane arrived yet? Will it leave on time? Will there be room on it? The smiles, the courteous nods. Inshallah.

The old man's keffiyeh sat on the side of his head at a party angle and one sleeve of his grubby white robe was rolled up, revealing a skinny, bare shoulder. She looked away, embarrassed by this elderly nakedness.

In Algiers a woman had stretched out a begging arm, the skin wrinkled, the elbow bony. When Stephen had bent to put some money in the dessicated claw and then turned to take Sten's hand, she had shivered with distaste and pulled away.

'What's the matter?'

'Nothing.'

'Nothing? Sure?'

'Sure.'

'Want to go back to the hotel?'

'OK.'

On the way, her attention was caught by the window of a boulangerie. The cakes were ranged for display: gateaux with intricate patterns and exquisite trellis work, tiny pastries with cherries gleaming through the glaze, iced biscuits decorated with frosty slivers of crystallised fruit.

'Like something?' asked Stephen as she stared into the window.

This was shabby, dilapidated Algiers, its bakers' skills – learned from the French and displayed in half-remembered style – a dream of European elegance transformed into a misshapen nightmare. As she looked hard at the cakes on the shelves, Sten saw the flaws emerging like a developing print: the smudged cream, the tiny irregularities in the trellis work, the dried fruit curling at the edges. Heat and heaviness smothered her like a rug thrown over a mad dog and a wall of silence pounded in her ears, blocking out the noise of cars, the cries of street sellers, the shouting of children.

'*Kirsten*, do you want something?'

She shook her head and produced a mollifying smile.

'No thanks,' she said.

'Nothing?'

'Well, a drink, maybe.'

'Nothing else?' he prompted, looking down at her, smiling.

'Maybe.'

She wanted to be alone, to take off all her clothes and let the air touch her skin and renew her spirit. Stephen's attentions drained her. His hot hands left scorch marks on her body, his breath burned her face, his penis siphoned her fluids from her, leaving her dry and parched.

She stared listlessly at the cakes, then turned to walk away, not waiting for Stephen.

The El Sharak hotel, too, showed signs of a forgotten past. Curving upwards, the graceful stairway was bordered by a wall grubby with hand-marks. The black and white tiles on the floor of the lobby were chipped. The ornate plaster work running round the ceiling of their small room disappeared abruptly into the partition wall through which, each morning, they could hear the Cairo businessman clear his throat. When they'd first arrived, the washbasin had been speckled white and red – trace elements of the rice and pimento meal of the previous occupant.

They climbed the steps to the side door to avoid the desk-clerk, who always wanted to practise his English by reading Sten's passport. 'The meenistaire of for region affairs,' he boomed the first time. 'See how easy it is? I am educated. I speak English, French, German.'

'And Arabic?' Stephen asked, but the man shrugged. The French had not encouraged Arabic. It was a sore point.

One of the elderly cleaning women was leaving the hotel, hurriedly pulling her mask up to cover mouth and nose, her ankle-length coat trailing the ground as she moved, silent as a ghost ship, down the steps. Sten hated the masks. Once, standing at a street crossing, she found herself level with a car stopped by the lights. The young driver wore a crisp, blue and white striped, button-down collared shirt, open at the neck. His gold-ringed fingers drummed on the wheel and a gold watch ornamented his wrist. Shrouded in black, his wife sat beside him, hard, olive-stone eyes staring out through the narrow slit in the black, lace mask. Her cold, appraising look left Sten stripped.

She lay on the bed watching Stephen slip his T-shirt over his head, unzip his jeans and fling his cotton trunks into the air. And flinched when he flung himself on top of her . . .

'One thing about you,' he said, leaning across her for the cigarettes, 'you used to be *always* ready for me.'

'I wonder should we try the airport?'

'So how come?'

'How come what?'

'That now you're not.'

'Oh, I don't know. That's what it's all about, sex. Sometimes it works –'

'Maggie isn't either.'

'Isn't what?'

'Ready for me. Hardly ever.'

'Maggie's your wife.'

'It's only been lately.'

'What has?'

'You know, that you haven't been ready for me.'

It was true. Her whole body was dry. When he pushed into her, there were no warming liquids to smooth his way. She felt arid as the desert.

'Oh, I don't know,' she said, flapping the sheet to cool herself. 'I don't know what's the matter.'

The smoke from his cigarette drifted across their heads. Below the window, car horns hooted with growing insistence, nudging the women off the streets for the night. Within the hour darkness would give possession of the city to the men, the boys and the street cats. A faint sweet smell of rotting vegetation rose and slithered in through the shutters. Stephen elbowed himself up and stubbed out his cigarette in the saucer he'd been balancing on his chest: 'OK, come on. Up. You're right. Better find out what's the story with the plane.'

At the airport, the plane had arrived, yes. And yes, it would leave on time, inshallah. But no, there wasn't room for two, only one. It was a military plane and only by special concession. If they had travel documents stamped by the Ministry, perhaps?

'We're press,' said Stephen, showing them his ID, but the official shook his head.

'OK, you go,' said Stephen. 'I'll fax the office and tell them what's happened.'

'And what will you do?'

'Pine for you. Wank. Maybe take some shots of that beach north of the city where they were putting up defences yesterday. If I can get permission.'

'I wonder how long this'll take?'

'You'll only be gone three days maximum and then, when you get back, we'll go over to Marseilles and stay in bed for a week. How about that? We need to give ourselves time, don't we?'

'Three days? My God, three days in a desert, looking at a war everyone has forgotten about.'

'Listen,' he said, 'have you got everything? Passport? Water tablets? Have you the battery for your laptop?'

'Of course.'

She wanted to fling her arms out, send him spinning away from her. Just leave me alone, she wanted to cry. Leave me alone.

Instead, she kissed him on the cheek.

'Have you remembered your water bottle?' he asked.

She closed her eyes.

'*Now* what have I said?'

It hadn't been three days, of course. So far, it had been seven: three days waiting at the outpost and now four days here at the refugee camp.

'Tent city,' Shadeed had corrected her gently. 'It's only temporary, but it is our home until we can return to our mother-country.'

Shadeed was kindly, diplomatic, used to handling journalists and fact-finding politicians. The journalists kept the war on the pages of the newspapers. The politicians produced the money and, sometimes, the guns.

The old man called a woman to brush up the sand, checked the catch on the shutter, then shuffled off through the door. Raising the glass to her mouth, Sten emptied the lukewarm dregs of the coffee down her throat, concentrating on each last drop. It would be another two hours, at least, before they brought any more. She wrapped herself in a sheet and padded across the courtyard to the shower room, where she stood, motionless, as the tepid water flowed over her. As soon as she stepped out of the cubicle however, and started to pat herself dry, sweat bloomed on her skin like a fever flush. Irritably, she towelled the stickiness between her legs and wondered what Stephen was doing.

They woke her at three in the morning.

'We're going,' Shadeed said. 'Be ready in ten minutes.' In the lavatory, sudden fear – yellow and liquid – burst from her bowels.

The driver of the jeep was the same one who had collected her from the airport and she noticed once again the serenity of his profile: the straight forehead, the delicate nose, the lips – upper and lower – balanced in perfect symmetry. His wristwatch gleamed gold against the cuff of his khaki shirt and his black keffiyeh was wound neatly round his head, the swirls layered one on the other like waves, the tail tucked in firmly at some invisible but designated place.

When they camped that night, far out into the desert, the cook spread rugs around the fire, the soldiers sprawling on one side of it, smoking and talking. The driver sat slightly apart from the main group, cleaning his gun. Beside her Shadeed opened the flap of his tooled-leather cigarette pouch and took out a cigarette, fitting it into his holder and packing in the tobacco before lighting it. Then, on the first draw, eyes closed, he flipped the pouch closed with a crisp slap, leather against leather, and stretched out on the rug.

'We have two more days driving,' he said.

'What's the driver called?' Sten asked. She'd been trying not to look at him all day.

'Lamine. He's our best driver.'

'I've been watching him. How does he know where he's going? He seems to drive for miles and then he turns, for no reason.'

'No reason that *you* can see,' said Shadeed.

'But how on earth does he know when to do it?'

Shadeed smiled and shrugged. 'We're desert people. It's our way of life.'

'I just can't work it out.'

'No, of course you can't. You are not one of us.'

'I mean, I can understand at night. Then, he can navigate by the stars, but in the day time, when everything looks the same, mile after mile of sand. A bit of a bush, maybe. A rock. Then another bush.'

'There are stars in the sand as well, you know. Desert people are not blind.'

Shadeed had a wife and three children living back in the refugee camp. His parents and young brother had been napalmed as they fled across the desert to safety, and he lived with the certain knowledge that because his people had been wronged, one day this wrong would be put to right. If no one else, Allah would see to it. Sten envied him his certitude. She knew he was right, but she had no belief and there were times when his rocklike conviction irritated her. It took no account of the rest of the world, of what was happening beyond the desert. There were other wars, other disputes, other tragedies. There were train crashes, hijackings, riots. Governments had to deal with political coups, unrest, the stock markets. There were always other agendas. You're not the only ones, she wanted to say. Lacking faith herself, Shadeed's made her angry.

'We know there are other things happening in the world,' he said, 'but we are here, in the desert. We have to fight for our homes and our future.'

The silence was loud between them.

A burst of laughter came from the men on the other side of the fire. Two of them got up, arms around each other's shoulders, and walked out into the darkness. The cook came over to where Sten and Shadeed were sitting and said something in Spanish.

'He says tomorrow we'll have some of his very good bread for breakfast,' said Shadeed. 'He hopes you'll like it.'

'I'm sure I will.'

'He says you need to keep your strength. *Our* women are strong. They have strong legs.'

The cook nodded and smiled, then, leaning over, kneaded her thigh, feeling it for toughness. She was annoyed to find herself clenching her muscles, watching his face for a sign of approval.

That night, Sten woke and looked upwards. The sky was

throbbing with living light and for one fearful moment it seemed as if each point of starry brightness was pulsating, gathering speed before hurtling downwards towards her. Then she turned and saw the reddening of the fire. The pot oven sat in the midst of the glowing wood, its lid covered with embers. By first light, the bread would be cooked.

When she next woke, the men were stirring, moving quietly in the pre-dawn chill. Shadeed, standing by the fire, cradled a mug of coffee in his hands, watching as the cook tore off pieces of the steaming, crusty bread. Away to one side of the camp, the driver knelt towards Mecca, lowering his head slowly to the sand, private, as always, in everything he did.

They set off as the sun rose over the edge of the earth, balancing itself on the horizon like a distant world glowing with promise. The jeep hurtled across black, metamorphosed rock, the hardened enamel bouncing the heat back up on to their faces. High up on top of the food boxes the cook rode bare-chested, the tail of his keffiyeh streaming out behind him in the hot wind. Shadeed showed Sten how to wind the long scarf round her head and face so that only her eyes were exposed to the biting red sand and the rays of the white-hot sun. But the wind tore the tail loose, the whole thing fell apart and she was forced to wrap it round her head again and again, finally holding the end between her teeth.

The first stop was at noon. Sten gulped from the water bottle and Shadeed shook his head at her.

'Drink slowly,' he said, but she was driven mad with thirst and could pay no heed to his advice. Her tongue had erupted into a thousand, rubbery organisms weaving around her mouth in search of water, and when she drew air into her lungs, the heat of it suffocated her.

'I feel sick,' she said, and Shadeed boiled a small amount of water for her to drink.

They all took refuge from the noonday heat. Most of the soldiers crawled underneath the jeep, the driver made a canopy out of a blanket tied to the back of it and Sten lay down alone in the shade of the meagre thorn tree which had been their stopping point. Shadeed pointed to the glare-bright sky: 'Move here,' he said, patting the blanket, 'to the edge of the shade.'

Later, she understood why, for as the sun moved overhead, the thorn tree, struggling like a decorous matron to retain its modest circle of skirt, was left bare of shade.

She dozed, slept, dreamed that she was trickling sand into her mouth. The grains scratched and scalded her dry throat and left her feeling worse than before. When she woke, her mind was heavy with sadness. This war was never going to be won and these men – wives and children left behind on the edge of the desert – were doomed for ever to hope, buoying each other up with their desert camaraderie. Once, Shadeed told her, he and another soldier had got lost. They'd drunk the water from the radiator, then fanned out from the jeep, certain that their comrades would continue circling the desert until they were found. Another certainty. And he was right. They had been found, but by then the other man was dead.

'He died for the mother-country,' said Shadeed, but Sten felt he'd died because he'd got lost.

A slight movement over by the jeep caught her eye. Silently, the driver lifted his gun from where it rested on the dashboard. Raising and firing, all in one continuous movement, no time taken to aim, he plucked from the air a pretty, fawn-feathered desert dove. She watched his hands pick up the bird. Strong, dark hands, white nails clipped square.

And thought of their coolness touching her.

They searched the desert for another thorn tree to camp by, but found none, only a pile of Coca-Cola tins discarded by a previous patrol. That night, as the cook was making up the fire, a beam of light far away to the south swept across the night sky.

'The look-out,' said Shadeed. The look-out jeep unloaded food and water, more men. They'd brought a small black goat with them and one of the men held it as Sten stroked its silky fur.

'The desert gazelle, it's called,' said Shadeed, fitting tobacco into his holder. The goat's eyes were bright as diamonds, but beneath her hand she could feel it shiver. It was a pretty little thing.

'May I take a photo of it?'

'Of course,' said Shadeed.

She raised the camera to her eye and the man holding the goat smiled. Then, through the tiny window, she saw him draw a long knife from behind his back and swiftly slit the throat of the animal. She lowered the camera and watched the legs of the goat fold like sticks. Blood throbbed on to the sand. Then, horrifyingly, it manoeuvred itself to its feet again. The man with the knife smiled, shook his head, took a stone from his pocket, sharpened the knife and then drew it once more across the gullet of the goat. This time the creature sank to the sand and stayed there.

'We waste nothing,' said Shadeed. 'The stomach will be used for carrying water, the skin for making purses and these . . .' and he held up his cigarette pouch. 'The meat, of course, we will eat.'

He smiled at her. 'You like goat meat?'

'Yes,' she said, knowing it was a test.

That night, the men drew a lattice in the sand and played a game with stones and goat pellets. The driver watched them for a while, then raised his hand. One by one they played against him, slapping their pieces noisily on the sand and shouting encouragement to each other while he sat quietly studying the game, his courtly fingers tossing the stone in the air before placing it with deliberation on his chosen square. The olive skin on his face was smooth in the firelight and she imagined stroking it. Only when he had beaten the last contender did he smile, and Sten had to turn away from the gentle sweetness of it, feeling herself swell and moisten with desire.

The march out to the desert front line came the following night. When the moon had gone down, they set out, the driver taking the jeep across the desert in low gear, edging it smoothly from one look-out post to the next until they reached their rendezvous. There the commander-in-charge led them out across the sand in single file, signalling swiftly for them to fall to the ground whenever a flare was sent up. Over to the east, the regular nightly mortar exchange had begun, sending ribbons of exploding light through the sky. The commander whistled softly, guiding them along to the huge wall of sand that acted as the front line.

When a flare went up suddenly, perilously close, Sten flung herself to the ground, flinching away from the image of her white legs tattered by machine gunfire, her blood seeping into the sand as fast as that of the goat she had eaten the previous evening. She thought briefly of Stephen, but already the commander was up and guiding them on with a tiny zit-zit sound.

When they got back to the look-out, Shadeed was waiting by the jeep.

'You're satisfied?' he asked. 'You see how close we got to the enemy lines? Soon, we will go over the top and claim back our motherland.'

Sten nodded.

'I've got it all,' she said, patting her notebook, wondering how much she could use, how much she would have to invent. Nothing had happened. Not really. She had, she knew, been taken on a publicity exercise. She had got nothing. There *was* nothing, just a forgotten war.

She wondered if Stephen was still waiting in the hotel in Algiers.

As the sun came up, they lay down to sleep by the jeep, exhausted by the night march. Later, in the heat of the day, the driver took them back to camp. Sten felt numb with thirst.

That night the glasses were laid out in the sand: four for six people. The ceremony was the same as it had been every other night, except that this time it seemed to take longer. Greedily, she watched the cook pour the tea one at a time, then hand round the frothing glasses. She was given hers, the soldiers watching as she drank swiftly, concentrating on the liquid as it slipped down her aching throat. The cook took her empty glass, rinsed it with sand, then poured a glass for the driver. She looked down at the sand, thinking of his mouth closing on the rim.

The first glass of tea was always strong – as strong as life, they said. Then the cook added more sugar for the second brew.

'You remember – what this one is called?' Shadeed asked.

'As sweet as love?' she said, and he nodded.

Tonight, the second glass seemed too sweet and she sipped it carefully, drop by drop. Through the firelight she could see the driver sitting, slightly apart from the other men, looking into the flames. The sleeves of his khaki shirt were rolled up to his elbows, which rested on his crossed legs. His feet, in leather sandals, were brown, cleaned by the sand. Last night, when he had helped her climb up into the jeep, she'd inhaled the sandalwood smell of his skin.

The cook handed round the third and last glass of tea – the signal that the day was ending. The third glass, they said, was smooth as death.

She took as long as she could drinking this last glass. Soon, they would all stretch out on the rug while she, the only woman, lay decorously at one end. There would be nothing more to drink until dawn and already her mouth was dry.

The cook threw a bit of tree stump on to the fire and it flared, lighting the calm face of the driver. His eyes were still, unblinking, seeing something distant in the flickering flame. His lips were like plums, deep purple and soft, and Sten's mouth watered, for she knew that if she could sink her teeth into them, her thirst would be quenched.

NED LENIHAN

Candid Photography

A photograph. That's all it is. Seven inches by five. Colour, with a glossy finish. Not hand-printed, by the look of it. Slightly underexposed – some facial detail's in shadow.

Foreground comprises six young men, in varying degrees of athletic pose. They're in focus. So's the grass in front of and around them. Weakens the effectiveness of the portrait, this large depth of field. The subjects, four of them kitted out in red shirts and black shorts, are lined up adjacent to a marquee. Composition's poor: people, in short-sleeves or skirts, stand about with drinks in their hands and distract the eye.

Left to right, that would be Mullin in the tracksuit bottoms. His hair is naturally blond, parted in the middle, wavy, and healthy in a way that – to me at any rate – suggests orange juice, surf boards, muesli breakfasts. An immaculate set of dentures gleam at the camera. Light-meter must have exposed for these. A gold watch twinkles on his right wrist: Mullin had already retrieved his possessions from the team valuables bag.

Next to him, myself, of course, clutching an empty bottle of champagne.

I'm short and stocky. Look a little bored. No surprises there. My head's tilted, as if in defiance of the camera. Never did like having my picture taken. Tangles of coarse, black hair lay, uncombed, on my temple. My shirt hangs over my shorts. My colours are just about visible. University had intended to award these at a ceremonial dinner. I didn't show up. Sports administrator sent them on in the post. Sick of her nagging, I allowed my mother to stitch them on to my shorts.

Goalkeeper, keen as mustard, has his right arm wrapped

around my neck. Can't remember the name. He's laughing. About a week or so after, I dropped him from the side. A black, official team sweatshirt stretches across his 48-inch chest. Available only from the campus sports shop. At a ludicrous price. A pair of bright orange pads barely cover his tree-trunk legs. Despite his size, the ball often eluded him.

He's not wearing his protective face-mask.

'Don't take it off,' we used to joke. 'You look better with it on.'

His other arm grips Davey Lynch's forearm.

Lynchie worked in the Far East after teacher training. Received some postcards from him then. On the back, Lynchie's flamboyant scrawl recounted a life of sun, scorpions, snorkelling, MacDonald's takeaways, live sex shows. He sent a 'Happy Deepavali' greetings card once. Didn't explain the ceremony's significance. Typical of him. Never fully explained things. In his final letter – posted from somewhere in London – Lynchie didn't reveal why he'd tired of all that fun in the sun.

Unperturbed by the goalkeeper's eighteen stone. A cigarette smokes in Lynchie's left hand. His legs are crossed. A nonchalant right boot points to the baked ground. His black socks are rolled down to his ankles. His calves are firm and tanned. Mine are muscular but pale.

The tall, wiry frame of McNally slouches next to Lynchie. McNally grew sideburns, as wide as they were long, down to his jaw-line. Winter or summer, his straight, greasy hair curled at the collar of his donkey-jacket. Once – for a laugh – he hired a tux for an end-of-season dinner dance. Looked no different. Wanted that certain bohemian look. Fell more naturally to Lynchie: wispy beard, crucifix ear-rings, conversation to match.

Lynchie had the advantage of being a biker. Leathers, studs, zippers, knee-length boots – the works.

Never been on a motorbike before I met him. Hadn't a clue where to hang on. While the bike was in motion, worried that my legs were too near the spokes of the back wheel. First time I took a lift, Lynchie told me to clasp my arms around his midriff and squeeze tight on his leather jacket. Not sold on the idea. Gripped the bit of metal that arched up from the end of the seat behind my back – no mean achievement, particularly when a bike is hurtling along at high speeds. Whizzing through the countryside on the 750, Lynchie's shoulder-length curls flapping from under a full-face crash-helmet and into my face, wished we would reach our destination in a hurry. But not in too much of a hurry.

McNally drove a beaten-up Morris Minor. Whenever he could get it started.

On the extreme right of the photograph, good old reliable Thornton, or was it Thorburn? In any case, his thin lips are cracking into a smile of sorts. He is the only team member brandishing a hockey stick. Good quality. He used to apply linseed oil to the wood before the start of each season. Brought a spare along to every game. A very methodical character. Thornberry, that was him. Quietly efficient at the heart of the defence. No backtalk – got on with the game. Never a peep out of him in the dressing-room. Or on the bus back from away fixtures. A dull conversationalist. Wore soft contact lenses on the field, black bi-focals off it. Put in hours of study in the library on campus, but attained average grades. What was his most distinguishing feature? His hairstyle: it was neither long, nor short.

Everyone's hair is backlit. The manual that came with my 35 mm camera no doubt told me that, in photography, you should never shoot directly into the sun. Mustn't have read it very carefully. Hopeless like that. Even today, whenever I buy some new appliance, can't be bothered wading through a few pages of instructions.

Splashed out on the camera, along with a developing tank and black-and-white enlarger, soon after cashing my first grant cheque. Never been away from home before. Never had that much money before. Can be forgiven for not having the slightest clue how to budget.

Just about managed.

Reserved photography magazine with newsagents at that time. Colour pages carried adverts for things I could never afford. Plus nudes – impeccably lit – striking bizarre poses in outlandish locations. Portraits, still life, landscapes, seascapes – if Lynchie could oblige a lift, I'd have a go myself. Got through two rolls of film a week then. Thirty-six exposures, 400 ASA. Ate beans-on-toast a lot. So much for sacrifices. Worth it in the long run. So I thought. One day my magnificent portfolio of self-developed black-and-white shots, printed on hard grade matt paper for maximum contrast, would be hailed by the critics. Perhaps I'd cap a distinguished career by marrying one of the beautiful nudes that modelled for me. It had, after all, happened to David Bailey.

So I thought.

Bought a 28 mm fish-eye lens and a 200 mm telephoto in my second year. Enabled me to shoot subjects without their knowing. Still prefer the candid shot over the posed portrait.

But there's no money in it.

Didn't win the hockey tournament. Beaten *and* disgraced. Didn't win one game in the entire competition. Gallant, but doomed from the word go.

'It's not the winning but taking part that matters,' Lynchie muttered as McNally – the scruff landed an unsportsmanlike but well-timed punch during one heated exchange with the opposition – took his marching orders. 'I'm only here,' McNally corrected him, 'for the fucking beer.'

Beer and champagne, actually. Champagne won in a raffle. Duly passed to team-mates. Swallowed in greedy gulps. McNally's dad – grudgingly introduced by his son – pitched in with: 'What have you lot got to be celebrating?' 'Friendship,' is what the goalkeeper said. Toasted with his plastic beaker.

No one argued with him.

Lynchie, who was familiar with Ansell Adams landscapes and Bill Brandt social commentaries, said I had the eye for a good photo.

Not much evidence on this showing. Seem content to shoot

off snaps instead of striking images. Lined the boys up, set aperture and exposure-time, showed an obliging passerby shutter location, shook, uncorked – *unscrewed*, actually – took aim with the aforementioned bottle. Volunteer who peered through camera's viewfinder deluged in froth. Didn't press the shutter at exactly the right moment.

Moment's hesitation can make the difference. Between a good picture and a bad picture. Have since learnt to my dismay.

Done with posing, Mullin, McNally, Thornberry and the goalkeeper sloped off to the dressing-rooms. Lynchie and myself traipsed off in the other direction. Attending a modest presentation ceremony in the pavilion. I captained home side. Expected to proffer words of congratulation or commiseration to the finalists. Thank the organisers for their help, the sponsors for their support, the spectators for turning up on the day. Lynchie, my vice-captain – 'Who put the vice in vice-captain?' became something of a catchphrase that season – also expected to make an appearance. Sat through the presentation formalities and applauded dull but mercifully short speeches. Discussed aspects of the well-contested final with match officials. Shook the hand of the winning captain.

Back to the dressing-rooms. In silence.

Lynchie was different. Most students I met during my first term attempted to strike up a friendship by commenting on essential course texts I hadn't bothered reading. Remarking on the plight of the Palestinians, the black South Africans, the oppressed minorities I frankly didn't give a damn about. Lynchie kept his mouth shut. Limited himself to sardonic one-liners.

If there was nothing to be said – for instance, after the team's dismal showing in the hockey tournament – he said nothing.

A particularly hot day. Tournament played in a league format. Even the losers – us, most definitely – hung about in the July sun for most of the day.

Spirits high back in the dressing-room. Despite showing on the field. Hissing and gushing of shower-jets. Animated voices talked all at once on missed open goals, working holidays abroad, local summer vacancies, next year's accommodation options, the night's television.

Normally I opted out of communal showers. Preferred a good long soak in the bath, back in my room on campus.

Lavish dinner had been planned. In honour of a long-serving sports administrator due to retire at the end of term. I'd brought a change of clothes, rehearsed a few vague lines of eulogy. Could hardly be expected to impart these niceties reeking of sweat. Conceded that post-match shower essential.

Bundled dirty team-shirts into a kit-bag. Asked coach: 'Why do we have to wear nylon shirts in summer?' just before undressing.

Strange how a trivial comment can remain in the memory.

Lynchie had joined the rest of the team in the showers. While he scrubbed his face, his back, his thighs, I involved myself in a protracted discussion on the day's tactical blunders. While the goalkeeper bawled smutty limericks and chants, I wanted to know how different team selections might have helped us on the day.

One by one, showerers returned, towels wrapped round their waists, dripped little pools on the dressing-room tiles. All except Lynchie.

Finished chatting to the coach. Headed for the showers myself.

I'd seen Lynchie naked once before. Alone in my room, very late one night, photographing a bowl of fruit, experimenting with a number of lighting set-ups, when Lynchie and his girlfriend called. They'd been bopping at a party in the next tower block. Only popped in because – surprise, surprise – the booze ran out. Don't know how we got on to the subject of nudity. But Lynchie, who could be very persuasive when he wanted to be, dared his girlfriend to strip for a photo session. She didn't need much persuading. Things got pretty steamy when he joined her on my carpet. Pair struck some imaginative poses with my bowl of fruit.

Lynchie later hounded me for the best 10 by 8s.

Shower-water hot. Steaming, in fact. Lynchie in the thick of it, scrubbing himself clean.

Didn't intend to look. Lynchie was a fine figure of a man. Nature had been kind to him. Phallus didn't so much dangle as swing. Like the pendulum of a grandfather clock. Enviable proportions. Warranted a second glance. I looked. Discreetly. Organ juddered to life. For my benefit. My naked form – I was soaping my arm-pits by now – may have inspired it. Lynchie's warm smile, verging on a leer, certainly implied this. Not the most fluent conversationalist at the best of times. There I was, in a shower, aware of my friend's developing erection. At a loss for words.

Eventually managed: 'You picked a fine time to defy the laws of gravity.'

Not bad, considering.

The bike-rides, the confidences entrusted, the post-mortems on matches in the bar, the lunchtime rivalry on pinball machines – all seen from a new perspective.

Lynchie didn't apologise. Tried to play the situation down.

'Thanks for the compliment,' I said, 'but I don't swing that way.'

Couldn't stop myself from sneaking another look.

Tip of his organ quivered. It shuddered. It became engorged.

'Ever tried?' he leered.

'No. And I don't intend to start now.'

I'd have been all right if McNally hadn't come back. If he hadn't returned to retrieve his soap-on-a-rope. I would've had my back to him. Saw Lynchie gape. Turned my head round to McNally. McNally didn't bat an eyelid. 'Hello, big boy,' he said. 'Sorry for intruding.' First chance he got, McNally dished the dirt to the rest of the lads. Tried to explain. No joy. Packed the game in after that. Not Lynchie, though. Nothing bothered him.

And then. Last summer.

Out of the blue, one evening, the note slipped under the door of the shop. My shop-front, a bland window-display, chock-a-block with enlargements of grinning newlyweds (vignettes, soft-focus, not particularly good, barely adequate in fact). 'On my way to a holiday in the Burren,' the note read. From McNally. 'If you fancy a drink, I'll be in the pub across the road.' Heard years before that McNally had turned out a drunk, joined the AA, been on and off the wagon. Never drink much as a rule. Wouldn't have taken up McNally's offer, even if I'd seen the note in time.

Then it started. Two days after the note. Noticed locals stopped saluting me in the street, weren't returning my telephone calls.

The sordid details, I'll spare you those. What sordid details? Not as if I actually *did* anything. Rumours, nothing more. Gross exaggeration. A slur on my friendship with Lynchie.

Not good for business, this sort of thing.

A small community. Such a scandal will be the ruin of me. Whether I deny the charges or not. What parent, if they suspected, would let me near their child?

Don't do anywhere near as much PR work as I used to. Hate it anyway. All that hanging about at a function. Until four or five dull men in suits call me over to photograph one handing a cheque to another, while the rest of the group looks on. Used to do well in the summer. Weddings and first communions always good money-spinners. Cleaned up with confirmations at the end of every May.

But not any more.

The cowboys are moving in on my territory. Shooting on 35 mm format. The sort of people who'd look at you for using fill-in flash during daylight hours.

I'm a professional. They can't touch the standards I set. Whether I'm interested in my subject matter or not.

Lynchie will never see fifty. He may be dead already. Crashing at high speed, going up in flames with his bike – that's not too hard to imagine. Unless he contracts Aids first.

But me. What will become of me? Lynchie's comment in the showers that day best sums me up.

'You just take photographs.'
It's about time I started taking a few good ones.
But not here.

EMMA DONOGHUE

Counting the Days

Jane Johnson grips the rail of the *Riverdale*, watching the estuary water heave and sink below her. She counts the days: nearly five weeks since she boarded at Belfast, and the city of Québec is only one more day away. The provisions might almost have lasted, if it hadn't been for the heat and the maggots in the ham. The same journey took Henry eight weeks, last year, when the seas were high. Tomorrow she will be beside him.

Today she is beside herself. On this voyage Jane has discovered herself to be a most imperfect creature. For all her weather-dried red hair and her two children, she is as restless as a young goat. What has appalled her the most on this little floating world of the *Riverdale* is not the squalor, nor the hunger, but the dearth of news. No one has left their company, except for that old man who died of dysentery the other day. No one has arrived, unless you count the stillbirth down in steerage. The only gossip is the rumble of clouds and the occasional protest of gulls. The passengers have to spend their time guessing what is happening in the other life, the real, landlocked world, now split in two for them like an apple, where on one side people weep for them and stare into the horizon that has swallowed them up, and on the other side, other people stare back, waiting for the first glimpse. Or at least so they must believe, these passengers. Unless they are longed for, why are they here, clinging to the back of this wooden whale?

Jane reaches into her pocket for her cache of letters, and loosens the ribbon. They're too few; crumbs to her appetite. The first, bearing the unlikely postmark, *Canada West*, Henry didn't send till he'd been there a fortnight. He wanted to wait till he had good news to tell, *something encouraging*, he wrote, the eejit, as if she needed any message but his living scribble on the paper, between the edges that are black from a month crossing the Atlantic to her.

Henry Johnson leans against a wall in Montréal. *I am thinking great long to see you*, his wife says at various points in the creased pages. Her grammar makes him want to slap her, and take her in his arms, and cry.

He should be in the shop, helping with the dinnertime customers, but he had to step out to get a little air. Maybe the sunlight and the long shadows of the trees will settle him. Maybe he's just nervous because of the trip he must take tonight, down the sinewy St Lawrence to Québec. When he gets back, at the end of the week, he will be a family man again.

Dear Henry when you and me meet we will have many an old story to tell each other.

He cannot understand why his stomach is churning. Such weakness is gripping his limbs today. He feels as if he will never straighten up from this wall. Its timber frame bears the claw marks of last winter's ice. A carriage clatters by; the crack of the whip rings in Henry's ears.

His nerves are spiders' webs beneath his skin. Have the months of wandering and working and living hand to mouth taken such a toll on him? Henry is an older man than the brash grocer who fled Antrim and his debts last year, but a stronger one, surely. The bad times are over; he is going to be the husband Jane has always deserved.

She clambered on to the ship at the warm end of May, with Alex behind her, his fists full of her skirt, and Mary heavy on her hip. By the first week in June, the air had thickened around them. Jane had begged from everyone who shared any of her names to make up the twenty pounds for this cabin. She and the children are sharing it with two aged clergymen. The air is fetid, but anything's better than home. At least on ship she doesn't have to jam the door against whoever might knock.

In such a year as 1849 it is better not to think about home. The town of Antrim has lidded its eyes. Most of those who aren't dead have been evicted; the rest count farthings or starve behind closed doors. What overwhelms Jane, when she lets herself dwell on it, is the sense of anticlimax: they held themselves together through four years of blight, and where is their happy-ever-after?

Down in the steaming gloom of the cabin, Jane hunches on the bunk with her eyes squeezed shut, and tries to find her better self. At least she and her children have some bedding, not like some of the passengers, who sleep in the spare sails. Besides, what right has she to make a fuss about leaving for a faraway country, when her uncle did it years before her, and her nephew, and her brother, and her two sisters? And her husband. She let Henry go on ahead; thirteen months he's been without anyone to wash his shirt. What kind of wife is she? She jolts the crying toddler on her lap, watching dark water punch the glass. What kind of a woman would be more loath to go than to part, more afraid of the journey than the separation?

Sometimes Henry's letters are so obstinately cheerful that they hurt her throat. *I have had rather a rough time of it*, he remarked after the storm off Liverpool. The paper was stiff with salt; the water had spewed through portholes and nearly sunk the ship. Is his bravery a fiction, Jane sometimes wonders? When he wrote to assure her that he had not panicked like the papists who threw holy water on the waves, whom was he trying to comfort, or convince? *I knew if we were to go down I might as well take it Kindly as not as crying wouldnt help me.*

They all think him a cheerful character: the other fellows in the shop, his Frenchie landlady, the farmers he lodged with in exchange for kitchen work, down by the Great Falls. Henry Johnson cultivates a reputation for cheer. The way he sees it, it's good manners to Providence to at least seem grateful.

It would surprise him to be told that he is eaten up with anger.
Or rather, that anger serves him, eats up whatever stands in his
way: tiredness, inertia, despair and loneliness. Ploughing through
six-foot snowdrifts, anger has burned in his gut and kept him
warm, or warm enough to keep walking anyway.

Henry credits Providence with bringing him so far, but it
could be argued that it was anger that did it, anger that dragged
him away from Antrim in the first place. Anger has brought
him halfway across the world; he hopes to seed the soil of this
vast country with it.

Something is burning in his guts now, but he doesn't know
what it is. His fingertips ache; he presses them against the wall,
outside the shop where he should be serving customers. He fixes
his thoughts on Jane; everything will be ordinary again the
minute she disembarks. Lying in Carrickfergus gaol, he used to
conjure her up in the shadows: her stiff apron, her sandy hair
coming out of its net, her huge laugh. *Dear Henery. I hope your
not reflecting on the past but always looking forward.*

His letters make casual mention of *six weeks walk* and *five
hundred miles*. Some of the places he writes of or from have a
familiar ring – Lucan, Hamilton, New London where Jane's
sisters are – but others are like strange fruit in her mouth:
Niagara, Montréal. Québec is her destination, but she had no
idea how to pronounce it until she asked the clergyman on the
opposite bunk. All she knows of this new world is words on a
page.

The river is beginning to narrow around the ship. Jane stares
at the green hills, the fields dotted with cottages and the
occasional spire that hooks the light. *I felt almost as if I was
getting home again*, says an early letter from Henry. But other
times the strangeness of the place shows through his lines. He
speaks of vast waterfalls, Indians, syrup leaking from the trees.
He tells her that they need bow to no one in this country: *The
Servant eats at the Same table with his master.* But on the outside of
one envelope he scrawls, *Bring the gun.*

*

The afternoon has dimmed around him and still Henry cannot move from the back wall of the shop. He hasn't felt this queasy since the days when he used to be a drinker.

There is doubt in these letters from his wife, tucked between the lines of devotion. Jane reports that his mother hopes he will come back to the old country; that her parents advise her not to make the crossing yet; that she only wishes he had found a permanent job and could send money. She offers with one hand and takes back with the other. *If you fall into your mind and would wish me to go to you I will, let the end be what it may.*

He turns from the wall and is sick into a bush. Its dark leaves quiver. Some foreign species; he doesn't know its name.

Wringing out Mary's rags in a bucket of seawater, Jane tries to imagine the country ahead of her. The ship sways, and brown water slops from the bucket on to her skirt. She wants to howl. But she will go up on deck and let it dry in the sun, then brush any lumps out. She hasn't time to be weak. She won't be a burden. What is she bringing Henry, if not a capacity for endurance?

The hard fact is, she needs him more than he needs her. For the past year, he has been an adventurer; she has been paralysed, a wife without a husband. Sometimes she hates Henry for going on ahead, for being able and willing to do without her in a strange land. But this is how Jane knows her kin, by an occasional flash of a resentment so intimate that she never feels it for outsiders: the maddening itch of the ties that bind.

Henry wipes his sour mouth on the handkerchief Jane embroidered for him two Christmases ago. It must be his old bowel complaint come back. He leafs through the worn letters for some magic phrase to calm him. But what his eyes light on is *You might write to me far oftener than you do.* Can she imagine what it is like to be here so many thousand miles from home, with no one to offer him a cup of tea or a word of sympathy?

The hard fact is, he needs her more than she needs him. He suspects Jane of enjoying her new independence; more and more, she writes to him after making decisions, not before. Anger swells in his throat now; he can taste gall all the way down. But he recognises this rage as a symptom of distance, the lengths love has to go to, the tautness of a marriage stretched like a tendon across a wide ocean. It costs them one and fourpence, paid in advance, to send each page.

The children are clamouring for some biscuit, despite the weevils. It won't kill them to wait just one more day. Jane squats down and holds them tightly round their waists, as if to squeeze the hunger pangs away. Alex and Mary both have her pale red hair; their three heads huddle together like a litter of foxes.

Across the deck she sees those two women who came on at Liverpool, clinging to each other mutely as if they expect to be washed overboard at any moment. One of them bends over the water to be sick; the other one waits with a cloth to wipe her mouth. Jane envies them each other. She is so weary of the feel of children, even her own beloved children; she wants a shoulder high enough to lean on, arms as hard as her own.

Henry is trying to walk back to his lodgings. He bends down again and retches on to the dusty ground as if voiding himself of thirteen months of self-pity. A passing lady withdraws her skirts. A priest tells him, in broken English, to go home. Henry is too weak to answer. He lets his head hang, and skims Jane's letters through blurred eyes.

Excuse bad writing and inditing, she wrote, as if every word were not a gift.

Henry averts his face from the page and throws up again, though there is little left but bitter air. If he purges himself of all his past errors, maybe there will be space for happiness to come flooding in.

His bowels have begun to churn. He tries to run. When shit sprays into his breeches and he doubles over, he is ashamed.

But no one is paying him any attention; those who rush by on the darkening street are on some business of their own. Henry tucks the letters into his shirt and pulls his braces and trousers down, squatting to empty his bowels on the cracked street. There is no end to the pain; the dark water keeps exploding from him. His solid flesh has become a bag of filth.

At some point he fastens up his trousers for decency, for some kind of containment, and staggers down the street. But the cramps bend him in two, like low blows from an invisible enemy.

Twilight finds him lying in a puddle of his own fluids, too weak to apologise when a woman stoops over him. She backs away, shouting something in French. He thinks he recognises the word for anger. Who is angry? Then the woman shouts it again, and he recognises the word like his own name.

As the light fades, Alex chatters of hunters and bears; Mary kicks at the railings and wriggles as if she wants to slip through into the sea. *You and them has never once been out of my mind and heart since I left you.* Jane has taught the girl to say *Dida*, the first name she knew for her own father. Mary has no idea what the word means, and plays with the sound as a bird would. Neither child is old enough to understand that they have left the only country they have ever known, to settle in a new one. They will be Canadians; Jane mouths the word to herself. It is not a matter of choice. What choice have any of them made, when all they know is what they are running from, when Henry with his exasperating enthusiasm is leading them into the dark?

Cholera, that's what the woman said. Henry nods slightly. He is folded into a hospital bed like a leaf pressed in a book. The diarrhoea is finished, and so is the vomiting; he has nothing left to offer up. He has given every drop in his body to this alien soil.

Cholera, anger made flesh, the dull burning fuse in the guts, the bile spewing through the bodies of those who stay and those who go. A disease familiar to those who are herded from country to country, from city to city, drinking and washing with the same water.

This ward is filling up; the nurses run like messengers bearing secrets. Each new arrival is doled out forty drops of laudanum. Henry can tell, by looking at the others, that his cheeks are concave, his eyes are sinking in their sockets, and he too has taken on a blue tinge, as if they are all part of the same boiling sea.

He closes his eyes. He shuts his ears to the moans and retchings and convulsions all around him. In his mind, he reads fragments of letters. *Our best Days are before us.*

It occurs to him for the first time that he is dying.

It comes as a sort of relief. He feels near to sleep.

He knows he should pray. His God is unsentimental; he sits in judgement. There is no time left for Henry's old prayer, the one he directs as much at his wife as at his Creator: *make me what I have not been yet, a good and providing husband.*

At dawn, Jane is up on deck again. They have come to an enticing green island, its slopes furred with beech and ash. Blue strings of smoke rise from the sheds.

Grosse Isle is its name, she hears; it is where the sick must disembark. The ship pauses only long enough to set down the two grey-faced women from Liverpool. Jane watches their little boat bob towards the shore, with as much relief as compassion. She feels her health like a rich coat around her.

The sun is high when she glimpses the walled city on the promontory, pushing into the river like a sentry's gun. The fiction on which she has lived for a year is about to come true. At the sight of its towers, Jane begins to let her feelings flood her. Hasn't she been brave long enough?

Soon Henry will be walking beside her, carrying the children, pointing out landmarks as the sun touches them, but with eyes only for her. He will make up to her for all the waiting. She leafs through the letters, hungry for a sentence she remembers, the sweetness of his admission that they should never have let themselves be parted, *but dont be discouraged Dear Jane.*

This morning for the first time she lets herself taste how hungry she is, lets the children see her cry. But she shakes back the tears so she can see the busy docks, the ladders that will set them free from their prison ship.

Henry floats up from unconsciousness and wonders what Jane will do when she steps off the ship and he is not there. *PS Dear Henry do not neglect to meet us at Quebec.* Which will win, panic or anger? There is no letter he can write to tell her the end of the story. She will have to deduce it from his absence, interpret the suspicion in the faces of the French on the quay, read death in the yellow flags that mark the medicine stations.

Where will she go? Surely the Emigration Agent will take pity and pay her way to New London. Henry prays she'll come safe through the plains shaking with heat, the summer storms, the waist-deep mud of Toronto, and reach her sisters before the winter and a cold like she's never known. How long before she hears for sure that she is a widow at twenty-six? Until then, will she keep writing letters, he wonders? No, she's a practical woman; she wouldn't write without an address. That's how he picked her: as a fellow-traveller in a whirling world, a rock in a hard place.

Leaning over the rails, Jane imagines the improvement; that slightly hunted look will be gone from her husband's face. What a cocky letter he sent: *I am 14 lbs heavier than I was when I left and I Can go into the bush and chop a log.* But so much will be the same: his dark eyes, his sweep of hair, the way his hands will close around hers.

Maybe he'll have brought some food with him.

How will she live, thinks Henry through his fog of fever? Will she and her sisters go into trade together? Or will she find some slow-moving neighbour to take on her and the children, some Irishman twice her age who'll be husband and father both?

Will she still count the days she has to live without him in this country?

He'll be there on the dock. Henry is always there at the end of her journeys. *Without you I will settle myself no place*, he wrote in the letter that persuaded her to come at once, not to wait a month later, because you never knew what might happen. *And Jane Dearest anything I can do Shall be done to make you happy and forgive anything wrong in the foregoing.* Every letter is a promise, signed and sealed; they all end, *your faithful and affectionate husband until death.*

His skin is cold and wet like a fish; the only water left in his body is on the outside. Henry licks his shoulder. He is sinking down below all human things. He is sliding into the ocean; he won't wait till her ship meets the land. He will sport around it like a dolphin, he will make her laugh louder than the gulls.

He shuts his eyes and swims down into the darkness.

Jane peers at the landing stage where the crowds are milling. That speck of black, standing so still, that must be him. His eyes, sharper than hers, will have marked her out already. What distances cannot be travelled by the gaze of love?

Simply A Leaf

The official stared at me. I could see her bring out her mental smileometer, attempting to ascertain if there might be a hidden trace of humour on my face.

'I'm not a wife,' I reiterated. 'I haven't been a wife for quite a while now. And although I'm very glad to have a house, I wouldn't fancy being married to it.'

'What will I put down under "occupation"?' she demanded.

'Leave it blank,' I said. 'That's what I'd do if I were you.'

'I've got to fill in answers to all the questions on this form.' She smiled at me, begging me to understand her onerous bureaucratic duty and to co-operate as fully as I could.

'You could put down "unemployed",' I suggested.

'May I have your card?'

It was my turn to be perplexed.

'Your UB card please?' she elaborated, her patience beginning to thin.

'UB?'

'Yes,' she spat out. 'Your Unemployment Benefit card.'

'I don't have one.'

'UA then.' I had become a tedious burden, I could tell.

'Your Assistance card. May I have it now please?' It seems that she thought that because I said I was unemployed I should have had a card to carry around designating me as such for all the world to see.

'No, you've misunderstood,' I told her politely. 'I am unemployed, but I don't have a "dole" card. I've managed on my savings so far. I've never been on the dole.'

'Then I can't enter you as "unemployed",' she wailed,

glancing apprehensively at the rapidly forming queue behind me. I noticed that the woman two down was elderly and on crutches.

'OK, OK,' I said, relenting. 'OK, be my guest. Put down whatever you want. I don't mind.'

It wasn't true, of course. But there was little else I could do at that time. I watched the woman quickly scribble something down. She was in charge again.

'The neutron star is as massive as the sun. And it is so dense that a pinhead of its material contains a million tonnes of matter.'

I was reading a scientific magazine, but my mind wheeled, at this critical point, from the stars right down to the earth. It was the pinhead image that did it, grounded me right beside the ancient Chruch Father, Thomas Aquinas. You see, it was he who suggested that dozens of angels could dance on the head of a pin. Wasn't he imaginative? And did he not possess extensive powers of observation? My friend Dorothy had told me all about this.

'Just because you can't see them is no reason to dismiss them,' she'd said in response to my raised eyebrows.

'Oh, I'm not. I'm not.' I wanted to be kind to her concerns. 'It's just that they are rather insubstantial, are they not?' I made a swinging movement between us with my left arm as if to slay all the imaginary angels resident there. None fell. And she was not impressed.

'Thomas Aquinas was a great teacher. He was making a profoundly spiritual observation when he said that forty angels could sit on the head of a pin.' It seemed that this was her summary, her high-powered précis, her entire presentation to me.

'Did he see them there?' The question might have appeared slightly offensive and smart-alecky, but I did not intend it to be. My multi-directional enquiries could not be adequately answered by her one-eyed words. Better narrow it down, I thought, to a slimline, tangible thing.

'What do you mean?' Dorothy squeaked. She was offended, but I would not backtrack.

'Well, I was only asking if he had any empirical evidence for his assertion.'

She hesitated and I took advantage. 'I mean,' I added, 'when and where did this Aquinas chap observe forty angels cavorting together on the head of a pin?'

It was then that she told me it wasn't that kind of knowledge at all.

'St Thomas Aquinas,' she enunciated carefully, as an obvious antidote to my disrespect, 'St Thomas Aquinas was a theologian and not a mathematician.'

'What's an angel?' I asked, deciding to try another angle, becoming more awkward now.

'Neither man nor God,' she said.

'Good,' I retorted. 'You've just told me what an angel is *not*. Now tell me what it *is*.'

'A Spiritual Entity,' she creaked, unsure of herself again.

'Ah, yes, but then, so are we.'

'But we are human.'

'So what?'

'Angels are not.'

'Nor animal?'

'No, of course, not animal.'

I was determined to press ahead. 'In what particular form do they exist?' I enquired.

'Incorporeal form,' she told me. 'They are spirits. They exist without a body.'

'Ah.' Once more I was inspired. 'Aha, now you've admitted it.'

'Admitted what?' She was flustered. I think she regretted the entire conversation.

'Admitted that this Thomas Aquinas guy was a chancer.'

'I have done no such thing,' she said, using her Senior-Infants voice against me. Maybe this was how she saw me, as an intractable six-year-old.

'But you have just stated that angels have no bodies.'

'Yes.'

'How then,' I flung at her, 'could Thomas Aquinas, or any other divine, have counted them together on the head of a pin?'

I was not reconciled – and that brings me to another negative aspect of Dorothy's personality – her preachy manner, ultra smug, in fact. It was all right for a state-sponsored, twice-pensioned National Teacher to say 'Be reconciled to your lot', but she never agonised each morning over what to do with her day. She wouldn't have me do it either.

'If you try to kill time,' she once quoted, 'you will damage eternity.'

Actually, I agreed with that pronouncement – as an abstract statement, that is. But it did not apply to me. I'd had sufficient difficulty coping with this realm and did not concern myself too much with 'eternity'. And as for 'killing time', if it appeared that way to Dorothy, it was because she did not appreciate the romance of my struggle to learn Russian or the integrity of my striving to invent something cheap, wholesome and desirable for the peoples of the world. That reminds me. I could have answered 'inventor' to that officious clerk yesterday. It would have sounded impressive. It would have been legitimate. I am an inventor. I made an integrated series of disposable house-hold items once. I mustn't say what they are because I have not yet taken out a patent and I'm certain they'd be popular if ever I managed to get them off the drawing board and into the nation's kitchens. If the important people could see working models, they'd be impressed. I don't know why I forgot to say that I was an inventor. On the other hand, I might have told her I was a student of Russian. That would have made her come down hard on her already hard-bitten nails. But it also is true. I have courted it all for years, the magic of St Cyril's alphabet, the chunky and soft sounds, the challenge, the chat. One night during class I'd even dared write a note in Cyrillic script to fellow-student, Darragh:

YA OCHEN LUBIO VASH, TAVARISH TALOUR

(I LOVE YOU VERY MUCH, COMRADE TAYLOR)

I'd written, forcing each character slowly and lovingly out with critical reference to the Standard Cyrillic outlines in the textbook before me. I was pleased to receive a prompt reply. A note swiftly placed in my fist as I left that night said simply:

SPASIBA YALINA. KHARASHO

Darragh had thanked me very much. But he never returned to that group again. Maybe I had frightened him. Maybe he had gone to Russia. I don't know.

I drifted, seated, and lolling gently on the garden swing, the spring juices of the earth a blend of perfumes about me. If a bud, despite everything that here and now is evil, grew into a leaf, I would know. And I would call it a leaf – simply a leaf. It was essential to be able to identify things. When my daughter was smaller I had taught her to recognise animals. In her little room I'd posted cut-outs on the wall, and I would lead her around to each one and she'd exclaim, cat, cow, dog, chicken, horse, donkey, fox. I added a second dog later. It was a different breed and smaller and lighter in colour and I wondered what she would say when she first saw it. She said dog, dog, lovely new dog.

'Are you single?'
　'No.'
　'Married or widowed?'
　'No.'
　He frowned at me.
　'I told the girl she could put down whatever she liked.' I was getting careless now.

He regarded me with contempt. '*She* has not got the authority to do *that*,' he declared.

'Oh.'

'You see, Missus,' he advised, 'I'm going to . . .'

'I'm *not* a Missus,' I pointed out, interrupting him.

'Well Miss . . .'

But I darted in again. 'Nor am I a Miss,' I said.

He produced an extremely audible, almost primal sigh. People in the office fixed their eyes directly on me.

'It's Ms,' I told him, Ms.

'Ms! What's that then?' He clamped his upper lip firmly down over his lower one and his canines showed. He reminded me of Bugs Bunny. I had to strangle a smile.

'Oh,' he said, 'it's funny, is it? Tell me then, what is this amusing Ms?'

'It's not amusing,' I told him, assuming an ultra-serious demeanour. 'Ms is just like Mr. It's been in use for several years now. It's a description of a female adult.'

'Not in my book it's not.'

'What exactly is in your book?' I flared.

'It's not on the form, Missus,' he said. 'On the form it says Mr, Mrs, Miss, clear as day. Now if you are not a Mister,' – he spelled out the long version of the word – 'if you are not a Mister, then clearly you must be a Mrs or a Miss.'

He eyed me for feedback. I believe he was taking pleasure. I saw him enter the word Mrs beside my name. Then he drew a clear sheet of blotting paper over the entry and damped it down. This time there was no indecision. Obviously he had the authority required to do that.

That evening I needed to relax. I chose a bubble bath. When I had drawn a full quota of water and added a generous tumbler of bubble-making stuff, I pulled my head right down to the water to hear each individual bubble pop and crack. It was like an orchestra tuning up. And as the music subsided, the colour spread, rainbows captured in every conceivable shape. But these, too, proved to be ephemeral and they disappeared as I moved about and inadvertently doused them down. I drew my shoulders on to the plastic pillow and automatically my legs floated. I lifted one leg from the water and it felt unusually heavy. I quickly restored it to the comfortable, liquid surface again. Is it not easy to believe, I asked myself, that water was our first world and that I was once – in the ocean – once – billions of years ago – no, not me – but a very remote and tiny ancestor – an amoeba – a blob – a single-celled piece of cosmic plasma – feeding – replicating – budding – branching? They are still there in the ocean, the identical descendants of our common ancestors. We made a different journey, that's all.

The phone rang. I heard Dorothy attend to it.

'Are you dry?' she yelled through the door.

'No. Who is it?'

'It's Aoife.'

Aoife is my daughter. She's at college in the States studying anthropology. She must be phoning to say what her plans are.

'You talk to her,' I said to Dorothy. 'Find out her schedule or ask her if I should ring her tomorrow.'

Dorothy returned to the phone.

I'm splashing now. I'm seven again. I watch the fine spray from the shower target my thigh. I observe what happens when I put a fist over the shower head, the tingling in my hand, the overspill as the pressure builds up.

'Aoife's off to Mexico tomorrow,' Dorothy reported back at the bathroom door. 'She says she's going there with another girl and some chaps. Field study, she calls it.' There was a faint drone of disapproval in her voice. 'She says not to ring. In a week or two, when she's settled in Mexico City, she'll ring you.'

It's not always easy to appreciate other people's worries, to enter other people's worlds. At breakfast next morning Dorothy was pensive and tense. She held up two forks to me, and several spoons and knives.

'Why,' she asked, 'is it only the tips of forks that corrode and not the spoons and knives as well?'

If this had been a serious question, I suppose I would have attempted to answer it. But it wasn't. It wasn't a fun question either. It was a diversion, that's all. It was D-Day for Dorothy. At 10.30 a.m. she would have her final interview for the post of Principal of her small, five-teacher school. At thirty-seven (she's two years younger than me) and the longest-serving and most experienced member of the staff, it was obvious she would have no difficulty at all. She was acceptable in other ways too. She knew her place. And she also knew the place of Augustine and Aquinas. Indeed, I reminded myself, she was familiar with the intricacies of Aquinas's speculation on angels gathered together on the head of a pin.

There was a red-haired man in front of me in the grey, public office that day. He, too, was registering for temporary work. Before ten o'clock, when the queue began to flow towards the various hatches, he sat by me. I was reading. I always bring my own reading material to waiting rooms. I am currently intrigued by the coastal counties of the west.

'Kerry is a bizarre place, behind time in a real sense, for here, in the most westerly land in Europe, the mean time of Greenwich in summer is out of place with the reality of Kerry by one hour and forty minutes.'

This had never occurred to me before. I read it and was appalled. Could County Kerry not be itself? Why did this wild and wonderful place have to be standardised like that? The man beside me was looking over my shoulder at a beautiful colour-spread of altocumulus clouds over Brandon Bay. His long, red hair tumbled down his shoulders and almost touched my face. I restrained myself admirably, for truthfully, I'd have loved to have filtered that hair through my fingers.

'Fantastic-looking place.' He grinned at me and with a quick lick of his tongue cleaned the roots of his beard. He must have noticed that there was some butter there.

'It's in Kerry,' I replied.

'I lived in Kerry for sixteen months,' he confided.

'Oh, really.' He was a real Dub. 'Which part?' I asked.

'Beyond Dingle. I worked and lived there for sixteen months.'

'What are you?' I asked and immediately regretted the question.

'A thinker,' he replied, nonplussed.

'I mean, what did you do there?' I quickly realised I had compounded my folly.

'I philosophised,' he said. He was smiling, no, maybe laughing at me. 'Except for the two weeks,' he added enigmatically, 'when I was without my bicycle.'

'Oh,' I said. It was all I could manage.

'You see,' he explained, 'my bicycle was buckled in a little accident.'

I'd lost the drift of the conversation and was no longer in control. I decided to keep my mouth shut and he obligingly ploughed ahead.

'It took twelve days to get a new front fork down from Dublin,' he continued. 'While I was waiting for it, I had to walk.'

I nodded.

'I didn't do well with the thinking then.' He was smiling to himself, recalling some special aspect of the past. 'You see,' he said, coming right back to me, 'I'm lost without my bike. The pedals operate my brain. When I walk on the soles of my feet it cuts off the circulation to my head.' He relaxed, assuming that I had understood, that everything was now crystal clear.

'What are you looking for?' I asked. 'I mean what type of work are you offering to engage in?'

'Philosophy, of course,' he replied. 'It goes without saying.'

'Anything else?' I asked, tentatively. I was beginning to see things his way, to open up to his world.

'Well, I can make currachs.'

'Oh,' I interrupted. 'Did you learn that in Dingle?'

'No, I never learned.'

He noticed my surprise. 'But I did make several currachs while I was there.'

'I don't understand. That's skilled work. Surely you'd need to learn it from somebody, be an apprentice or something?' I asked.

'I didn't,' the red-haired man volunteered. 'One night I dreamed I was making a currach, step by step I dreamed I was making the entire thing, and from that day on I was constructing currachs with the native men.'

'That's extraordinary.' I did, incredibly I did believe him.

'What have you put down under "Personal Work History"?' I asked. I felt I had known this man for a thousand years.

'Just thinker/boat builder, darlin',' he replied.

'There's not much currach construction going on in Dublin,' I said, speaking gently so as not to discourage him.

'I know,' he said. 'Don't you think I don't know? And I'm not sure there's much work for philosophers either.'

I was home early and was sitting, sipping a small sherry, when Dorothy returned. There was a casserole cooking in the oven. Her face was flushed and her eyes danced in her head.

'You got it. I know you've got it.' I was pleased for her.

She kicked her winter boots in the air and flopped on to a bean bag.

'Yes. I did. It won't be official for another week yet, but yes, I've got it.' She snatched another breath. 'You are now speaking,' she announced, 'to the new Principal of St Stephen's National School.' I kissed her on the cheek and she hugged me. I poured her a glass of dry sherry.

'Am I glad that's all over,' she said. She stretched out her long legs towards the log fire. I like logs and the smell of burning wood.

'How was your day?' She asked this when she remembered me.

I told her about the woman on the radio that morning who claimed that all the song-birds were disappearing from the land. I told her I believed that had happened during the Famine because little birds like sparrows and larks were eaten. I told her I had looked up the etymology of the word 'steadfast' and that it was a Greek word meaning 'strong' and 'persistent'. I told her what Co Kerry had to endure.

'I mean how was the job-hunting?' she asked.

'We registered,' I told her.

'What do you mean "We"?'

I hadn't realised I'd made a plural statement until she queried it.

'Myself and Kevin,' I replied. 'There's this man,' I added before she had time to ask, 'there's this beautiful man I met there – his name's Kevin – and he and I registered at the same time.'

She wanted to say something else, ask a supplementary, in fact, but I forestalled her. I'd remembered something important. I went into the kitchen and filled a tiny vase with cold water.

'He's upstairs,' I told her, as I carried out this delicate operation. 'Having a wash. He'll be having dinner with us.'

'And what on earth's that?' Dorothy asked as she watched me take my prize from a cup, put it into the vase and place the vase in the centre of our dining table.

'Oh that.' I tried to sound offhand. 'You mean that?'

'Yes, that.' She dropped the word, like a useless nothing, downwards towards the floor.

'Kevin picked it for me today,' I told her. 'It's a leaf . . . it's simply a leaf.'

SEÁN RUANE

Coronach

In memory of my father
Patrick Ruane
1925–1992

My Father's only enemy was *corvus corone cornix*, the 'grey' or hooked crow. After forty years of hostilities he had still never managed to down it; and with the recounting of the path of each stray stone or bullet, the bird rose higher in all of our minds until it soared in the rarefied air of the mythical: it was old as archaeopteryx; more huge than any roc; and its hangman's hood made an ungraspable phoenix of it, as invisible now to the shotgun as once it had been to the catapult.

To such an impressive invincible foe, Dad must always have remained the barefoot slingshot from the West; but because in affairs domestic and business he had come to enjoy as indomitable a reputation as the predator among prey, we were certain that the adversary would one day be overcome and banished. For the moment, however, this masked goose-stepping tyrant patrolled the periphery of our thoughts as arrogantly as it marked the well-kept hedges of our farm in Meath. Avian arrogance and human awe seemed justified at the time; for, in the long unsuccessful struggle against the bird, Dad had inadvertently shot three non-combatants. The first of these was my Uncle Joe.

It was the Christmas of the 'Phoney Emergency', with childhood in Mayo several removes from the experience of total war. Joe was helping my Grandfather to fix a stone wall in the bottom field; and Dad, nearby, had been left in charge of the antediluvian shotgun. He rested the weapon in the crook of his arm so he could put his hands in his warm pockets, away from the cold steel barrel and the wind. The worn wooden stock slid forward a few inches; so Dad jerked it back towards himself with his forearm, and the old gun went off, peppering with holes the already ragged arse of Joe's trousers. Blood rushed from the openings like possessed pigeons from a dovecote, and to ease Joe's pain, his Father threw him into a boghole. Fortunately, the gun was too weak to have caused grave injury; and now, in America, Joe will reveal to anyone with the stomach for it evidence of wartime heroism on the 54th parallel.

The second victim fell when I was seven. It was a large pied bird, muddied enough in March to be mistaken for the crow. Dad ran home with it, and as he put splints on the damaged leg and wing, told me again and again how it diverts enemies from its fledglings by pretending to be hurt. Then he washed the blood and mud from its body, revealing an iridescent plumage of glossy green and bronze, set off by brilliant white patches and blue-black throat and breast. He nursed it devotedly for seven nights and days, and before conjuring it back to the skies, he allowed me to stroke its crest and call it *pilibín*. I marvelled that he had his own magical name for this strange creature for which the encyclopaedia could offer only 'lapwing', 'peewit' and the hilarious '*vanellus vanellus*'.

Less fortunate than these survivors was a white racing pigeon, caught between the bead of the shotgun and the culmen of the hooded crow. As the dark bird spidered away and the innocent fell at our feet, Dad and I looked on amazed, an alchemist and apprentice observing the first albedo. Dad phoned the pigeon's owner, a wittering man from Cardiff, who requested tearfully that the bird be given a decent Christian burial. With the defiant guilt of Pilate, I slid its leg-ring on to a new Saint Brigid's Cross which Dad then pushed into the soil of the shallow grave. I knew that from the top of some ancient oak clotted with the black nests of rooks the hooded crow was looking down on our foolish ritual of expiation. Now that it had avenged for its family the public humiliation of the Ark, its dark thoughts could turn once again to carrion, or lambs' eyes, or the soft feet of calves as yet unborn.

The pigeon fell in spring 1979 during my final year of primary school, and Dad didn't shoulder his gun again until the next New Year's Eve. It had been snowing heavily since the morning of the 30th, and in the year's last hours of daylight the sky was still casting down millions of dying asphodels. I was sitting inside, wondering whether I should start the book entitled *Metamorphosis*, which my brother David had bought me for Christmas, or re-read quickly the Turgenev novel for which the final notice from the library had arrived. My memory of the Russian's references to pigeon and lapwing, jackdaw and rook, helped to decide the issue; but before Yevgeny Vassilyevitch could step from the carriage, I had turned from the page to the greave-deep snow outside, where my Father stood stock-still and armed.

Through the condensation on the window, his strong profile was further pronounced. I outlined his firm chin and corniced eyes, but the image wouldn't hold; so I drew a cartouche around him and blocked it in. This only blurred the statuesque figure, and in frustration I wiped the rest of the glass with the back of my hand. I was opening the window for a better look when the indistinct hunter raised his gun against the grey sky, and shot. The glass shuddered, as in a storm, against my fingers, and in the distance a lone bird jerked and plummeted, helpless as a hooked fish reeled before the 'priest'. Its line of descent brought it to earth within ten yards of the marksman, who remained in the firing position for a long time after the shot; man and gun together like that had the outline of a startled bittern. At last, Dad lowered the muzzle to the snow and made his way over to the bird. As he inspected it, a murder of rooks collected, low in the sky behind his back. The cortège curved silently upwards, and flew to the point in the heavens directly above him; then swooned in vortex, calling raucous curses down upon his bare head; breaking and rejoining ranks as they fell; rising suddenly away from him and wheeling in disarray to their wood. Dad watched the masked Chorus to the distant trees, studied once more the fallen bird, and then turned back towards the house.

I left the sill and ran from the room. My wellingtons were too small for me; so I had to wait inside the open back door until Dad had removed his with the help of the threshold. Wearing these boots, I swaggered – rook-like – through the snow, trying at first to step in the deep prints Dad had left, but soon giving up the game as it slowed my progress, my stride being longer than his. In the bitter wind, the bird's body was flapping like a broken hollow-stayed umbrella. It was not until it dabbed the snow that I saw it was unkilled and trying to reach with its quivering crowbill the lead in its sky-grey back. Yes – it was definitely a hooded crow. It was so frightened; so clearly beyond help. As if it were a sad memory, I held it tenderly for a moment where it lay; then I stood up straight and closed my eyes and stamped its life and shape away.

After my father's sudden death years later, I remembered how I'd met him, eye to striate eye as he returned from the whited field that day: his rifle was bowed, and in his left hand was an unspent cartridge.

A Glossary with Some Notes

title
coronach Irish funeral-song; cf. Scott's poem *Coronach*, an elegy to a king.

paragraph 1
forty Here used not only literally, but also indefinitely to mean a very long time (as in, eg, Genesis 7:4 (the story of Noah's Ark); Shakespeare, *Sonnet II*).
it was old as . . . more huge than Elision and solecism.
archaeopteryx Primitive reptile-like creature with wings, from 125 million years ago.
roc Gigantic mythical bird of eastern tales, able to carry off an elephant.
phoenix Traditionally, a symbol of that which cannot be grasped.

paragraph 2
slingshot from the West Goliath came from the East to meet the future king.

paragraph 3
'Phoney Emergency' New collocation: Phoney War 1939–40 + Emergency 1939–45.
antediluvian Very old; from Latin *ante* + *diluvia* (before + Flood).
stock The wooden butt of a shotgun.
dovecote Pigeon-house.
54th parallel Line of latitude through Mayo; echoes the Korean War's 38th parallel.

paragraph 4

pied Of two colours (especially black and white), irregularly arranged.
pilibín Irish wood for lapwing.

paragraph 5

bead Small knob in the fore-sight of a gun.

culmen Small knob at the point where a bird's beak meets its head; prominent in the hooded crow.

at our feet Adumbrating the manner of the death in paragraph 8.

albedo Any whitening of a dark substance, eg in alchemy, where the 'black raven' is said to change into the 'white dove'.

Pilate . . . leg-ring Pilate himself composed the legend posted over the crucifixed Christ.

humiliation of the Ark Cf. Genesis 8:6–12; (*v.* **forty** and **ante-diluvian**).

paragraph 6

asphodels A kind of lily (symbol of death) which grew in the Greek heaven, Elysium.

Metamorphosis Story by Kafka, which is Czech for 'jackdaw'.

Turgenev novel *Fathers and Children* (1862) – as with *Metamorphosis*, above, the book-title points up a central theme of the story.

greave Armour for the shins.

stock-still (*v.* **stock**).

paragraph 7

Through the condensation . . . back of my hand The child tries everything to make the father remain heroic and kingly.

corniced eyes A cornice is (*architecture*) a horizontal projection crowning a building; and (*snow*) an overhanging mass of snow. The word 'cornice' is probably from Latin *cornix* (crow).

cartouche Term from hieroglyphics for the oval ring in which was enclosed the name of a Pharaoh. Egyptians believed this protected the royal person. For other regal references, *v.* **coronach** and **slingshot**.

plummeted From *plumbum* (Lat.) = lead; plummet = weight attached to fishing line.

'priest' In Ireland, the mallet used to finish off fish when they are caught and spent.

line of descent Another definition of the word **stock**.

a startled bittern will stand quite still, with its long bill pointed upwards.

murder / cortège (of rooks) Standard collective noun for crows / my alternative which fits their alignment, their funereal function, their colour and their call.

point in the heavens directly above A definition of the word 'zenith'.

masked Chorus Members of the earliest Greek Chorus wore masks. I also had in mind the fact that Sophocles dressed his Chorus in black when he heard of the death of Euripides.

paragraph 8

I left the sill . . . stride being longer than his. These lines show the change which the relationship between father and son has undergone.

sill / threshold Like **archaeopteryx** and **Metamorphosis** and the definition of 'zenith' (above), these may help to point up a rite of passage theme.

hollow-stayed umbrella To enable them to fly, birds have developed hollow bones.

dabbed Pecked; brushed with colour.

crowbill A medical forceps for extracting bullets, etc

a hooded crow For the first time in the story, the indefinite article replaces the definite in the appellation of this crow.

paragraph 9

father's For the first time in the story, the word is not capitalised.

striate eye (*v.* **corniced eyes**) Stria are (*architecture*) grooves in a column; or (*snow*) slight marks or ridges on snow. The crow has a striate eye because it has 'crowsfeet'.

whited Made white (*v.* **albedo**); freed from guilt. Also cf. Matthew 23:27: '*Ye are like unto whited sepulchres, which indeed appear* *beautiful outward, but are within full of dead men's bones, and of all uncleanliness.'*

cartridge A shotgun's ammunition. The word is related etymologically to **cartouche** (above).

WILLIAM WALL

In Xanadu

Ah but you got away, didn't you babe,
You just turned your back on the crowd . . .

Leonard Cohen, 'Chelsea Hotel No. 2'

1

We slept fitfully then, uncertain of the slipshod hills of winking streets and bloody crosses, the streams of the rivers that wound through everything, throwing that uncertain light in the eyes, on the buildings, as far as the sky even. And when we did not sleep, we lived along the streets, in the bars, in the groves of the College. Staying awake was not difficult. There were nightclubs, dances, flats and bedsits, even glorious starry winter nights. There was walking the hills where the streets wound in and out like water. And there was talk. Everyone talked about music, some talked philosophy or poetry or science. All of it, once the light was gone, in the grey pain of the next day, seemed utterly banal, utterly false. But we were convinced that memory played tricks. We were convinced that no one remembered exactly what had happened. That we had said things that surprised even ourselves with their beauty, ideas that ravished like Cinderellas, but which had now slipped away without leaving even broken glass, or had unaccountably transformed themselves into ugly sisters.

It all changed when Eileen died. It was during our last term, just before exams. She was coming up to College from her

sister's house, where baby number four had just been christ-
ened, when an articulated lorry pulled out across the road. The
Mini was too small to slip underneath, and when the roof came
off, it took the top of Eileen's head with it.

Even though there are no endings really, even though each
story is a continuum out of which we pluck what we call stories,
which our own skill tricks us into thinking complete and self-
sufficient, even though there is only one full stop, nevertheless,
that death was a terminus at which all of us stopped, and from
which we set out again later in different directions. We never
looked back.

I met Kevin as I climbed up the hill from the Gaol Gate. He was
sitting propped against the steel bars of the College, his coat
raised around his ears. His head hanging. I could see, even
before I recognised him, that he was drunk.

– Did you hear what I did? He was looking up at me. I
wondered if he could see who I was.

– Kevin?

– Jesus, man, he said.

I helped him up and he leaned heavily on me. Where was he
going?

– Man, he said, I haven't a fucking clue. Know what I mean?
Your place or mine?

He laughed loudly and repeated it several times. Your place
or mine.

It wasn't far to my flat. On the way he argued with me about
directions, insisting that I lived somewhere else. As we passed a
garden with blackened hydrangeas bulging out through the
fence, he leaned over and vomited noisily. When that was
finished, he threw his head back and said – That's better
anyway. I felt I had to get that off my chest. You know what
they say . . . Drink it down it'll do you good and get it up you'll
feel better!

– What were you saying? You said you were after doing
something?

– Shit. Don't remind me.

He got up again and we struggled on. As we walked he told me.

– It was Kelehan's lecture. You know. The influence of *Beowulf* on Einstein's Theory of Relativity or something. Jesus, I hate Anglo-Saxon. Anyway, he started off with the slides again. The whole place in darkness at the flick of a switch. Presto, like. A moment of awed silence. Then – the Ruthwell Cross.

– What else!

– Every bloody lecture has a slideshow, and every slideshow starts off with the Ruthwell Cross. Anyway, the spirit moved me for once. As soon as I saw the Ruthwell Cross, and all the nuns with their pens poised, I couldn't stand it any more. So I shouted, I quote, an obscenity at the darkness. Only Kelehan was standing just behind me with the fucking remote control button.

– What obscenity?

– Ah, I just said fuck the Ruthwell Cross or words to that effect.

– What did he say?

– He threw me out. Blasphemy *et cetera*. The nuns were very upset apparently and were demanding an apology.

– Did he say that?

– Or words to that effect.

– What did you say?

– I said the nuns were entitled to be upset. I said it was a despicable thing to do, but that I was under a lot of strain at the moment and I hoped they would accept my apology in the spirit in which it was intended.

– So?

– So I'm only barred until next week. The nuns took a maternal interest in me and recommended a good prayer group, so I went off and got pissed out of my mind.

– A perfectly natural reaction.

By now we had reached my flat. He threw himself down on the couch and began to snore almost immediately. I went to bed myself and slept until the early hours. When I woke eventually to go over to a lecture, he was sleeping like a baby and the flat reeked of stale beer and other people's clothes.

Later he was awake. I fried sausages and eggs and bread and we ate it listening to the one o'clock news. The price of beef, it seems, was going through the floor. Now I cannot remember why, but I remember we smiled knowingly – Beef is not going to go through the floor around here, we were saying. Students do not come in for such luxuries. We spoke for some time about food. Eventually Kevin asked me if I knew Eileen. But everybody knew Eileen.

He said he had a date with her and did I think she'd go far. Everyone knew Eileen was easy. She would sleep anywhere for anything. There were dozens of people who boasted having slept with her.

– The best thing about Eileen, he told me, is that she has a car.

Then we spoke about campus politics. We were agreed that the new Union president was a cretin. His campaign had been one of carefully printed literature and well-organised public meetings. He was Ógra Fianna Fáil. Trust Fianna Fáil to organise it down to the last detail. We had distributed carelessly typed pamphlets for a left-wing candidate who had secured about six per cent of the vote, but retained the undying respect of the student body.

– So when are you meeting Eileen, I asked.

– In about an hour. Here.

– Here? How does she know you're here? Jesus. You were waiting for me last night!

He grinned.

– Well, he said, I could also fall asleep on the road. I did it before. If you didn't come along.

He had cleared the table and aired the room, and generally made himself useful around, so I didn't object. Now, while I transcribed notes I had borrowed, he washed the ware. The clatter of dishes and the smell of soapy water reminded me of home. I could almost sense my mother standing behind me, facing out through the deep windows at the geraniums or the snowdrops she husbanded through the winter. The sense was painful.

Soon Eileen came. She was one of the College beauties with an unusual face that looked dull in repose but was attractively mobile. When she smiled it seemed to go into shards, like glass or facets of a kaleidoscope. She had a raucous voice, and a fund of obscene stories. They left together in her car, and after they were gone I settled down to serious study. They did not come back, and so, after dinner, I went to bed with a book.

When they did come back, I heard their voices calling me through the letterbox. They were outside in the rain and I could hear the engine of the car running and wipers dragging across the screen. I wanted to pretend I had heard nothing, but they just kept calling, so in the end I let them in to drip around the floors of the flat. Eileen switched off the engine and left the car parked where it was, half in-half out of the road. They were both drunk, and possibly high as well, and in high spirits. They had brought a six-pack and a bottle of cheap wine with them – Hirondelle I remember it was called – a two-litre bottle. Eileen told jokes and recited verbatim snatches from *Annie Hall*. Kevin recited a poem. We put on Leonard Cohen and listened while we drank. Eileen said 'Chelsea Hotel' always reminded her of herself. The bit about getting away and talking so wild and so free. She said she felt she talked too much and we both said no, that it was great to meet someone who talked as much as ourselves. So then she stood up and sang 'Chelsea Hotel', standing with her hands by her sides and her head thrown back in the attitude of a folksinger. She sang it like a ballad, a song of bitterness and pain. When she was finished, she slid in beside the table and drank what was left in her glass with a flourish, but we didn't feel like clapping. For a time we could think of nothing to say.

Eileen began to cry quietly, cradling the glass in two hands. She said we were nice boys, and why was it that she couldn't always go out with nice boys. Kevin said he wasn't sure he liked the idea.

Then they danced for a while and I sat on the floor.

I stayed on the floor when Eileen and Kevin moved to the couch. I think I may have passed out or drifted into sleep, because when I woke up they were making love. I sat there for a moment watching them, mind clarified by unconsciousness, and saw the languid movements that are the language of the body, the small silent lock that a man and a woman turn, that brings intimacy and pain, safety and rejection. It seemed to me for an instant that I was watching the coupling of mythical creatures – a Paris and Helen, a Deirdre and Naoise. Then the mood passed and I felt the sour wine on my tongue, acid tumbling in my gut. It was five o'clock on a winter's morning and I was cold.

I got up and opened the curtains and the lights had gone out all over the city. Houses were shut down. Nothing moved except the couple on the couch behind me. I left quietly and went to bed. Later I heard Kevin in the toilet, and later still I heard Eileen singing in the kitchen. I remember thinking they were here to stay and I would have to make sure my landlord didn't find out. Thinking of my landlord, I drifted into an uneven sleep, in which I returned periodically to near waking to hear the strange sound of someone else's morning.

But Eileen and Kevin never really moved in. Every morning they made plans about where they would go next. The fact was Kevin had no place of his own. He simply hadn't bothered to look when the rush of advertisements came out in September. He had drifted from friend to friend since then, kipping on floors and armchairs, sustained by late nights and beer. Now, instead of moving in, his belongings began to accrue, each day bringing something forwarded from another doss. The last to come were books – scattered, lent, forgotten. The hated *Beowulf*, *King Lear*, Coleridge's poems, Berryman and Roethke, MacDiarmaid. Abused prodigals, they took their places and were as unassuming as they could be while at the same time exuding an impression of permanence. When the books arrived I knew I was stuck with Kevin. For a vagrant, he surprised me by the extent of his baggage. Eileen, on the other hand, had nothing to impede her, as if anything heavier than a change of clothes would have fatally burdened the red Mini.

Most of the time they were useful. Kevin cooked well. Eileen was fanatically clean. Sometimes I arrived home to find they had prepared something exotic. Smells filled the flat, the hissing of pots, the burnt smell of spillages. On one occasion all three of us wrote an essay I had to hand in the following day.

What I found difficult to bear was the way their intimacy took control of the place. It was everywhere. Eileen's pants hanging out to dry. Underclothes lying on chairs. Tooth-brushes, hairs on the furniture, notes. Even worse because less tangible was the air that filled every corner. I began to feel as if I was living their lives, as if I was an element in their complex union, a temporarily unused organ. The time would come when I would be again called upon to respond autonomously to stimuli, when expected reactions would be demanded of me. In the meantime I must agree to be tended and ignored.

One day I came in from a walk along the river and knew immediately something was happening. The door to the living-room was ajar and through the opening I could see they were on the couch. I went straight into the kitchen. As soon as he heard me, Kevin came out. He was wearing a vest and shorts. One sock was still on.

– Hi. You're back.

I said I hoped I wasn't intruding.

– Jesus, man, it's all over now. Are you making tea? Bring us in a cup when it's made, will you?

– Fuck off, I said. I was annoyed. But I made the tea anyway.

They sat up when I came in. They seemed to be careless of their nakedness in a way I had never seen before. Eileen was naked, but had covered herself with his army-surplus jacket. I could see a single white breast, banded above and below by a faint suntan. As she moved her hand to take the tea, the skin stretched and softened, and the nipple quivered when she moved. Kevin stroked her arm as we spoke.

– We've something to say man, Kevin said. Eileen giggled.

– I'm not pregnant or anything.

– You're going to be engaged, I said. It will be in *The Irish Times* and it will be a long engagement until Kevin can get a job to support you. It was a joke, but they didn't laugh. All right, I said, you've decided to go steady.

This time they laughed. Then Kevin looked sheepish and Eileen poked him obviously in the ribs. He spoke slowly and carefully in the way they must have planned.

– Look, he said. Jesus, I mean here we are, right? Living in your flat. I mean, it's generous, you know. Above and beyond the call of duty. You don't owe us anything. So, Eileen was saying – we were both thinking – that we ought to split the rent. Three ways, fair enough. And we owe you a few weeks. No bull, three ways exactly. Eileen has the waitress job, and I have the grant. What about that?

I didn't want to say I would prefer it if they left because I knew they would, leaving an irreparable gash in the fabric of my days. But I knew if I let them pay, I would be stuck with them. I said I couldn't possibly let them pay anything. They argued a bit, then suddenly they caved in and Eileen reached completely out of the sheet and grabbed me by the head with both hands. Tears swelled in her eyes.

– You're just beautiful, she said. You're so beautiful. She dragged me against her and I felt the warmth of those breasts and the smell of bodies and lovemaking. She said – We have a surprise. We're planning a trip and we want you to come along.

– A trip?

Kevin said – We're going to drive down to Dingle. Stay in a place down there for a couple of days and drink ourselves blind. Talk Irish and all that meaningful bullshit. Eileen is doing Irish!

– Where are we going to get the money?

They laughed.

– That's what we're telling you. We have the money. The grant, right? And Eileen has her job. It'll be incredible.

It was settled. We were all going to Dingle as soon as it could be organised.

That night there was a party to celebrate the decision. They went around the College all day announcing the trip. The story was fantastic enough to attract hangers-on. I caught up with them at half past ten in Starry's and was given a small whiskey and a pint of Carling. A medical student I knew was singing 'Peggy Gordon' in the style of The Dubliners, including the Dublin accent, and Eileen, fully clothed now, Indian style, with beads and bracelets, was listening intently, her mouth slightly open, a pink tip of tongue between her teeth. Kevin was arguing at the bar, with pursed, frustrated gestures. I was stopped as I went to find a stool, by James Keane, a young poet. Almost incoherent with drink, he accused me of being bourgeois and soulless. Then he began to tell me a joke about a condom and a thermos flask, breathing rapidly in my ear. I remember the punchline was *Sure I'll be on the job for twelve hours* and it was a good joke. I said I would have to remember that one and he laughed loudly.

Kearney, one of the department tutors, an MA student, was kicking me in the ankle as I stood there, so I left the poet and sat beside him.

– That was an awful fucking essay you gave me, he said. I could have done without that.

I didn't tell him it was a three-way production. I explained that I was caught for time, and that having Eileen and Kevin staying with me was an exhausting trip. He winked suggestively and said – I'd say you wouldn't get a wink of sleep with those fuckers, hah? At it all night. Eileen is fine half!

– A whatayacallit *ménage à trois*. Fuckin' hell! And he groaned suggestively.

Now that Eileen and Kevin had become long term, I was surprised by the number of people who hadn't slept with her. It was as if the relationship that had developed had called their bluff. Not that anyone came up to me and said hey, I never slept with Eileen, I was only joking. It was obvious enough, though, in the way they spoke about her. Kearney, for example, had once boasted to me that he had screwed her three times in one night on the back seat of her Mini. I remembered that, because I remembered asking whether it was possible to make love in the back seat of a Mini, and he had made the same wink and said something about the Kamasutra and acrobats.

Somebody had a guitar, and in the public bar a box-player was found, who for a tray of Guinness played until closing time. When we were put out, I told them to follow the crowd to my place.

A lot of people were dancing in the living-room and the air was heavy with smoke. In the bedroom people were sitting around drinking quietly. Here and there a couple grappled desultorily. It was in the kitchen that the serious drinking was happening. The six-packs and wine bottles were ranged on the counter and the sink was full of empties and caps. A confused Kearney was jammed against the sink by a dark-haired woman who kept saying he was invading her personal space. The medical student, who was drunk and surprised to find himself at a party where he knew nobody, was singing snatches of 'Raglan Road'. The guitarist was sitting cross-legged on the kitchen table, apparently taking up little space, and picking out the notes of a tune the box-player was giving him.

I was looking for Eileen and Kevin, but couldn't find them. Instead I found a girl I knew sitting on the end of the stairs drinking from the neck of a bottle of Paddy.

– I'm going to kill myself, she told me, matter of factly. It's a cry for help, of course. I wouldn't do it if I didn't need help.

I said – If you kill yourself here, it'll be embarrassing.

She looked at me blankly. I said – I'll have to explain to the landlord how I found a girl on the premises who isn't mentioned in the letting agreement.

– Fuck off, she said, and went back to drinking.

I sat down beside her and after a time she passed me the bottle.

– Do I know who you are? she asked. I told her we knew people and who I was. You're OK, she said. Anybody who knows my friends knows me.

Her name was Terry.

– Want to dance?

She smiled crookedly and winked.

– Fucking drink, she said. No good.

She got up and walked unsteadily ahead of me into the living-room. When we began to dance she wrapped her arms tightly around my neck and put her head on my shoulder. I put my hands on her back, inside her shirt, and we danced like that for a time. Then we went into the bedroom and sat in a corner. There were fewer people there now, and somebody had made a joint. It passed slowly from finger to finger, and when it shrank it was held on a pin. It was wasted out before it reached us, so another was rolled. I pulled deeply, holding my breath, and heard the ritual quiet bells. Blindly I passed it on, but she didn't smoke. Instead it began its passage once more, a glowing tip circling like a rosary, until it expended itself in warmth.

The conversation was haphazard.

– Oh, great hit, someone said and some poeple laughed tenderly.

James Keane, the poet, declared that Dylan had betrayed us. The revolution, he said, could do without Dylan. Terry began to sing 'It ain't me, Babe' and everyone listened intently. After two verses she stopped.

– I don't smoke shit, she said, because I like to keep a clear head on me. Shit only screws you up.

– Oh no, I said, you have it all wrong. It's the other way round.

A chorus approved me. We were all upset.

– No, Terry said. It's always the same. Anyway, if you're going to smoke you have to be happy, right? Everyone nodded.

– Well I'm not happy. How could I be happy? I'm going to fail my finals, right? My dad'll beat the shite out of me. I'll be destroyed. My best friend split with me last night. I mean, I'm totally fucked up, right? That's it.

– Hey, somebody said, there's a law. Your old fella can't beat you.

Someone else said – So why don't you do it, Ter? I can see it on the headstone: She took her life as lovers often do. Don Maclean, he added informatively.

– Anyway, she said, I don't give a shit.

– Any chance of a shot at that bottle, Ter? Reluctantly she passed it on, and it went around and came back almost empty. She swore loudly and shut up. When the joint came round next time, she took it. I turned around to watch her, and as I watched I realised this was her first time. An excess of affection took me, and I wrapped my arms around her and hugged. She seemed to diminish in size as she pulled on the joint and the red tip intensified. She spluttered and coughed as she inhaled, so everybody laughed loudly. Afterwards she sheltered against me and smiled broadly at everyone.

Later I heard the red Mini outside, and Kevin and Eileen came in. They were aruging and their voices could be heard even before they got out of the car. I got up to see them and it was only then that I realised the party was over. The kitchen was empty. A single couple was still dancing in the living-room and the box-player and the guitarist were finishing off what was left in the wine bottles. I told Kevin and Eileen they had missed a great party and left them to evict the remnants. The poet was asleep on my bed so I woke him up and threw him out. Then Terry got up to go.

– So? she said. So thanks anyway for the party.

– Please don't go, I said. Were you really going to kill yourself?

She smiled. – I'll stay as long as I can sleep in my clothes.

I agreed and she got inside the blankets quickly. I stripped to the Jockeys and we curled against each other in the cold sheets. Our hands warmed each other, and slowly she allowed me to touch her. She had small soft breasts and when the nipples hardened they sprang away from the touch. Some time later we made love and fell into a deep and untroubled sleep. When I woke in the morning she was gone, but had left a note.

It's Sunday, in case you didn't know. Gone to Mass. Back for breakfast. Don't get up. Terry.

2

Kearney arrived on the pretext of giving me back my essay. It was a wet Tuesday evening and we had just managed to coax a fire into life in the living-room grate. It was the first time we had ever lit a fire there. That was Terry's doing. At the moment he called, she was kneeling in front of it, face and hands blackened and smelling of smoke.

– I brought back your essay.

– Come on in. You know Terry?

– Oh, I know Terry, he said, managing to make it as suspicious as possible. How have you been keeping, Terry?

Terry told him to fuck off and carried on with the fire. Now she was holding the front page of *The Irish Times* against it and the draught was roaring in the chimney.

– Listen, I really came over to ask if you knew anything about Kevin.

– Why?

– Well, for starters, I didn't get an essay from him for weeks. (I knew Kevin almost never turned in an essay. He had long ago decided he could do without the ten per cent they represented on the paper.) But apart from that I hear he's gone off the rails a bit. Knocking around with Eileen. You know the way it is, they're bad for each other. That's what I'd say.

In truth, I had seen little enough of Kevin. He slept here most nights, sometimes Eileen did too, but since Terry came I had kept up a regular attendance at my courses and so I was often out before he got up. The same was true for Terry. We often attended each other's lectures in fact. I wasn't sure what his condition was. But Kearney's interest was strange.

– I'll tell him you were asking about him. He'll be surprised.

– Overwhelmed, Terry said. A brown circle was forming on *The Irish Times*.

I said – Watch out, Terry! And almost immediately the paper caught fire. She dropped it straight into the grate and bundled it in with the fire-tongs.

Kearney looked like he was planning to stay, so I said I had work to do, thanked him for dropping back the essay and got him out.

– He makes me squirm, Terry said. There's something behind all this. That bastard hasn't an ounce of humanity in his body. He reminds me of my ex-boyfriend.

– The one who drove you to suicide, I joked.

– That bastard. And it's no laughing matter.

I cooked and Terry talked. If I remember rightly, it was a chilli or a curry. It was mostly beef we ate. You could buy steak for almost nothing down in the English Market because of the Foot-and-Mouth outbreak. I can remember the onions watering my eyes because Terry made a thing of wiping them with the sleeve of her blouse. I could smell her scent even over the smell of the onions.

She told me about her father, a schoolteacher in a small country school. She said everyone hated him, and hated her as a result. He would creep up behind them as they were writing, and lift them out of their seats by the short hairs of their necks. That was his favourite trick, she said. And she always had to be best in her class. He started to beat her the day she went into first class, and to the day she left home he would take her pants down and flail her with his belt. If she struggled, as she rarely did, he would drive her around the room, sometimes even with a stick, or a brush handle, once even with a knife. If she escaped, he would take it out on her mother, so that in the end it was easier to take what he gave.

She learned never to shout or cry, because none of her friends knew. Nor could she tell them. The humiliation for a seventeen-year-old of being beaten like a child was too great to bear. She was sure that once the initial sympathy had worn off, she would merit only their contempt. And out of this certainty grew another – that somehow she deserved it, if only because she never tried to escape.

The older locals respected him as much as the younger ones feared him. They called him The Master to his face or in his absence. It was an axiom in the parish that The Master puts manners on the young pups. Not only did he put manners on them, but he found them work as well – farm labouring mostly for the boys, if they didn't have a farm of their own, and shop work for the girls. People could point to his creations as upstanding members of society.

But that wouldn't do for his own child.

– In the beginning he worked me till I hated him, but in the end I worked myself to get away. Then I hit this place and I just blew up. I suppose I'm completely fucked up now. I'm going to fail my finals and he'll kill me.

Terry often said this, and now, as always, I comforted her as best I could, but I sensed something else in the way she said it, something that was beyond comforting, beyond restitution. It was as if failure was a kind of faith, as if she were simply repeating her belief like a prayer. And sometimes it seemed like a perverse hope. Nevertheless she went to lectures and wrote essays regularly. During all that time she never missed one, never tried that trick with the bottle of Paddy again. And I take pride in that. We kept each other on the level in many ways. We stayed at home a lot, drank cheap wine from Galvin's Off-Licence, glutted on cheap beef from the English Market and made love in front of the fire or went to bed early and made love in bed. We were tender to each other, both hurt, both healing in our own way. We were lonely and needed each other. I suppose we were simple, or naive, having no thought for time and what it might bring.

She loved to drink while we made love, red wine like blood on her lips. And in her passion she used to say everything and cry like a child. Often as we approached the height she would beg me never to hurt her, and her trust overwhelmed me.

Once I asked her why she continued to go to Mass when she was living in sin. Insurance, she said. Fire insurance. We both laughed, but I knew there was something more behind it. She got up every Sunday morning, sometimes she crept out so as not to wake me, sometimes even she was back before I noticed she'd gone. One evening she went to confession and afterwards she talked about going back to her own place – a bedsit in the suburbs.

– But I need you, I told her. I won't be able to do without you. I'll fail my finals.

– You don't need me as much as I need you, she replied, and anyway if anyone is going to fail their finals it'll be me.

I said she was behaving irrationally, that if there was a God he couldn't have any objection to us. I wanted to say that, no matter what God wanted, I wanted her to stay. I wanted to say that God must be a cruel bastard if he would send each of us back to our separate loneliness after all. But mainly I wanted to hold her for ever, not to let her slip out of my fingers, out of my life.

But she didn't go. Instead she began to feel guilty about our lovemaking. She would be reluctant for a time, capitulating reluctantly, afterwards sleeping uneasily. Things were not made easier by the fact that Kevin and Eileen were quarrelling a lot now. We still rarely saw them, but at night we could hear them from the next room. I knew they were both drinking more than they had been. They would stay out till the small hours, then ramble home, waking us as they came in, the house filled with the crazy pattern of their voices.

We tried not to know about it, but Terry became increasingly uneasy. And I began to feel that the house was somehow polluted, tainted, and that our love was being corrupted by the presence of Eileen and Kevin.

One day, after they had a particularly bad row, Terry decided
we had to get them out.

– They're freeloading on you. They're using this place as a
dosshouse. You have to put them out. Jesus, they'll destroy you
anyway. Take a look at yourself! You look like you haven't slept
in a month. Which, as a matter of fact, you haven't.

– I can't do it, Terry, I told her. Kevin is my best friend. I can't
do it.

– Well, what about what he's doing to himself? She's a bitch if
ever I saw one. Everybody knows about her and Kearney. She'll
eat him up.

– What about her and Kearney?

Terry looked at me as if she had only now realised what a fool
I was.

– Everyone knows she's with him when she's not here.

– Jesus, I said, I never knew you listened to the sca.

It was meant to be cutting.

As it happened, I met them both at a meeting shortly
afterwards. It was an Ógra Fianna Fáil meeting, and we had
gone along to heckle. There was a big crowd there, and there
was a lot of enthusiasm and rhetoric. A student called Mac-
Carthy was speaking when I arrived. He was talking about the
great intellectual and moral loss that had befallen the party.
That was because Dev had died that autumn, after a decade or
so of blindness and deafness as President of the Republic.
MacCarthy kept referring to him as The Long Fellow as if he
knew him casually. Anyway I heard shouting from the far end
of the hall, well away from the exit, and almost immediately
Kevin and Eileen burst from the crowd and rushed the podium.
In a matter of seconds the speaker was pushed aside and Kevin
was shouting about Pol Pot. When the party lads began to jostle
him offstage, he suddenly shouted that Dev was a wanker and a
woman-hater. Somebody lashed out at him and blood blos-
somed at the side of his nose. Eileen shouted and somebody else
hit her. They were dragged down into the crowd and gradually
the mayhem reached the door. When they were ejected, I

followed and found Eileen gasping for breath, and Kevin sitting on a step. Inside the uproar was dying down and MacCarthy was voicing the spirit of the nation, and lo and behold, who also spilled out but Kearney. He spoke quietly to Eileen while I held a handkerchief to Kevin's nose. They laughed over something. When Kevin was ready to get up, Kearney was gone. Kevin said – Where's that fuckin' shifty bastard Kearney?

Eileen shrugged.

Apart from a bloody nose and a few bruises, Kevin was OK, and Eileen was only winded. I took them up to Ludgate's for a pint. Bill Ludgate wasn't too happy about serving me, but I told him it was medicinal and that we'd be out as soon as health had been restored, so he left us alone. We went into the small room where there was a blazing fire.

They talked all that night about the trip to Kerry. They hadn't forgotten it. It was still on. That is, if Terry and I would come along. They wouldn't go on their own. The only problem was money. They were after going through Kevin's grant, more or less, and Eileen was getting fewer and fewer hours in the take-away. A lot of it went on drink, but they had bought books as well, and clothes. Kevin had a fantastic pair of boots, and Eileen had silver earrings. If they could get enough money together, they'd take off tomorrow, enough for petrol for the Mini and a few nights' B & B. They'd hit Kerry like a hurricane.

Terry, according to Eileen, was the most wonderful woman in the country. I was incredibly lucky. She mentioned John Lennon and Thomas Hardy by way of comparison. I had noticed before that Eileen's field of reference was very broad. Now she told me she hoped Terry was a good fuck because I deserved it. *She* was, she said emphatically, which was more than Kevin deserved, and anytime I could change places and she'd have the better bargain. By then we were all very drunk. We made our way back to the flat with a couple of six-packs and woke Terry up.

Kevin had some dope and we drank and smoked until we all felt elated and exhausted at once. I seem to remember Eileen and Terry singing something in duet, Kevin gave a fireworks display by turning out the lights and twirling a lighted cigarette very fast so as to make magic shapes in front of our slow-motion eyes, and I recited the first part of *Kubla Khan*, a poem which had never failed to get a response in such circumstances because everyone knew it was supposed to be about an opium dream. Terry and I went to bed very late and woke in the same mood of elation. We stayed in bed all morning and went out about two o'clock to get something to eat in the Kampus Kitchen. There Eileen tracked us down, demanding we pack our bags. We were going to Kerry.

3

None of us had enough money to stay in the guesthouse, booked by Eileen as the cheapest dive in Kerry. Fortunately we had brought sleeping bags as a precaution against what Eileen called Kerry Damp, a kind of rising dampness which she claimed infected every bed in Kerry. We spent the nights sleeping in turns, twisted impossibly into the back seat of the Mini. We woke up in a different place each morning, but always facing out to the taunting clarity of the Atlantic air. Our clothes got damp as the dew slipped in through the leaky bodywork, and our bones got cold and stiff. On the third morning the Mini refused to start, but fortunately we had parked at the top of a headland, so we pushed it until it spat smoke and jerked away from us. Naturally we all fought like sharks, and like sharks the suggestion of a hurt to one of us drove the others into a frenzy of cruelty. We made it worse by drinking in the pubs until the very last moment, unconsciously or consciously postponing the minute when we would have to look at the Mini and say – Well, whose turn is it?

The days were different though, as if a malevolent spirit settled on us at lighting-up time. The days were crystal clear, brilliant with light shattered off the sea. We bought cooked chickens and beer and ate them on the sand, tearing the chickens apart with our hands. Afterwards we played football with a beer can or walked along the foreshore. There was the privacy of the marram and the warm joints of sand between the rocks. And there was always so much to make up, so much to say, and it all gave the days depth and turned them into idylls.

Once we talked about our childhoods. We had all been Catholics, Terry in a way still was. Eileen came of party stock – Fine Gael, farming and the confraternity as she said. Kevin and myself were both solid middle class, middle Ireland. We marvelled at how badly our conditioning had gone astray.

– Here we are, Kevin said, flaad out on a beach in Kerry, littering the place with chicken bones and empty cans of Harp.

– Not to mention the sex, I added.

– The sex, he said, is only fucking outrageous.

– And not a whiff of that shithead Kearney.

I said nothing. He wagged his finger at me.

– I know your type. I know what you're doing, you shagging literary wanker! Thinking about God. Or better again, not thinking about God!

– If the fellows at the office could see me now!

Eileen sat up suddenly. She had been stretched out with her hands over her eyes, the winter sun glaring down on her.

– What difference is there? she said. Sharply, there was an edge in her voice.

– There's a world of a difference, I said. Jesus.

– So you smoke dope, she said. You make love in the grass when there's no one looking, so you read Sartre and all that other shit. But deep down you're the same. So is Kevin. So am I.

– None of us are the same, I cried. I was hurt by what she said. – None of us are the same as our parents.

– Prove it, she said.

– How? If it isn't obvious anyway.

– It isn't obvious. There was a smile shimmering at the edge of her lips now. I'll show you how.

She stood up and looked at the sea. Then slowly she took off her clothes and kicked them into a bundle. We lay there staring at her until she stood totally naked, so that we could see the winter raising gooses on her sides. Then she began to walk slowly down to the sea, without stopping, without looking back. I remember with absolute clarity the sound of the waves tumbling on to the sand and broken shells at the water's edge, the colour of her hair against the light, the way her ass dimpled at the thighs when her leg swung back. We were enthralled.

She stepped in gingerly, testing, then she turned and it seemed she was coming back, but she stopped again and went in, and didn't stop this time until she plunged in head first.

We were excited by her courage and ashamed not to follow her. Her beauty paralysed us. We stared frankly, but nobody spoke until she was dressed again. Then she said that if we hadn't the courage to do that, we couldn't say we had left it all behind. Soon she began to shiver, and being nearest I gave her my sweater. As I laid it on her back, I felt my arms were enclosing an incredible animal, as pure and as fearless as a unicorn.

– You know, she said, Terry is the only one of us who is different. Look at her. She's totally naked.

I looked at Terry then and saw that she had been crying. Her face was streaked still, even as she brushed at it. She and Eileen embraced, their arms locked tightly into the flesh, and Kevin and I, sensing that they were beyond us in some way, got up and kicked a can around on the sand between the rocks and the sea.

That night was warmer than the others, the kind of pet night not unusual in the South. Clouds had come in and there was a suggestion of rain in the air. Terry and I walked along the headland and sat staring out at the blackness of the horizon, listening to the waves roll along and expend themselves on the rocks. Occasional phosphorescence winked at us.

– She's beautiful isn't she? Terry said.

I was cautious.

– This is a change! I said. Where's the Whore of Babylon we were talking about a few days ago?

Terry looked fixedly out across the rocks. After a while, as if I hadn't interrupted, she said – And she has no shame or inhibitions. She's lucky. I wish I was her.

– You're wrong there, I said. Not to want to have shame. It's eating her up.

She thought I was dramatising.

– Just because she drinks too much all the time?

– And smokes too much and fucks too much. And all that. But that's not why I'm saying it. I mean it. She's dying.

– Of shamelessness. Terry roared with laughter. She laughed so much she fell back against the heather, the better to laugh at the sky. I waited until she was finished and had wiped the water from her eyes.

– So, I joked in a German accent, ze cause of death? The Shvine hat no shem!

– I suppose, Terry said, serious this time, I suppose she's a kind of whore all right. But everybody wants a whore, isn't that right? Isn't that what Freud said? Everybody has to have two women. One is a virgin and the other is a whore. One is innocent and trusting and dependent and the other is danger-ous and desirable. One is for sex and the other is for home.

I said – Freud thought that was a disease.

– So what? Some people need their diseases.

– Nobody is really like what Freud thought they were.

– Some people are, she said. Oh yes they are.

We heard their cries from across the strand on the way back and Terry looked intently at me. For the first time I found her gaze unbearable. But they were fighting and the car looked as if it was going to collapse, or else the handbrake would slip and the car would drift down into the water. If it had done so, they would certainly not have noticed.

It was probably that night, as we strove to sleep in the cramp of the car, four of us, sprawled against each other, between the fretwork of the steering wheel and the immense mound of the door handle, legs on the handbrake, arms over heads, the gear lever always in the wrong place; it was probably that night that she told us about her sister.

– Margaret is her name. And she's four years older than me. Wild too. All the girls in our family were wild, even though I'm the worst. She used to sneak out to go dancing at Redbarn, when my parents thought she was still in bed. She had a special miniskirt for the occasion, short almost as far as her ass. She kept it laid out under her mattress, so it was always ready when needed, as she said. She used to walk the mile to the main road in a pair of wellington boots, with this miniature mini under her ordinary skirt, and when she got to the crossroads, she used to hide them in a hole in the ditch until she came home again. Then she'd put on her high heels. A minibus used to drive round the villages and the crossroads to pick people up for the dance. There were showbands there, Dickie Rock and Joe Mac. Everybody loved Joe Mac because he used to tell dirty jokes and do rip-offs of people. And the guy who drove the minibus was an ageing teddy-boy – slicked hair and pointy toes and all. He used to make passes at the women in the bus – it was always women, I don't know how the fellas got there. They had cars I suppose, or bicycles. Margaret used to say that the smell of a woman's underarm was all he wanted. When he'd get them to The Barn he used to ask the girls to let him smell them and if they let him, he'd go off happy into the trees.

– Anyway The Barn was this huge dancehall on the edge of a huge sandy beach and all the couples used to go down into the sand. That's why my father never let Margaret go to the dances. So she used to sneak out. Well, as I said, Margaret was the wild one. She used to tell me every morning who she went dancing with last night. And if I was really lucky, she'd even tell me what he did. All I remember was a lot of hot French kissing. Sometimes, if he was the rushing type, he'd shove his knee in between her legs and that'd probably satisfy him. He'd go back to his farm in the hills and cream off for a month thinking about it. It was all push and shove, roving hands and slaps, and tickles and bites. I used to think, I was thirteen or so at the time, that if sex was like that, I'd rather play Camogie.

– I used to hear the minibus coming back, and if it was a calm night with a light breeze from the south, I could hear fragments of their voices going across the fields. I used to stay awake on purpose to hear them. The countryside is lonely at night for a young girl. Nothing to break it up except the sound of a dog barking or a fox, or a distant car.

– One night she came straight into my room to tell me about it. She'd finally met a someone she actually liked. He was an accountant in a firm in Youghal. After that she slipped out all the more often. I was amazed that she got away with it. She'd tell my mother she was going upstairs to study, that was the year of her Leaving Cert., and then she was going straight to bed. Then she'd get out through the window and meet him someplace in his car. Several times I thought about telling, in fact I threatened it more than once, but always something happened to put her back in favour. She might say that Dominic – the accountant – had sent me a box of chocolates, it was always Irish Rose, or she'd let me in on some detail of what they were doing. I remember when I first found out it was gone beyond the French kissing. It was a casual remark of hers, that he hated bra fasteners or something, or that he had cold hands, but it set me thinking and dreaming. For the first time I began to consider what a man's hands would be like. I went through all the usual discoveries then, in the space of a few weeks. Or at least it seems like that now. And during that time I developed an obsession about spying on them. When I was able to stand it no longer, I followed her one night. It was springtime, and it wasn't so dark as it had been, so it was easy enough. I saw them in the car together and I saw the fake struggle she put up. I saw him lift her sweater, and I saw his head go down on her breasts. She threw her head back and her mouth opened slightly, and even from where I was hiding I could hear her breathing. I lost my courage, and ran home as fast as my legs could carry me.

– Of course, the outcome was inevitable. Thanks be to Christ for the pill! She got pregnant and he married her with very little persuasion. They make a nice pair. Good to each other and everything. Three children. She was the youngest Lady Captain of the Golf Club a couple of years ago.

Eileen said nothing for a while. Then she slapped her fist off the dashboard.

– I hate that fucking bitch! she shouted. And her prick of a husband! She had the neck to tell me I should get a grip on myself! Jesus fucking Christ! She said I was throwing myself away!

We went to Considine's Pub and Ballad Lounge most nights we were in Kerry because there was good music, and they had a square of timber in the middle of the floor where you could get up and dance. Eileen and Terry knew all the dances, mostly polkas, and they spent an hour or two dragging us on and off the floor and showing us the steps. Kevin came off badly from it, but I began to get the hang of it, at least to the extent that I was in the right place at more or less the right time.

One night we found ourselves in an argument with three men at the next table. We were talking about O'Riada. We were saying that he had put life back in Irish music. That people like The Dubliners and Planxty would never have got off the ground without him.

I had had a drop too much and felt sentimental and inspired. I said his love of music killed him. That Ireland was a sow eating her litter. I think I may even have quoted Kinsella's elegy – *I am in great danger, he said* . . . Certainly I was lyrical about it. Anyway the talk turned to the Provos, as all talk of culture in Ireland must eventually turn. It transpired that the men we were talking to *were* Provos. One had been over the border. The older one had been out in the fifties. He reminisced about jumping ditches with a bag of guns to avoid the Special Branch car that was coming to take him away.

Naturally we kicked ourselves under the table and put our heads down into our pints and paid attention to the music. True or not, trouble would be big trouble if it came. There was no sense in drawing the local Provos down on us.

But Eileen suddenly produced a block of hash that nobody knew she had and began to offer it around.

– Look, she said to the one who had been out in the fifties, you can put it in your pipe! I never tried it that way, but I'd say it's brilliant! Even if it isn't a waterpipe.

She was brittle and dangerous like that, as dangerous for us, at least, as the men were. But the fifties man scowled at us and turned his back. One of the others called us fucking hippies, and did we know that it was people like us that were sapping the courage of the Irish people? Drug addicts and degenerates. Over the border, he told us, they'd kneecap us. Eileen told him she knew a Kerryman who thought that kneecap him was the Irish for I don't know, and tried to explain the joke when they didn't laugh.

For the rest of the night we managed to keep her under control. She danced a lot, increasingly wild, drawing attention to herself more than we wanted, but she kept away from the Provos. They drank their pints and stared at her from time to time. I met one of them in the toilet and he looked out of it. He was leaning his head against the wall of the urinal to steady himself. I remember he pissed down the leg of his trousers. I began to relax. As drunk as that there was no danger in them. After that I started to enjoy myself again. I took Eileen out for a waltz and she pressed against me as if I were her lover, and I couldn't keep my hands still. She looked up at me once and I said – I can't help it Eileen. You're so beautiful.

And she just smiled and told me to carry on, and if she didn't like it she'd have stopped me long ago.

– But take your time, she told me. I like it slow. Remember that.

At closing time we took the remains of our pints out into the open and finished them off in the shocking cold of the street. It seemed to us that the air and the stars cleared our heads and we talked and talked out there until the cold got inside our clothes.

The Mini was parked along by the quays and the three Provos were standing beside it.

– Jesus Christ, Kevin, they're waiting for us.

– We can't run now, he said. They'd catch us.

– Good night lads and lassies, the fifties man said.

Someone, probably the drunk one, had puked on the front windscreen. The third was standing on the bumper and bouncing up and down.

– Why couldn't you buy an Irish car as you were at it, the fifties man laughed. A Ford. Made in Cork where you come from yourselves. This oul yoke'll never stand up to the climate around here.

Eileen saw the car and exploded.

– Get off my fucking car, you bastards. I'll fucking kill you.

She rushed them before we could stop her and the fifties man had her in his arms in an instant.

– Fucking hippy! He was very strong. Listen boys, he told us, why don't you shag off and leave the ladies here. Or even if you want to take the other one, we'll keep this one. Sure we could see straight away the kind she was.

– Yah, said the drunk, she's a whoor alright.

– A fine half, the third added conversationally.

Kevin went for the fifties man with fists flailing and then the drunk stepped in. He was lighter than I imagined he would be, fast as a cat. His blow struck Kevin on the cheek and seemed to lift him backwards slightly. A second blow caught him on the ear and he fell down. He retreated quickly from a badly aimed kick and the drunk laughed.

– I destroyed the car, he said, but you know the way it is. Sure a feed of drink can't be always good. I always said Considine's stuff was sour. But I'm a lot better now. I got it off me chest.

– I'm getting a feeling about you, me lassie, said the fifties man. Down here.

He shoved one hand between her legs and she started to scream. He tried to shut her up, but she bit him. I could see the others were panicking.

– Jaze, said the third man, shut her up or she'll have the guards out!

Terry began to scream then as well, and Kevin and I shouted for all we were worth. Lights began to go on in the cottages along the quay.

The fifties man shoved Eileen back and the others began to run.

– We know where you are, he told us.

He punched Eileen on the breast and shoved her against the car. Then they were gone. We could hear the thump of their feet echoing from a side street. They were gone so quickly I almost didn't notice.

Eileen cried all the way back to Tráigh an Fhíona. Kevin drove and Terry hugged her in the back seat. She had to change her clothes because of the smell, and since she had washed some things in the sea that morning and they weren't yet dry, she had to put on some of everybody's. Then we all sat out, wrapped in our sleeping bags, and talked. Eileen broke up some cigarettes and rolled a third of the dope into a joint and we all smoked. We smoked another after that and it calmed us. We lay back and looked up at the stars, and ribbed Eileen about not telling us she had it before. Then we pooled all the sleeping bags and got in under them and fell asleep locked in each other's arms. The dew woke us, and our clothes and sleeping bags were wet through. It was six o'clock and dawn was still a long way off. We got into the Mini and drove home, as much for the warmth of the heater as to escape.

4

Terry

My father is here. I heard a knock at the door. Jim is out, but it isn't his knock. I know it's Daddy. He has a firm knock, practised. A hand that knocked on doors to complain about truancy, or to say he had found a place for someone. The

Master's hand. The first thought that comes into my mind is, will he beat me? I don't know what I would do if he beats me here. Once, when I was about fourteen, he heard I was smoking. The nuns told him. We used to smoke in the toilets and we always had a first year to keep watch. But the first year ran away instead of warning us and we were caught. For the others it was an embarrassment, the fear of being kept in at night, extra homework. But my father was waiting for me when I came home. He had a letter in his hand and I could see the convent motto, probably hand-delivered by the same first year that ran away. He caught me by the ears and pulled me into the kitchen. My mother was sitting at the table as pale as a sheet, folding and unfolding her hands. He stood me up against the sink, and he seemed quite calm. I didn't look at his face, but he seemed to be different, without rage, almost sad. I wondered if I was going to escape this time. Then, without warning and in total silence, he began to strike me – in the stomach, on the chest, on the shoulders – careful as he could be not to leave marks, though he didn't always succeed. Then in a pause he was telling me, quite calmly, that he was suffering for my sin of disobedience, that what I had done was a shame to my family, that he regretted having to hurt me, that to spare the rod was to spoil the child. When I was crumpled up against the sink, he kicked me and tried to stand me up again. I didn't cry loudly because my best friend was waiting for me out on the street. She might knock on the door at any moment and someone would have to explain to her, or he might even make me go out and tell her to go away, and she would see quite plainly what was happening to me.

Nothing ever came out of those beatings. I never became resolved about leaving home. I never grew suddenly courageous like someone in a film or those powerful women who ring in on radio talk shows. In a way I became more cowardly, more shamed, more hypocritical. When the whole school discovered that someone's father had gone to England and was living with some woman, I threw in my lot with the jeerers. I took as much pleasure as I could out of making veiled remarks to her and sniggering afterwards because she didn't seem to notice. I laughed when a friend got pregnant and I pretended to be helping her so as to get the inside information for the other smokers in the school toilets.

And my father never became contrite and tearful like the psychology books say. He never apologised to my mother or me, or anyone else that he harmed. Instead he got a heart attack one day as his class was doing a geography exercise, and had to retire at the early age of sixty-three. Retirement didn't suit him and he spent his time stalking up and down the village and writing letters to the newspapers in Irish.

I almost never see him. When I have to go home I do – Christmas holidays or for a family funeral. Not much else to draw me back. There is always the excuse of my studies, which he seems to accept. He has never enquired about my results. When I say my holidays end at such and such a day, he doesn't raise his head from the newspaper. My mother looks away and doesn't speak.

Now he is sitting at my table, drinking tea from Jim's mug, looking caved in a little, slightly hollow-faced. He wants to know who I am sharing my flat with. He looks around in the pause that follows his question and precedes my answer – a pause too long I know, but I have not prepared an answer, never even expected to have to give one, don't know whether I will tell him or tell him a lie such as I have grown used to telling.

His eye rests on Jim's dark green jacket and I see him calculating that such a jacket could never fit me, even with my taste for outsizes. (And as I see all this, I see Jim's hunched back in the jacket and the way he turned his face towards me, myopic and bland, as if the book he was studying had robbed him of reality.) Then he notices that the mug has Jim's Mug glazed in green along the side opposite the handle. He puts it down quietly and looks at me. Waiting for an answer.

Why should I answer him?

Why should I tell him one word?

Fuck him.

I could tell him Jim will never be back.

I could say I think Eileen has him. That I've seen them dancing together and that her body is incredibly beautiful and that I don't blame Jim for wanting her instead of me.

– His name is Jim. (Why should I protect him?)

He straightens up. The quiet look is there again. He reaches down into the pocket of his overcoat (does he have a cane?) and his hand slowly fishes up a handkerchief. He blows his nose.

– You're going to come with me. I took the precaution of finding a flat for you, not quite so near the College. I would bring you home to your mother this minute except that I have invested so much in your education and you might as well finish it. The landlady is an elderly widow, a Mrs O'Donoghue, the sister of a man from home. I was instrumental in procuring a place for her daughter in the Civil Service, so I can trust her completely. A good Christian woman. I hope you haven't lost your head completely? You're not, aha, expecting? Mrs O'Donoghue drew the line at that. She has no wish to draw shame on herself.

He blows his nose again. In the time he is speaking, he keeps the handkerchief poised in front of his face, casual, cold. But I see now that there's a tremor in his hands. Parkinson's disease, I think. Somebody told me all old people get it. In this case too late. Certainly not fear.

– Don't pack anything. In case your – paramour (he coughs and laughs a small, tight laugh) – should barge in on us. The man who owns the mug. I'll come back myself.

He drives me about two miles as far as a place called Summerton Avenue or Summerton Close. Unbelievably the house is called *Xanadu*. A small, fat woman opens the door. She has bad teeth and even as I shake hands with her I smell rather than hear her words. My room has a single bed with not enough blankets, a kettle on a tin tray, and a cup and saucer. A large wardrobe with a mirror on the door, a straight-backed chair. I am to eat my meals with Mrs O'Donoghue, the keeper of the keys. I may not leave the house or enter it without her permission. The door closes at nine-thirty, ten on Saturdays. No Drink. No Men. No Pets. No Food in the Rooms. My father will drive up once a week to make sure I'm still here. Mrs O'Donoghue will telephone if there is a breach of discipline. She knows everything. No secrets.

As soon as they go, I climb into the wardrobe and close the door. There is a comfort in the smell of darkness and camphor balls. In the fact that outside the darkness is a mirrored door. After a time I get out and pull the blankets off the bed. I take them into the wardrobe with me. I roll them into a ball behind my back and go to sleep.

What I'm really worried about is what happens when she's finished with Kearney. I mean I can hold out indefinitely. But I saw her dancing with Jim. He couldn't keep his hands to himself. And she liked it. I could see that too. She's animal in a way. She just needs to be stroked in the right places. Like my dog. If you scratched him under the hard part of his ear, he would go quiet and his eyes would go glazed, almost hooded. I've seen her like that too.

Jim would like to fuck her. He won't do it as long as I'm around. But he becomes attached easily. Look at the way he took to me. He kind of grows on people, like ivy. After a time, to break him loose you have to rip things out. If she goes for him, he'll take her, I know it.

Then what will I do?

Mrs O'Donoghue doesn't know I managed to smuggle some shit in here last night. I waited till she went to bed and I smoked it all. I bombed out totally and I thought I could see Jim and Eileen in bed.

She has one of those model bodies, like they hang clothes on in shop windows. Her breasts are bigger than mine. I think I have arrested development. The strange thing is that while I was watching them, I was enjoying myself. I wasn't jealous at all.

Does this mean I would like to go to bed with her too?

I have sex on the brain.

Because I'm not getting any.

What about Mrs O'D?

Mrs O'D says the sheets on my bed are the ones she laid her late husband out on. Wilful waste, she says, makes woeful want.

Saw Jim.

– What happened? Terry?

I was a bit out of it. Mrs O'D doesn't recognise the aroma of cannabis resin. I've cut a square hole out of *A Critique of Pure Reason*. I get the hit by snapping the book open, inhaling quickly and snapping it closed again. Almost nothing escapes. Who showed me how to do that?

– Terry?

I can remember telling him to fuck off, himself and Eileen. I can remember him going too. In the light of a little reason I can see I was wrong. But who cares!

I have been permitted a visitor. Because she was female. Needless to say it was Eileen. Mrs O'D told her I was studying too hard altogether. That she wasn't happy about the bags under my eyes. She told Eileen she could stay the night because Eileen said she had driven up from home. She even put cushions and blankets on the floor.

– Let's get locked, Eileen said.

I tapped my nose. Mrs O'D would guess. Instead we smoked from the square hole in Kant's *Critique*. Eileen made love to me, of course. I expected that. When she began to take my clothes off, I felt suddenly powerful, as if I had willed it. I felt as if every muscle, every nerve ending, was so electric, anything they brushed against would implode. So I touched her perfect body as tenderly as I could, not wanting to destroy her.

The act itself disappointed me. It was pointless, singular, unforgiving, but afterwards my head was comfortable and at home against the crook of her neck. It would have been the perfect end if Mrs O'D had come in with a nice tray of tea and toast to find us naked together, a siren and a child, asleep in her funeral sheets.

KATHERINE O'DONNELL

Emotionally Involved

Clare is propped up on a high stool at the bar counter. Her skinny body twists as she sucks hard on her cigarette. I can never get used to the way that her hands are always shivering very slightly. She speaks in a very low murmur, hardly opening her mouth. Her eyes squint and blink past me. It always feels as if she is not talking to me, but is allowing me to hear her talk to herself. She is so honest that it's embarrassing, but I'm addicted to that thrill of being a voyeur of her fears and dreams. I feel honoured and disturbed by the intimacy. She really could have been pretty, being so petite and blonde, but everything in her troubled features and gestures asks you not to look at her. I sit at the counter with her, leaning in towards her to hear her talk, and trying to avoid her smoky exhalations.

'On one particular day,' she says, 'an old lady was placed by her relatives in the institution where I work. The old lady was very frail and had become confused in her thinking. She had the severe misfortune to come into the hands of a cruel attendant. Like all successfully cruel people, this attendant is very clever, and she fools some people and frightens the rest of us who know she is a sadist. By an accident the old lady was left solely to the attentions of this attendant. Some people do not like being tortured.'

She flicks her cigarette a few times and stares abstractedly at the ash as it falls off into the ashtray. Then she says: 'I work the night shift, and as I'm pushing open the heavy oak doors to enter the white hall and begin my night of work, I hear a strong voice shouting. I find the old lady, her eyes peeled open in shock, shouting. The attendants leaving brief me. "There was trouble when her urine bag tube was being inserted. She was an unmarried woman." They use the past tense. "There was blood on her sheets. We have brought all the doctors and the priest to her. We have given her as much sedative as she can take. We have placed her as far away from hearing people as we can."

'"Rape!" is what the old lady shouts: "Rape!"'

Clare is silent for a couple of minutes and I wait patiently for her to continue. Sometimes, if I interrupt her stories with comments of my own, she just says 'Yes' and then smokes silently, entirely unable to continue, no matter how much I try and coax her. We both remain in the silence then, unhappy, until she starts to talk again or I say a quiet 'Goodbye.' I'm afraid to hear the rest of this story, but it would be worse to have her stop. I've learned not to make comments, but to wait through the pauses for her slow communication.

Clare continues: 'All night the old lady cries. I position a small radio transmitter at her bedside, which carries her voice to the receiver I wear on my hip belt. Her cries follow me through the night as I work with Mary, the other attendant, turning and washing and cleaning the sleeping bodies of the old women. During the night, the tiny little old nun in the long white habit comes to the old lady's bedside and sits there tending her throughout the night – mopping her brow, moistening her lips and reciting constantly a low and powerful flight of prayers. In the early morning the old lady is stil crying, although her voice is weakening.

'When my work is over, I gladly switch off the box on my hip and shut off her cry and the nun's prayers. I walk out through the heavy oak doors into the autumn dawn across the city. I walk up the steep hills to the narrow building where I have a bedsit, and I climb the long and wide flight of stairs to the very top of the house. I let myself into my room. A dusty layer of faded velvet curtains blocks the daylight from stealing through the tall, high window. I crawl on to my mattress, which is tucked into the back of the room where the ceiling slopes down to the floor, and I curl up as small as I can under my blankets. I try to sleep through the day, but all I hear is the old lady's constant cry.

'On my way into work, walking down the steep hills at twilight, I stare at the wet slate roofs, silver in the late sun. I watch the smoke from the evening coal fires bathe the city rooftops in a wispy fog, and I find myself repeating the old lady's word, over and over with each and every downward step.

'The attendants leaving brief me.

'"We have brought all the doctors and the priest to her. We have given her as much sedative as she can take. She has been crying all day, although her voice is cracking, she still cries. The little old nun has been with her all day. We are going crazy with her, all except that attendant who has been singing through her work. The nuns say they believe that there can be no blame involved, but we would not be surprised if that attendant got a promotion to supervise the laundry."

'Throughout that next night the old nun prays and the old lady cries. Her voice leaves her, but still she mouths that word. The halls echo with her silent moving lips. All the old women lying in their white beds know that something is wrong. All night the other attendant, Mary, and I move through the halls turning their stiff bodies, one by one. We change the sheets and wash the backs and between the legs of those who soil themselves. Many of them are crying, even in their drugged sleep. I like working with Mary. We have worked together for some years now and I like working with her; we work swiftly and she never says anything.'

As Clare is talking, I'm hearing that old lady shouting.

Clare goes on: 'We clean the dentures which have been placed in the mugs at their bedside. I scrub the pink plates free of yellow scum. I pick the even smiling teeth free of undigested creamed food. The old women are upset, so there is a lot of work to be done, chasing through the halls to answer their cries. I usually like to feel how quickly and silently, how efficiently and expertly, I move through the halls to anticipate and tend to the old women, but this night I become confused in chasing the moans. I turn the box on my hip belt off. My uniform clings to the sweat at the small of my back. I put my hot face to the cold old walls. I press my ear to the wall. I put my finger into my other ear and rock there for a while, trying to remember what it is I should be doing.'

Clare doesn't know that you can't admit those things. She pushes up the sleeves of her light grey cotton top and turns her palms up on the bar counter. We both stare at the inside of her forearms, her pale skin and long blue veins. When you stare at her she really is so pretty, but it's like a secret because nobody notices. She sees me looking at her and she hunches over, wrapping her arms across her midriff.

She drifts back into remembering the hospital and says: 'Hannah calls for me in the night. She generally snores through the night, lying flat on her back, with no pillow; her toothless jaws and bearded chin playing a fluttering and sucking accompaniment to her dreams. She often laughs loudly and gives friendly shouts in her sleep. "Darling, darling, darling child, where the fuck are you at all?" Her hands wave the air in a search for me. "Here, sweetheart," she says and hands me her glass eye, covered in part with green strings of mucus. She slips under her sheet and is asleep. I disinfect her too blue glass eye and leave a note for the morning staff.

'Towards dawn I go to her, the old lady, and I put my hands on her cold old hands, which clutch the white blanket to her neck. "Rape!" she mouths. Her eyeballs are so expanded in her head that there is room to push a meat skewer into her open pupils.

'"I know who raped you," I say to her. "I will stab them." She stops for a moment and then her lips move over the word.

'I don't know if I sleep during the day or not. If I do sleep then that old lady and her cry is the sole substance of my dreams.'

Clare, Clare, Clare, Clare. Clare, would you stab somebody who hurt me? That's the only thought in my head. I hate this when I crash into being in love with her. She continues to talk so slowly and precisely as if she's remembering the lyrics of a song.

'When I go into my workplace the attendants leaving brief me. They are tired. They both stand with their arms folded, leaning against each other. One is very large, her sleeves are pushed up tight over her fat forearms. The other is skinny, her hip bones pierce through her tight white uniform. She is very pale and has blueblack circles under her dark eyes.

'"It is still how it was with her. The praying nun has been with her all day. She is still the same," they say.

'I'm only just started work,' said Clare, 'when who should swing by but the cruel attendant. She hails the praying nun with: "Hello, Sister, how are you?"

'"Oh, Kathleen, aren't you very good to come by again," says the nun.

'"Ah sure, not at all, I'm just after finishing my day at the laundry and I thought that as I'm passing the door I'd call in and see you both. How's the poor old cratur this evening?"

'"Much the same."

'"Well, God help us, all we can do, I suppose, is to pray for her."

'The old lady is beating the thin white blanket with a bony fist. She has her eyes fixed open and staring on the cruel attendant. I'm standing at the door looking at her, looking at the cruel attendant. The old lady eventually gets to rasp: "Rapist."

'Kathleen laughs a clean, loud laugh that lifts right up from her belly. She inhales and smiles with a deep magnificence that lights up her flushed face.

'"She's soft in the head," she says.

'"Yes," said the old nun. "Yes."

'But I could see that the nun was made anxious by the presence of the cruel attendant. The cruel attendant made a move towards the old lady. She went to stroke the old lady's head.

'"Stop," I heard myself say.

'She stroked the old lady's head.

'"Good night now, love," she said, and kissed the old lady's forehead. She left in good cheer.

'"It's not good to get too emotionally involved," she said to me and Mary on her way out, "but it's hard to help yourself, isn't it?"

'It was a long time before the old lady stopped shaking.'

I point to Clare's coffee cup and raise my eyebrow. 'Yes,' she says. I wave to the barman, who is at the end of the bar reading the sports pages, and I get two more instant coffees. I get him to slip a measure of whiskey into mine. I need the comfort of it. I've never been in this bar before. It's right downtown in the heart of the shopping district, tucked away on a nondescript side street. Last week the clocks were turned back an hour.

Outside it's raining and the Saturday shoppers are scrambling in the early dusk to finish their errands before nightfall. There are a few covert drinkers sitting alone in the stained-glass gloom, staring at the bottom of their pints or the burns in the carpet. Decades of cigarette smoke envelop everything with a soft orange film. Nobody I know would ever come in here. It's a perfect place to meet Clare.

Clare is talking: 'I like working with Mary. We have worked together for some years now. We work swiftly and she never says anything. She has two girls and at our break she likes to knit for them. She works at night so that she can be at home to send them to school, and so that she can be there when they return. I sometimes ask about her girls, Michelle and Danielle. It's not that I want to hear about them, but I sometimes like to see how her face changes; she becomes flooded with love and she talks on and on. I try and pretend to listen, but she stops when she realises I'm just staring at her. She must work because her husband has not had a job in years. He used to collect her in the mornings. He used to stand leaning against his red car and he would say "Hello" and "Good morning" and such to the prettiest nurses. He is very handsome, nearly beautiful, which is surprising because Mary is awkward and does not know how to be beautiful. I knew that her husband had left her because the other attendants had asked me if Mary had said anything to me. I was glad she hadn't. "He is such a good looker," they said. "He probably has a lovely new girlfriend. The bastard." That's what they said.'

Clare played with a packet of sugar, crunching the granules through the paper with her coffee spoon. 'I was sick with the old lady's cry,' she said, 'and I wanted to see some love. I ask Mary about her girls, Michelle and Danielle. She starts to cry. I watch as she cries so hard that she starts to sob. I go to the linen press and get her out a small, soft, white towel. She stops crying quickly, like a switch has been turned. She stares at me like she's looking through glass and then she shudders and she stands up and we begin to work.

'We work for many hours. Just before dawn properly begins, I stand out on the fire escape to smoke a cigarette and look at the stars. They are most brilliant when there is a thin line of silver-blue in the east. I like to smoke when the air is so clean in my lungs and so cold in my bones.'

This is an image of Clare that I find easy to picture. A skinny young woman in a thin white uniform, standing on the fire escape of an immense Victorian building hidden behind high walls; a building with windows so high up that the people inside can see nothing but small frames of sky. It was the workhouse in famine times. Clare, a skinny young woman on a fire escape, sucking deeply on harsh tobacco in the cold night air just before dawn.

Clare continues: 'As I'm out there having my smoke, I'm listening to the box on my hip belt and I'm hearing the nun's novenas and the old lady's breath expelling her cry. I hear Mary come into the room and start to talk with the nun. Someone turns off the receiver. I can hear no more. When I go back inside, the tiny little old nun comes to me and says: "I have arranged that her sister comes to visit her tonight. She will be here very shortly."

'"What? No. That's too upsetting. It's stupid. Why did you do that, Sister?" My anger bursts all over the word "Sister".

'"I am doing all I can," the nun says, "and nothing is helping. Maybe her sister can reach her. Now why are you so angry with me?" she asks.

'Because I feel so useless, is the reply I cannot utter.

'"Go and do your work," she says, patting my clenched hands.

'I go to Mary and say: "Mary, is the old lady not too upset to have visitors? Her sister will be very upset to see her in this state."

'Mary says: "It's the not being heard that is killing her."

'"How do you know this, Mary?" I ask.

'She presses the heel of her palms into her eye sockets. She says: "I don't know if it's going to work. I don't know if it's going to work." And then she said: "The worst of the damage was done in making them too terrorised to tell. God forgive me, I knew that something was very wrong but I was innocent."

'I stayed with her until she had the glass look in front of her eyes again.'

After a while Clare slowly began again: 'Well, the old lady's old sister comes to visit, a taxi brings her to our place. She is very petite and wears a tailored navy blue wool coat and a blue silk scarf at her throat. She carries a navy blue leather handbag and she wears navy blue leather gloves and shoes. Her silver hair is in a permanent set. She is crying.

'"Rape!" the old lady mouths. I've been raped, she wants to tell her sister.

'"I know, I know." The old lady's old sister holds her and rocks her, crying. "I'm so sorry," she says, "I'm so sorry."

'The old lady died peacefully on the following day. I was surprised to realise that she was a very beautiful old lady. The little old nun and the old lady's sister were very pleased with her peaceful death. They felt that she had made a good recovery. I don't know what Mary thinks, but I try and believe them.'

Clare's fingertips shook lightly on my wrist. 'But do you know what, Ger?' she said.

'What?' I asked.

'I've been missing that shouting old lady. I wanted her to keep shouting. For all of us.'

Location, Location, Location

'Is there anyone here?

'No, no.' The woman steps out into the aisle. Clutching my paper in my hand, I squeeze past her and slide down the seat into the corner.

'I'm going in a second anyway,' she tells me, drinking up the dregs from her cup and fumbling in her purse.

The waitress appears and tosses me her cloth. Before, she used to go through the obviously doomed attempt of leaning across two customers to try and round up the squashed peas and salt granules on the tables in front of me. Then one day she tossed me the cloth and somehow it seemed to work. We do it every day now. I tidy my patch as well as possible, even lifting up the little upright menu and cleaning under it before handing the cloth back to her. She returns it to some secret scabbard on her person.

'Are you having soup?'

She always asks me that and I always decline.

'Thanks, Angela,' the previous diner says as she leaves.

There is a menu, but I always go for the special.

'Ehh, wait till I tell you, there's . . .' Angela scrunches her eyes, 'ehh, pork chops, liver and bacon, steak and kidney pie, home-made burger . . .' Her pneumonic drill runs out of power. '. . . ehh . . .' she fishes out her note-pad, 'oh right, chicken, ham and stuffing.'

It's not bad actually. Three-fifty for soup, dinner and dessert and a cup of tea if you can fit it all. Great value. If there was anything to save your money for in this bloody town.

I plump for the pork chops. 'And a glass of water, please.'

I fold open the *Argus* and trawl desperately for events. First stop is the listing for the three-screen cinema. No change there. Any plays coming to the Town Hall? Doesn't look like it. I see Mickey Callan and Sandra Harty were out and about in the Seanchai last Friday night. And if the caption is accurate, and I have no reason to doubt it, Ben Wallace and Joe McBride enjoyed the night in the Rugby Club last Saturday. I come face to face with the Marist Confirmation class of 1956 and I put the paper down despondently.

I am beginning to wonder whether my job here will prove to be a snake or a ladder. I mean, I thought Waterford was a one-horse town. Jesus, this place makes Waterford look like the Calgary stampede.

Angela skids my glass of water across the table and follows it with a dinner-plate. 'There you are.'

I fold the paper and sandwich it between the menu and the salt-cellar. God, I'm depressed. This place is dragging me down. Ahh . . . I take an indignant drink of water. That's hot.

I cough and take a serviette from the dispenser on the table. I was trying to explain it to the mother and not getting too far. 'A market town,' she enthused as if I had not already served six long months. 'Have you found the library yet? Is there a Lions Club up there? Do they have the Round Table up there, remember the Round Table, Eamonn?' Grunt from the Dad, whose memory of Arthurian escapades seems less affectionate.

How can I put it into words? No planes fly over this town. There's no action. No soul, no romance about the place. The people here would slap Gene Kelly in galoshes, pack him home before he caught his death, the silly article. The town is into dour, grey reality.

I cut my dinner into strips and add salt. And it's not as if work is anything to write home about either. The worst thing about tax is not only is it dull, but it's bloody tricky too, a lethal combination. So much for getting experience of criminal law. The days are just dragging by.

But what if I expect too much? This is what she said and I was sufficiently defensive to indicate to me that there may be truth in it. Maybe nobody really likes their job. But you have to earn a crust somehow. Good to get the work. College was all about good times, but that's finished now. Maybe she's right. The salad days are over.

I take a mouthful of pork. It's not a cheery thought. That it's not just the venue. Maybe even if I get out of here inside a year and get a job in civilisation, it'll be the same. Maybe this is what nine to five is all about. Maybe this is life. Maybe baby.

Ever notice how the claim 'This book will change your life' sells books? Big time. Everyone wants to change their life. Is this why half the country watch the Lotto draw religiously, worry-beads of sweat on their brow, hoping against hope to get six figures? The fact that it is statistically more probable that a bolt of lightning will come in their window and burn 'G–R–E–E–D' on their glistening foreheads doesn't seem to bother them. Everyone wants to leap off the treadmill.

I take a forkful of creamed potatoes. They can't do potatoes up here at all. At least I had some decent spuds over the weekend. Is that pepper, I wonder? I empty some grey molecules on my palm and, reassured, chuck them at my dinner.

And I'm treading water like the rest. Weekends on friends' floors in Dublin, their VCR winking at me, wishing away the days in between. Twenty-four and so much more. What am I waiting for? To win the Lotto? To meet the right girl, settle down? Twenty-four, time to get serious.

Ulp. Is that it then? Is the game really up? What happened to the world I saw through Disney-tinted glasses as a kid, that world that seemed to hold so much promise? Maybe it was just a pie-crust promise.

'Jimmy, you boy you.'

'Francie, you hoor.'

Two builders arrive in a bustle of noise.

'What about the Clans on Sunday, Francie?'

'Ah, who's asking you, y'aul bollicks.' They exchange banter with the other diners.

'Is there anyone here?'

I get my fifteen seconds of fame. 'No, no, you're grand, work away.'

I know these two boys myself actually. Well, I've sat beside them before. The old fella with the open shirt in all weathers is Francie. The young guy down from me, well, he's at least thirty but his chest hairs aren't silver, that's Michael.

These are big lads. They have the full dinner and still want more: they eat like Irish navvies. I don't feel a lot in common with them, being from Lilliput myself.

'Well, boys.' Angela doesn't keep them waiting.

'How's it going, sexy?' says Francie, who obviously sees something in Angela that I don't.

'Wait till I tell yez, there's chicken, ham and stuffing, pork chops, liver and bacon, steak and kidney pie . . . and home-made burger. No, the home-made burger's gone, sorry.'

'No shepherd's pie, Angela, no?'

'Not today, Francie. Sorry 'bout that.'

'Not to worry, not to worry. I'll take the chicken.'

'And yourself, Michael?'

'Shepherd's pie, Angela, please.'

'There's no shepherd's pie,' says Angela, looking surprised.

'But I thought you said . . .'

'I was just asking her, that's all.' Francie looks at her with his eyes raised to heaven. He's delighted. I know he ribs Michael that he fancies Angela. He worked this out purely on the fact that they're both under thirty-five and unmarried. Romance is an actuarial calculation for these old lads.

'What were the others again?' asks Michael.

'Ehh, liver and bacon . . .'

'Aye, liver and bacon, that'll do rightly. And a glass of Coke, Angela.'

'Glass of milk for you, Francie. And yourself?' This is Angela's way of acknowledging that she sees me here every day: 'yourself'. If I open up on them with a machine-gun some day, she'll probably have a few theories on me, but they'll have to supply her with my name. 'Are you having dessert?'

I look down at my dinner. She's right, I have had enough. 'What do you have?'

'Wait till I tell you, there's lemon meringue pie, semolina and jam and rhubarb crumble and custard.'

'Do you have any ice cream? Yeah, I'll just take that so, please.'

'Tea or coffee?'

I always refuse either. I hand my plate across to Angela via Michael and go back to my paper. 'On the Town': this is some class of a social column. Basically they give a guy twenty quid to go on the batter and then he constructs a column with the names of all the people he can remember stumbling across highlighted in bold print. Best thing in the paper, according to locals.

'There's your soup, lads.'

'Friday night, being the night that's in it, I always like to head down to the Seanchai . . .'

'What time do the banks close for Easter?'

I look up in surprise. The question comes from Francie. 'Emm . . .' Why bother correcting him, one suit is the same as another to him. 'Four days,' I answer from my own knowledge.

'Aye,' he says and goes back to trying to butter a spongy slice of bread.

Oh well, so much for that.

'And who should I meet just back from Germany but **Una Corbett** *and her charming companion* **Helmut Dietenheimmer** *. . .'*

'There you are.' Angela plonks my ice cream in front of Francie, who whirrs it on. I wince as the first spoonful gives me a sharp pain behind my eye. It's actually straight from the machine, so it's fairly cold.

Michael leans forward to Francie and jabs a thumb behind him. 'He'll be getting his meals out for a while, I'd say, what?'

I casually look behind Michael's shoulder at the thick-set

customer at the take-away counter. I haven't seen him around town before, but he's wearing a suit, which narrows things down.

'Did you not hear?' Francie rolls a slice of bread into a cone and inserts it in his mouth without difficulty. 'She's taken him back.'

Michael looks at him in surprise. 'You're joking me. But I thought . . .'

'Aye,' Francie swallows without pausing in his speech. 'But he talked her round. He's two of them on the go now.'

Teresa, the owner, comes out to your man and serves him up his dinner on a plate covered in foil. He accepts it and makes some remark. I've never seen Teresa crack a smile before, let alone laugh with that kind of enthusiasm. The guy must be fifty at least.

'Jesus, he's some boy, Brady, isn't he? Ha ha.' Michael shakes his head with a detectable note of admiration. 'Smooth-talkin' old hoor.'

'Ah, don't be talking. This young one's supposed to be some bit of gear too. Consuela or something funny like that.'

'Sounds sexy.'

'Twenty-three years old. He's set her up in one of those new apartments. She still thinks he's going to leave the wife.'

Michael shakes his head and sprinkles his soup with pepper. 'I don't know how he does it.'

Francie rubs thumb and forefinger together. 'Money, boy, that's all it is. None of them want to turn their back on that.'

The beast gives a last bantering benediction to the staff and heads out. I can see him crossing the street and unlocking the door of a flash-looking car.

'Ah well,' Michael swallows a mouthful of soup. He seems to notice I'm listening and smiles at me impersonally. 'It was getting married so young that set him off.'

'Go on, you.' Francie reaches out and gooses the passing Angela. 'Don't mind him, Angela. He's only talking.'

Angela swats Francie with her cloth. 'What are you saying now, you trouble-maker?'

I stand up and burrow for the right change. Francie gets out into the aisle and wrestles with Angela as I try to put the change in her palm. 'Oh, Angie baby. You know I love it when you treat me rough.' The other diners roar their approval of the lunch-time theatre.

'Bye now,' I say, absenting myself.

'G'luck,' says Michael.

'Cheerio.'

I come out into the bright street and look up squinting. Well, that's something anyway. I need something to put this town and all its cynicism out of my head. I look at my watch. 1.40: twenty minutes. Head for water.

I always do that when the sun makes its rare one-day-only appearance in Ireland. If I were a painter, my easel would wear a groove on a river-bank.

By the time I get down there, the game is already under way. The sun plays a card from its golden deck and turns up the Jack of Diamonds. It twinkles roguishly before me as I stand and watch, transfixed. I've seen the old side-walk sharpie pull this trick so many times before, but I still can't figure out how he does it.

The light skates across the water like a lady-boatman. On the other side of the river, which I feel I could cross in five strides, a line of cherry-blossom trees release their petals to the gentle coaxing of the April day. A little pink snow descends. In a country without a summer, this is the best part of the year. In even another week, the leaves will gain ascendancy and the last blossoms will have flown away. Beauty is transience.

I walk along the water's edge and the shoal of sunshine follows. I moon-walk backwards unexpectedly, but I can't fool the sunshine which backtracks with me. I do this for a while, back and forth, like a child in a hall of mirrors. I see some cherry petals being carried gently downstream; they look like they're looking forward to seeing the sea.

I come to a park-bench by the water's edge. I look around me, feeling vaguely like I'm breaking a rule, then I feel the mostly green wooden boards. Still a little damp from yesterday's drizzle; cherry blossom petals from a nearby tree huddle together in a puddle on the slats. I sweep them off and some cling to my fingers. I lower myself down on the *Argus* and, closing my eyes, raise my face to the sun. The inside of my eyelids are coated orange with vitamin D. Gosh, I feel kind of sleepy; must be the big meal.

A gentle breeze tickles the back of my neck. I open my eyes again, unable to do without the sunshine. There must be something in sunshine, a mood-altering chemical, a kind of solar serotonin. I feel great. Behind the tops of the trees, a block of red-brick apartments peeks out, its shadow surmounting theirs on the water. They look lovely, not the least out of place, with their little balconies with wooden railings and sun-seats. Pretty. I put my hands behind my neck and bask in the reflected glory. I could even take off the jacket.

I take another look at the sun and, throwing caution to the breeze, remove my jacket. There is a curious feeling to doing this, kind of like removing the old dog-collar. I fold the jacket awkwardly over my forearm and rest it on my knees to keep it out of the wet. Another gust of wind picks up and there is a pink blizzard. A petal flutters down and crash-lands on my shoulder. Another follows and lands a little futher down my sleeve. I sit stock-still, doing nothing to disturb them. They lie where they've landed like confetti on a groom's shoulder. I sit in rapture.

It really is beautiful down here. I might even bring sandwiches tomorrow if it's fine, eat them here. There's an idea.

I wet my finger and pick up one of the petals on my shoulder. It's such a fragile beauty, wafer thin like the Host. Jesus, where did that idea come from? I look at my watch again. Five to. Yerra, I didn't get out of the office until ten past anyway. Time enough.

What's that? I hear something, something unexpected. I close my eyes and listen. I hear car-horns in the distance, but this is from the other side of the river. It's kind of indistinct. It's music, is it? Is somebody playing a radio in one of those apartments?

Then I see it. I can't believe I didn't see her before now. There's a girl sitting on the railing of one of the apartment balconies. She has long dark hair and is wearing a white T-shirt and blue jeans. Perched side-saddle on the railing, she's playing the guitar. Would you believe that? Playing the guitar! That's what the sound is.

I sit there with my mouth open like a frog looking at a fly. With the cascade of sunshine on the water, and the cherry blossoms swirling against the blue sky behind her, the whole scene is just . . . amazing. The beautiful young girl in the cool darkness of her casement, her elusive melody issuing forth on the breeze . . . This is a loveliness older than time. It's so beautiful, she is so beautiful.

I sit for a moment just drinking the scene in. How could anyone feel down in a world like this? I walk a little down the bank to try and get a better view through the trees. Who can she be? Where does she come from?

And then I realise: it doesn't matter. She's a tonic. Just when I'm totally teed off with this town and everything in it, I get sent this. Even if I never find out more about her, I'll have this moment, this sight, to keep pressed between the pages of memory like Wordsworth's daffodils. I am charmed by my own cupidity. This is great, I can face going back to work now. There is some glamour in the world after all. Everything's going to be just fine. I look up adoringly at this raven-haired girl. She symbolises potential, a wealth of possibilities. I'd give up a kingdom for this girl.

It's her. My heart hits the pit of my stomach, dumph, like a kitten hitting the bottom of a sack. Ah, it can't be, I won't let it. The town's grey hand reaches out and smudges my pastel idyll. 'Don't mind your princess shite, that's Brady's bit of fluff. Set her up in one of those new apartments, so he has. Sexy bit of gear, hah?'

How can I be sure it's her? She's a good-looking girl, could be about twenty-three. And that's an apartment. Two and two are four, Einstein. No, it's just my luck, that's all.

I sag down on to the bench like a punctured football. An unpleasant seeping feeling tells me I've missed the *Argus* by a fraction. I leap to my feet, fit to scream. The girl's barely distinct melody continues to waft across the water. A siren recedes into the distance.

Well, look, what does it matter? She's still a beautiful vision. It was a romantic notion, the first you've ever had in this town. But it spoils it, it just spoils it, all right? I think of that sleazy old bastard and I find myself actually kicking the stanchion of the bench. I can just hear him too. 'I know now, all this time I was searching for something, but I never knew what it was. Not till now . . . Not till I met you . . .' Don't give me this conversion crap: Damascus sees its first instance of road rage. You don't deserve her, there's no poetry in your heart, not like me, even if it is only a Wordsworth poem I did for my Inter.

I sit down again, this time carefully, and put my chin on my hand. Shit, I'm more depressed now than if I'd never seen her. And I still have to go back to work.

'Scotty.' A little dog, straight out of the ad for Black and White whisky, is snuffling against my shoe.

I pooh-pooh the owner's apologies. 'No, no, he's all right.'

'The weather's got him all excited.' The owner is a distinguished-looking old gent, with a 'tache and an Englishy accent. He tugs his lead but Scotty doesn't seem to want to be diverted.

Carefully shielding my jacket, I lean down and tickle the little dog under his neck. His dog-tag jingles. 'Lovely little fella.' I look up at his owner. 'I'll tell you, I know what it's like to be on a short leash myself.'

We laugh heartily. I pat Scotty on the head and stand up.

He gives the dog a proprietorial pat himself. 'It's not a day for working, is it?' he beams. I wonder if he's retired.

'Glorious, isn't it? It makes all the difference.'

'The summer's on the way for sure.'

We stand beaming at each other, two citizens of a country where the weather is genuinely conversational material.

'That would be a lovely place to live, wouldn't it? Right on the river.'

He flushes and I'm suddenly afraid I've offended him. But no, he's pleased. 'I live there myself, actually. Hold on, Scotty, we're going in a second.'

'You live there?'

'Oh yes. They are very nice too. How about you, you're obviously working in town?' Scotty is barking enthusiastically for some unfathomable little-dog reason.

'Yeah, I'm a solicitor's apprentice.' I put on my jacket and straighten the collar. Better get going.

'A solicitor, you say. Aren't you a great lad?' I look at my watch as he continues. 'My niece Sandra is starting in the Ulster Bank on Monday. What's wrong with you, Scotty?'

Scotty is still barking and wagging his little tail furiously.

'Oh look, it's Sandy.' The old man waves across at the building. To my astonishment, the girl waves back. 'That's her now. She's staying with me for a few days till she finds a flat. Say hello to Sandy, Scotty.'

I pat the persistent little terrier on the head as the late Consuela vacates the balcony and comes down to greet us. Oh well, what's a town only the people in it? What do you say, Scotty?

Woof woof, says Scotty.

I think I know where he's coming from.

Where Do We Go from Here?

I walked into Jackie's house the way I always walked into Jackie's house, through the backdoor without knocking and into the kitchen. The same way she always walked into mine. We were next-door neighbours and friends. And friends, as we always told one another, had no need to knock, had no business doing that sort of thing.

Jackie was standing by the cooker, lifting a saucepan off the front ring, naked as the day she was born. Milk boiled over the edges in large creamy bubbles, like something you would see in an Aero ad. She turned around instinctively when she heard me enter, and stood there facing me, making no attempt to hide her shame. If she had thought about it for even a fraction of a second, she would not have turned towards me, she would have turned away. I know Jackie, and I know that's what she would have done. But she didn't get a chance to think about it. She heard a sound behind her, and some reflex, some instinct, from way back in her primitive past, way back before people probably even wore clothes, caused her to turn swiftly on her bare heels on the cold tiled floor to face me. And it was probably that same instinct that held her hand steady as she did so, preventing any of the boiling milk from spilling on her bare flesh.

I should probably have turned my back on her, but once she had turned, and once I had seen all there was to be seen, we both understood it was too late for that. Jackie stayed where she was with the corners of her mouth downturned, her lips pulled in tight against her teeth, with an expression of sad resignation. Like someone who, having forgotten to close the downstairs toilet window before going on holidays, returned to discover that the cat had got in and eaten their goldfish.

It would almost have seemed like an insult to have turned away then. It would have made us both feel even more conscious of her nakedness. Worse than if I was staring systematically at each of her body parts. I became aware of my lips and realised I was copying her sad expression. She raised her eyebrows, wrinkling her forehead.

'Now what do we do?' she asked.

She stood there for a little longer, holding the saucepan out in front of her. It hid the lower half of her right breast from view. I watched the milky bubbles shrink, like balloons deflating, and slip back down behind the enamel side.

I shook my head. Partly in response to her question and partly because it was all that was left to do.

Then Jackie slowly turned back to the cooker and put the saucepan down on one of the cold rings. Although she had put the saucepan down, she still held on to its handle. She had goosebumps across both her buttocks. They reminded me of two small pale gooseberries. I saw her head shake to one side and her black hair flick across her left shoulder, then settle again.

'I probably should dress,' she said. She turned her head and half-smiled at me. 'There's hot milk here if you'd like a glass.'

We sat at the table in the kitchen, drinking the hot milk. Jackie had on a white cotton T-shirt and jeans. The bright sunlight from outside shone through the window down on top of her. It shone through the thin material of her T-shirt revealing her white brassière beneath it. I turned my eyes away.

Jackie looked up at me and smiled, spreading her lips wide, exposing her gleaming white teeth beneath them.

'So now you know,' she said.

I took a drink of milk. It was still too hot, and it burned on the tip of my tongue. The way it came out, she made it seem as if I had always wondered what she would look like with no clothes on, although I don't think she meant it that way. I think it was just something to say.

'So what do you think?'

Again she made it sound as if she was wanting me to make an appraisal of her body, but once again I knew this was not what she meant at all.

I shrugged.

'We're friends,' I said. 'It doesn't matter.'

She nodded.

'I know. You're right.' She took a sip from her glass. The hot steam rose out of it across her face like a mist, as if she were about to disappear into a dense fog. She put the glass back down on the table. Tiny webs of moisture were threaded about her eyelashes. 'It may even be the best thing that could have happened. Isn't that so?'

'It almost could,' I said. I felt a rim of milk gather above my lip. And before I could help myself, I licked it away with my tongue, all too aware of how suggestive it might have looked.

The reason I had called on Jackie in the first place was to ask her to go with me to a concert in the Guildhall. Some members of the National Orchestra were touring with an evening of chamber music by Beethoven. It wasn't really something either of us was passionate about, but we were trying to learn. We both felt that we were lacking a certain amount of culture in our lives, and we were eager to make amends for this. We weren't getting any younger.

We had gone out together on evenings like this before. We enjoyed each other's company. I had even gone ahead and bought the tickets. But now I was no longer sure I should ask her. It just didn't seem appropriate. But we had been sitting there for ages without speaking, and that didn't seem appropriate either.

Usually if I was looking for something to say, I'd ask her about Tom. If this was one of the periods she was seeing him or not? She had been going out with him for over four years now, in an on/off sort of way, as she liked to put it. He liked her a lot, there was no doubt about that. He had asked her to marry him on one occasion. That's when the first 'off' part of the relationship began. Jackie laughed when he asked her. She didn't mean to. It happened more out of embarrassment on her part, and she had told him this many times since. And although he knew it was true, it still upset him sometimes.

Jackie liked him a lot too. She just didn't think she liked him as much as he liked her, and she didn't feel good about this. She didn't think it was fair on him. She really wished she could like him more.

'I don't know what's the difference between our feelings for each other,' she said. 'I can't put my finger on it. But it's there all right. It just won't go away.'

When she talked about Tom to me, it was like he was in the next room, as if it were just possible he might overhear everything she was saying, and she always raised her voice slightly almost as if she wanted him to.

I liked Tom too. He was a good man. And I know he liked me. But all the same, when we talked we never really got beyond pleasantries. We didn't even attempt to. It would have been hard to know where it all would lead to if we did. We certainly never went out on an evening together. And no one ever suggested it.

'How long have we known each other, Jim?' Jackie held her glass between her fingers just as you would hold your face between them in horror.

I thought about it. Tried to recall exactly when it was we first met.

'It must be eight or nine years now,' I said. 'It was that time shortly after you moved in. Something was wrong with your electricity, and you came out to ask me if I knew anything about it.'

'And you didn't.'

'Not a thing.' I took another drink and placed the glass down on the table. I watched an inverted U of milk slip slowly back

down the side of the glass, leaving its mark behind like hot
breath on a cold window pane on a winter's morning. 'So
when was that?' I asked. 'How long is it since you moved
in.'

Jackie shrugged. 'I don't know. Eight or nine years.'

I laughed. 'So I was right then.'

Jackie barely smiled. Sometimes she didn't appreciate my
humour. She just about tolerated it. It puzzled me though that
she didn't know exactly when she moved in. I would have
thought everyone would remember something like that. But
then I suppose there are things more important about moving
than assigning to memory exactly when it took place. Jackie
moved here to get away from a long-term relationship that was
trying to come to an end but was dragging its heels about it.
'Someone had to do something,' she told me.

'That's a long time,' Jackie said, looking over at me. 'You
must know more about me than any other living person.'

Somewhere half-ways down my chest I became acutely
aware of the heat that the last mouthful of hot milk had given
off.

'You know a lot about me too,' I said.

'More than anyone else?' she asked.

I nodded. It was true. I had told Jackie all sorts of things.
Things you wouldn't normally tell another person unless you
were drunk or paying for the privilege.

She finished off her milk, then stood up and brought the
empty glass over to the sink. Her jeans were faded and tight.
They fitted her like a second skin. I looked at the smooth shape
of her behind. I remembered how it had been earlier dimpled in
goosebumps. And again the light shone through her T-shirt,
exposing her brassière underneath. The shape of her unsup-
ported breasts clearly came back to me. But none of these
memories reminded me of the Jackie I knew. It was as if I had
been looking at a different person all along. And now when I
saw her there bent over the sink, staring out the window, in her
tight jeans and her white almost transparent T-shirt, I didn't

know who I was looking at any more. Jackie? Or a memory? Someone from my imagination? Or someone who had never existed at all?

She spun around quickly from the sink.

'Take your clothes off, Jim,' she said.

I looked at her. I could tell she was serious. She really did want me to take my clothes off. My first reaction was to ask why. But something farther back than that already knew the answer. And I knew I would have to do it for her. I knew that our friendship deserved that much. That it depended on it.

I drank the last of my milk down. Like I was drinking a shot of whiskey. And stood up. I pulled my shirt out of the belt of my jeans and began to unbutton it from the bottom up. I took it off and laid it over the back of the chair. Then I pulled my grey cotton vest over my head. I kicked off my shoes and pulled my socks off. Jackie leaned up against the back of the sink. She watched me intently. She still looked serious. As if she were watching a documentary on television, dealing with some subject that was important to her. As if she were hoping to learn something.

I undid the belt on my jeans, loosened the top button and unzipped the fly. I tugged them down to my knees and pulled them off, one leg at a time. Then I pushed my thumbs into the elastic of my boxer shorts and took them off. I put them with the rest of my clothes, then stood there in front of her. She remained exactly as she had been. She didn't say a word or alter her expression. I didn't feel embarrassed or uncomfortable, just a little bored, as if I were waiting for a medical examination to come to an end.

I stood there for a few more moments. Then I raised my hands out in front of me and shrugged. I picked up my clothes and began to dress.

Before leaving I told her about the tickets for the concert.

'When is it?' she asked.

'Tomorrow night.'

'I'd love to,' she said. 'We don't do half enough of that. But I've arranged to go out with Tom. It wouldn't be fair to cancel it now.'

'No,' I said. 'I wouldn't expect you to do that. There'll be other times. This Culture thing isn't going anywhere. Not without us.'

Jackie laughed. I turned to leave.

'Thanks for the milk,' I said.

'You're welcome.' She smiled. She looked very pretty. 'It was a good afternoon, wasn't it?'

'It was,' I told her. 'I had a very good time.'

I opened the door and went out into the yard. I smiled back in through the window at her. It occurred to me that we always had a good time together. That it was one of the things I most liked about her.

FRANK O'DONOVAN

Candle Gazing

If you look at the flame of a candle for long enough, it's going to blot out everything around it. The surrounding distractions go first until you are left with the darkness. Then the darkness itself seems to melt away and the focus is entirely on the white flame of the candle, the intense, flickerless white light just above the wick.

So it was with me and Jazzer when I was fifteen and running with the gang in Cork. I didn't know it then, but it was the kind of crush that tends to blot out everything else. As soon as the intensity of my feelings for her got a hold on me, I could think of nothing else, and the ordinary, everyday world seemed to fade away. She filled me up completely and it was as if she was inside me, squeezing my inner organs so that I felt uncomfortable inside my own skin. Thoughts of her occupied my every waking hour and took over my dreams at night. Loyalty to anyone and anything else went by the board. The takeover was so complete that I didn't know what was going on until it was too late.

Jazzer was already a central figure in the gang by the time I started to drift around the edges, looking for a way in. I was drawn to the gang, like a fly to a zapper in a chipper, because I had to get out of the house at night. My ma and da spent their evenings in our corpo flat on the estate, occupying themselves with a litany of complaints.

'What's on the TV tonight?' he would say.

'A load'a rubbish.'

'A lotta filth, I suppose.'

'Sure, you can't watch it after 10.'

'Ah, I'm sick of watching the oul' TV anyway. I'd rather be reading the paper.'

'That's just typical of you, always with yer head in the paper.'

'Isn't it better than watching the TV?'

'But what about me, who am I supposed to talk to at night?'

'What's there to talk about?'

'What's there to look at on TV?'

'Ach, I should never have married you.'

'Nor I you.'

It went on like that. Da's favourite theme was escape: from the house, the estate, the job, his life. She always listened, even though she was bored by it, but then complained by repeating his comments privately to me the following day.

My escape was out the back door, over the wall to the field behind the row of tall, crooked houses at the bottom of Fairhill. I skulked around the edges of the bonfire where the gang gathered, passing butts of cigarettes and makeshift reefers from hand to hand, spitting in the fire and talking through their arses about the things they didn't even get up to in their dreams. Snatches of talk floated up from the pool of babbling voices:

'I finished 'im off, I'm tellin' ya, hit 'im with a pool cue . . .'

'Dead 'n buried . . .'

'So he said he'd read me me rights before I made the statement . . .'

'That mad bitch Jazzer was out with . . .'

How often I had heard that handle before I saw her for the first time in a haze of bonfire smoke. Her dyed blonde hair hung down her back in uncombed knots and she wore badly applied mascara, eyeliner, lipstick and caked powder. That first night she was fighting with one of the other stellas. She finished her off, holding her by the hair at the level of her knees, crowing with delight when she shouted to be let go. She pushed her away and sat down by the bonfire, triumphant, lighting a cigarette. I was turned on and off at the same time. I mouthed the words 'mad bitch' when I saw her chainsmoking cigarettes, pulling on joints and heading off on Nick's motorbike, her hair streaming in the wind, as if she was riding a wild horse, bareback. She sped up and down Fairhill, sometimes taking off over the fields towards Gurranebraher with a cop car in wailing pursuit.

Like I said, most of the gang were bullshitters, but a few you had to watch your back with. Nick, the hard man and head honcho of the gang, was one, Jazzer another, and, the most dangerous of all, Dino. Nobody knew just how dangerous he was until it was too late.

I sidled my way into the gang bit by bit over a few months, until I was part of the jagged circle around the bonfire. Getting in wasn't easy. Cork was divided in two when it came to gang turf. The river marked the boundary between the north and south rivals, the Norries and the Sorries. Gang warfare in neutral turf was common. It was a close-knit, suspicious scene and outsiders weren't wanted.

I took my turn swigging from the spit-covered bottle of cider and retched over the butts that came my way. I was disappointed with the lack of effect dope had on me, until I stood up one night and fell head first into the smouldering bonfire, to be dragged out feet first to howls of laughter. I even had a few tussles of my own around the edges of the main action that nobody took much notice of, but to me they were part of the rites of passage: the smoky fire, the smell of wet wood burning and the acrid stench of the odd tyre, the heady atmosphere of darkness and the street life were part of my newfound world, light years away from the front room of our flat where my ma and da groaned through their endless bitching. While I was becoming a man on the streets of Cork, they were dying their slow death in front of an open fire.

Even now, so many years later, my heart still races with excitement when I remember it all. These days my life is lonely by comparison, and when I think back it is as if I am looking through the wrong end of a telescope. Street life must have softened our heads 'cause we believed we were free. The cops couldn't touch us. They passed by regularly and tried to break up the group around the bonfire, but it was a half-hearted attempt that fell into a regular pattern. When the cop car stopped, the gang swarmed around it to hear a gruff 'move on'. When the car pulled away, we launched into a chorus of 'We shall not be moved.' Sometimes they did succeed in scattering the gang for a time, but it re-formed, like a mist that has been dispersed, as soon as the cop car was out of sight. Nick and Dino had it all sussed. 'There's fuck all they can do about it,' was Dino's cryptic summing up. Yea, it was magic, being young and lawless on the dark streets of Cork City.

Dino and Jazzer took no more notice of me than they would of a stray dog. Sometimes they sat around the fire late at night when the others had dragged themselves off home or to wherever they were crashing for the night. Jazzer was Nick's girl, but behaved like a flirt when she was alone with Dino. She would whisper in his ear and playfully massage his shoulders. They spoke softly as the night deepened around them and their talk was intimate and unreal, as if they were planning for a future they knew would never materialise.

The summer came and the talk continued over the cold stones of long-dead bonfires. It hung in the air around them and it now comes back to me in snatches, unrelated chunks that barely make sense, because one conversation, which I can remember in full detail as if I were hearing it now, in this very room, blots out all the others. It was mid-June, after midnight, and they were sharing a joint. I was miffed because they did not offer me a pull. A stray dog.

'. . . but you're the one that's havin' it off with him. You're the one who's causin' all the shit, it's up to you,' Dino was saying.

'Yeah, but you have the contacts, you know who's who. You can get into the bigger stakes, ya know what I mean.'

'But what about Nick? I've known him since we was kids . . .'

'Look, Nick has no balls.'

'You'd know all about that . . .' said Dino and groaned from a kick.

'Ya know what I mean. I don't want to end me days in a shit corpo house with a few kids on the dole.'

I remember their whispered talks as if they were hallucinations and in my dreams the two are clearly separate: Nick who had charisma, and Dino, a ruthless, sullen bollox.

Nick was my hero. You could say he took me under his wing as I got deeper and deeper into the world of the gang. Because I was small and wiry he began to take me with him when he went housebreaking in Bishopstown and Sunday's Well. At first I was the lookout, but bit by bit he taught me the tricks of the trade. Getting into houses through small windows became my speciality. He even saved my skin once when a guy whose trouser pockets I was rifling woke up suddenly and took a swing at me in the darkness. Nick threw a duvet over his head and we were out of the bedroom window like a shot.

Dino and Nick had grown up together on Fairhill. My ma hated them both with a passion and warned me to stay away from them. 'They're gutty boys, good for nothings,' she said with an air of haughty confidence. This added a new glow to them in my eyes. Both of them did time in reform school and they had sniggered at the back of Cork District Court the few times they were up on minor charges.

Keep your gaze on the candle flame. Fix it for long enough and everything around the bright light will fall away into the darkness, until the sharp, white blade holds you transfixed. Some nights I look at this white flame until my eyes sting and begin to water. When I close my eyes the burning candle jumps suddenly out of the darkness behind my closed eyes, the way the images of the night that summer when it all came to a head jump out at me in dreams.

'Jesus, the fight started before any of us knew what was goin' on,' Charlie Ross was shouting in the babble of voices. The lads were in shock, their face muscles tight and twitching, while some of the girls cried openly, leaning on each other's shoulders. 'What the fuck's happened?' newcomers panicked for news.

Earlier, Dino, Nick, Jazzer and another few of the gang had gone to the 'Swallow and Gawk' pub for a few drinks. Dino had been slagging Nick because he was getting too soft. The more he drank, the closer he moved to the bone. 'Yer afraid, yer afraid to get into the big league,' Dino said.

'Shut yer hole, yah don't know what yer on about,' said Nick, pushing Dino away from him.

'C'mon Nicky, how's about we do a hold-up, with real guns?'

'Yer outta yer tree, Dino. Forget about it.'

'Yer a chicken. Cluck, cluck, cluck.'

Nick got up and went to the bar. Jazzer, who was sitting on the other side of Nick, kept silent during the exchange. Dino looked up as Nick returned with three pints in his hands.

'Ah, Jazzer wuz right about yah. Y'has no balls.'

Nick looked at Jazzer first, then at Dino; he emptied the pints over the two of them. Dino got up, overturning the table, and the two closed. The barman shot out from behind the bar with a broken pool cue and the rest of the gang jumped up from their seats. They parted the two and Dino fell back into his chair, shouting 'Allrigh', allrigh', get offa me, I'll leave him off.'

Jazzer left the pub and Nick sat at the far end of the bar with Charlie and three other members of the gang. Dino simmered in a drunken stupor, his head sunk over a pint. Nobody knew how it started up again outside after closing time. 'It all happened in a blur, the flyin' fists, the shoutin',' Charlie Ross said. 'We grabbed at Dino but 'twas like someone had greased him, he kept slippin' away from us, lungin' at Nick. The knife came outta nowhere, flyin' through the air.'

Then Charlie pulled a blood-stained knife out of his pocket, the knife Jazzer had slipped into Dino's pocket the night she whispered in his ear around the charred stone circle where the fire had burned during the winter months. The mother-of-pearl handle seemed to glow for a moment in the darkness before Charlie shoved it into a plastic bag and then into a hastily dug hole.

*

I couldn't face the funeral, nor the cops who came to the door looking to talk to me about what I knew. 'What's the world coming to?' my ma said after seeing them off. 'What would you know about what happened to that gutty boy?' I cut out the picture in the *Evening Echo* of a cop standing guard over a black plastic sheet that covered the spot where he had fallen, the dark patch of blood barely hidden.

These days Jazzer visits me in prison regularly. She brought me the candles, telling me to light one every night and gaze at it for a few minutes. 'It'll steady yer nerves,' she said the day she handed the packet of white candles to me over the visiting table. She must have read about it in a women's magazine. ''Tis also a sign of hope,' she added hoarsely. Lucky for me it was a slack time in the prison, so there weren't many others in the room. Lucky too that I'm in a cell on my own. Fuck knows what would happen if I was sharing and had to explain the lighted candle to some hardchaw Sorrie trying to get to sleep. 'Blow it out or I'll shove it up yer arse, lightin' an' all.'

Dino was done for manslaughter in the end and lost interest in Jazzer during his time in prison. He headed off to England as soon as he got out, never to return. Jazzer took the road she hadn't wanted to take but, lucky for her, she only ended up with one kid on unmarried allowance in a shit corpo flat. The father was one of the old gang, I think – but, anyway, he took off as soon as the news was out. I'm all she has left now, she's telling me, the love of her life. She has great plans for when I get out. We're going to live together in the flat, me and her and the kid who's nothing to me. I'm going to get a job and we're going to lead a decent life for once.

Pigs are flying past the barred windows of my cell. I still haven't plucked up the courage to tell her that I don't want to have anything to do with her when I get out, because of what she did on Nick. Or maybe I just feel bad that I didn't do nothing to stop Dino and Jazzer. I don't know. And, anyway, she doesn't look as well as she did back then. She looks more than her age, the way women can, and grey roots are showing under the dye in her hair. She has put on a lot of weight, especially around the hips and arse, and she has bags under eyes that are hollow and lifeless.

This time I'm in for housebreaking, six months. What am I supposed to do? I have to make a living somehow, I don't want to spend the rest of my life on the dole. Every night I've lit one of the candles Jazzer brought me and now I'm down to my last one. It's going to burn out soon and I dread the time when the guttering stub flickers for a moment and dies: the flame will go first and then a brief interval of nothing before the white column of smoke spirals and twirls upwards, drifting through the barred windows of the cell and into the oppressive darkness outside, leaving the acrid smell of the dead candle to settle in my nostrils.

ÉILÍS Ní DHUIBHNE

The Makers

David sits over a blue bowl of tomato soup, spooning it to his mouth with the caution he reserves for all foods that are not sweets wrapped in plastic, bought by himself in the shop. Even though he likes tomato soup, has indeed requested it himself, he isn't taking chances. You never know where a slimy scrap of onion or a gritty seed, a sliver of garlic, might lurk, waiting to invade your body, uninvited.

His mother watches him from the other side of the table. Three o'clock. He's just home from school. Since eight, when she waved him off, a minute snail in a navy tracksuit carrying his enormous schoolbag on his back, she has been alone. She has, in those hours, performed a few tasks: carried clothes from the washing machine to the line, watered geraniums in the conservatory. She has painted a picture, or rather has painted at a picture which has been long under way and which may never get finished, for all she knows, or, in her present mood of lassitude, cares.

She stares at him. The vermilion soup travels from the bowl to his mouth, slowly and surely, seven or eight times. It has passed the test. He is also eating white bread, taking the middle bit out and leaving crusts in two golden rings on his plate. There is a glass of milk in front of him and he sips that from time to time as well. It's an unusual day for more reasons than one.

'You like this soup?' she asks, in grateful wonder.

'It's all right,' he nods. He doesn't smile but his face is neither angry nor anxious, as it usually is, at mealtimes.

'Good,' she says. 'It's healthy – relatively.' Healthier than fruit gums, is what she meant. Healthier than gobstoppers.

'But I couldn't have the same thing every day, could I?' He opens his eyes wide. They are not particularly big eyes, but his habit of widening them makes them seem big. Their colour is a clean morning blue.

She is not sure of his drift.

'Would you actually eat it, if we had it every day?'

'Yeah.' He lifts the spoon one more time, then lays it firmly down on the cloth. There is some red soup in the bowl, but not a lot.

'I'd like chicken soup too,' he adds. 'I'd like to try that. And the farmhouse vegetable.'

'Great!' she smiles. Chicken soup. Farmhouse vegetable. Is he serious? She scrutinises him more closely. His head looks like a flower, a heart-shaped blossom, pink and white, with the petals of straw hair fluttering in his eyebrows. He'd hate to hear that description of himself.

He stands up. It's not nice to be stared at.

'When caveman discovered the wheel, did he make a wheel-barrow? Is that the first thing he made?'

'Gosh, I'm not sure.'

She can never remember anything about pre-history, which interests David more than any other kind.

'I'll ask Dad. I think that was the first thing. He watched a stone rolling down a hill, and then he put a hole in it and made a wheelbarrow.'

'Probably,' she agrees. It sounds likely enough.

He pushes the petals of hair from his eyes.

'Can I get my hair cut? Now!'

'Sure. I'll ring them. No time like the present.'

No time like the present. That is not her phrase; she's stolen it from David's father. And the present is not Marie's time, not any more. Recently she has moved to the land of put-it-off. She's taken up abode in the land of dreams. When she phones the hairdresser, there is no reply, much to her relief. She feels much too tired to walk all the way to the village, and back again, just to transform David from a flower to a scrubbing brush.

'Monday', she tells David. 'Maybe he's closed on Mondays? Like, eh, the National Museum.'

'Mm,' he agrees, pulling at his fringe. 'Or maybe he's cutting someone's hair and can't come to the phone. Try again later,' he orders. 'Try again in five minutes.'

'I will,' she promises meekly.

David goes to his room to do his homework and she goes to her room, also with the intention of working. When she gets there, however, her eye alights on her bed – wide, silky ochre, seductive in the soft glow of the afternoon. The cat is asleep in the middle of it, curled into a neat, firm ball of white fur, catching the sun.

Marie lies down beside her, and lets the sun warm her face.

Daddy got the 'flu on New Year's Day, as he had every New Year's Day for ages: the effect of too much excitement over the Christmas holiday. Marie's mother got it too and a few days later phoned and told Marie this in her sick voice, the voice that made Marie grit her teeth and arch her back, that made her snap and snarl and hate when she should sympathise and love. A cry for help, a litany of graphic details followed. Diarrhoea and kidney trouble, weak spells and sick stomachs, vomits. These were her mother's symptoms.

'And how is Daddy?'

'He's very chesty. But he's got the inhaler and he's doing his best. I think he'll be all right, please God. But we haven't had a bit to eat in three days and I woke last night and the sweat was pouring off me.'

'Have you had the doctor?'

'I rang him this morning. He's to come later.'

This was the third day of the new year. Marie was at work. As well as the painting she has a part-time job in a gallery in town, and it is there, in the middle of the afternoon, that she receives this call from her mother. Typical. Every year her mother makes this phone call. Marie has to drop everything and run to her rescue. Her mother is a person of exceptional optimism, energy and good humour when she is well. But even a pinprick of illness punctures her utterly, robs her of every vestige of courage. Death's door opens when a common cold tickles her throat. Marie thinks she knows the reason for this hypochondria: her grandparents died when her mother was four or five. But understanding the cause is not enough to make the effect easy to tolerate. What Marie's mother needs is Marie's sympathy. And that is just what Marie cannot give. She has none. Or if she has, it dries up into a hard ball of resentment and disbelief when these crises occur. All she can think of is time, and where she is going to find it. There is no time in this life she has made for herself to care about ailing parents. There is not time for anything except the next deadline.

Marie went to visit them the day her mother phoned. She bought tomato soup and fresh bread and lots of mineral drinks in the nearby supermarket, then walked to their house, her own childhood home. It was dark and spitting snow, very cold. But inside the silent, neat house was a cosy nest – they'd got central heating a few years earlier, and the old rooms, which had always been freezingly uncomfortable every winter until then, were transformed utterly.

They were together in their high lumpy bed, her parents. Her mother lay back against the pillows with her eyes closed. Her father was sitting on the edge, his legs dangling to the floor, working on his breathing.

'I tell him to get up. He's better off up. He'll never shake that phlegm off his chest if he lies down. But he gets tired.'

Her father smiled weakly at her. He had the merriest smile, and small wide cornelian eyes which often twinkled in amusement or joy. They did not twinkle now. He sat on the bed, his grey and red pyjamas neatly buttoned, labouring to do this most natural thing. His breath came in thick, sticky whoops.

'He's got the antibiotics. He'll be grand, please God.'

'And have you got antibiotics?'

'No. I've to take fluids. I'm dehydrated. That's what caused the weakness. All the ould vomiting, and the sweating.'

Her mother overflowed with liquids, darkly swirling. Words poured from her in a rich stream, tea from a spout. Dessicated inside, her silent father struggled for air, smiling, taciturn. The difference. So it had been, always. The melancholic and the choleric? Life does not yield such easy contrasts. Her father was not really choleric. His lungs were dry, after years of smoking, of working in air thick with sawdust, the dust of concrete and asbestos, but his temper had always been sanguine.

Marie made them soup and buttered the bread and poured the juice. They tried to eat. Afterwards she tucked in her father. His body which had been stocky and thick was thin, hollow, although the shoulders remained broad. His legs were so skinny that they made tears come to her eyes.

Her mother cheered up considerably after the meal, although she ate none of it. So it was always: all she needed was a modicum of attention, proof that she was loved, or at least supported, by her family. Her father did not need this proof. He was cheerful, with or without attention. He took life as it came, and didn't believe in worrying unnecessarily.

Marie pulls the quilt to her chin, stretches her legs, tries not to disturb the cat. She closes her eyes. Tiredness weights her stomach, drags her blood earthwards. Now that the days are long and light and fine, she feels there is no night, and one day blends into the next as charmingly as all the frilled trees in the gardens form great, cushioned banks and waterfalls of light, translucent green. Getting up in the morning is easy, and every day seems like a holiday, weightless, freefalling. All tasks – work, painting, housework – have grown simpler. But today in the heel of the afternoon this exhaustion descends, and all she wants is to shut her eyes and return to the dream landscape she had left behind her the night before.

Daddy's flu became pneumonia. This, too, had often happened. The doctor asked, 'Would you like to go to hospital?' and Daddy, who liked hospitals, said yes.

Marie went to see him on his first night there. He was sitting up in bed, wearing a white gown, with an oxygen mask over his face.

'How are you?' Marie hugged him.

'Grand!' he said, smiling broadly. 'This yoke is bloody marvellous. And I just had my dinner. I feel great, to tell you the truth.'

He looked happy. He was in a ward with about six people. One man read a book. Some were looking at newspapers. Two of them were up, perched on the sides of their beds, talking to one another. Nobody looked sad or very ill. Besides, there was no television. A blessing.

'The nurses are great. One of them is from Sligo. She's a lovely person, a really lovely person.'

He felt safe in this hospital, where he had often been before. The doctors, the nurses, the medicine, the oxygen – he knew they could help him. The ward was coloured softly, like the inside of an ear, and it did not have a smell. Marie loved it too. The high beds you could see under, the tight white coverlets like envelopes, the flesh-coloured curtains looped like loving arms at the ends of the beds. She'd only been in hospital herself once, to give birth to David, the best event of her life. So her associations were brilliantly rosy. Like her father, she loved the orderliness of the place, and she loved the cheerful workaday atmosphere. A hospital, they both knew, is a place where people come to be refreshed and rejuvenated.

'Your mammy didn't come today, but she'll be able to get in tomorrow.'

'How is she feeling?'

'Ah, she's still only middling. But she's going to try to get in tomorrow anyway. Is it still snowing?'

'It's stopped now. It's OK.'

'Are you on your way home from work?'

'Yes.'

'How is David?'

'Great. Still on his holidays.'

He talked and talked, through the oxygen mask, sometimes

removing it to emphasise a word or a sentence, to make himself plainer. His talk was all of ordinary things, of how he was feeling and what he would do next, of his medication. Sometimes he referred to the nurses, already counting them as friends after one day. It was talk without much substance, but he spoke eagerly and with excitement. He nattered, in fact.

This was a man who had never had one real conversation with Marie, in all the years she was growing up. He had always been kind, gentle, considerate. But he had not talked.

Instead he had made things – for her, for her brother, for their children: her cradle, modelled on one in which a queen of England had once lain as a baby. David had lain in that cradle too. Later, he had played with a painted train, rocked on a horse carved from pale, gleaming elmwood. Her father's communication had been with his hands, in objects built or made by them. Now for the first time, when he could not breathe without artificial aid, he wanted to communicate like other people, with words. Marie listened, pleased, her heart warming inside her. Her mother never stopped talking. Talk poured out of her, a torrent of commentary, conjecture, opinion. Sense and nonsense. And her talk, excessive, sometimes became wearisome. Marie knew she could listen to her father for ever.

'I'll probably come on Saturday,' she said. 'I've visitors tomorrow night.'

'Fair enough, Marie,' he said. 'Don't you be driving in here in this bad weather. I'll be grand,' he said. '*Beidh mé go breá. Slán leat anois.*'

She grasped his hand, which had been a huge paw of a hand, every finger thick as a thumb, and now was bony with veins gnarled and tumescent as an oak, purple as aubergines.

'See you soon,' she kisses him.

She doesn't want to talk Irish to him. His first language. His first language is a dialect that hardly anyone speaks any more, a dialect of east Ulster Irish, on its last legs. There are some people – Marie's husband, Karl, is one, and he is right about many things – who would say that it is because nobody shares

his first language that Daddy never speaks much. Marie is not
sure about this. It must be strange, all right, seldom if ever
meeting someone who really knows your own language. But
plenty of people overcome this difficulty. Karl, for instance, is
German, but he has plenty to say in English. And Daddy knows
English perfectly well, just as well as anybody else in Ireland.
There is more to it than that.

All her life Marie has been busy and energetic, working stolidly
if not brilliantly; a day when she has not learned or written or
painted or made something she considers wasted. She sits on
committees and boards, she does two or three jobs, she keeps
her house in order. She has passed heaps of examinations,
given hundreds of talks, participated in umpteen projects.
Besides all that she loves to cook and bake, to sew curtains, to
paint rooms and paper them, to walk and to swim. Her life is
packed with activity. But when people remark, as they often do,
'How do you get the time to do it all?' Marie feels annoyed, or
accused. Why? Who is accusing her, and of what? All she
knows is that she is not happy unless her hands or her feet or
her head are totally engaged. Baking bread or scrubbing floors
or walking five miles across a mountain. Painting is the best
thing of all. That is like harvesting corn with a sickle. It is like
designing a house and then building it, stone on top of stone,
with your own two hands.
    That is what Daddy did when he was a boy, eighty-odd years
ago. There is talk in Ireland of the terrible poverty of the past,
and Marie knows it is true. Her mother refers to it, tells her
stories, usually about other families, thankfully distant, miserably unfortunate cousins. Stories of toddlers gathering brosna
for fires, of no food and no money and no boots and no heat and
no hope. Terrible humiliations. Daddy never told such stories.
He did not think of his family as poor, although they probably
never owned any money at all. They were medieval. Not
cavemen, but medieval. In his house, the cloth was made from
wool which his mother and sisters spun. It was dyed rust with

lichens from the rocks, yellow with weeds from the ditches, deep brown with black ink from the bog. Their food was grown in their own fields, their meal thrashed in their barn. They fished in the bay and salted barrels and barrels of herrings for winter. Even their house they had built themselves, and furnished with simple, beautiful furniture, because his family were carpenters and masons as well as fishermen and farmers. Hunters, gatherers, tillers. Makers.

They always had plenty to eat and, it seems to Marie, warm and beautiful clothes to wear. And the house, as Marie pictures it, was also warm, electric with life – with the slap of the churn and the whirr of the wheel, with the hopefulness of baking bread. The Middle Ages. Only a few things in that house could not have been there if he had been born in 1312 instead of 1912. His father and mother could not read, even, and had never been to school. But they could spin, they could make clothes, they could make tables and chairs and houses, and fish with many kinds of hooks and nets. They never stopped working. And that is what lies behind Marie's life. Centuries of people buzzing about their work of survival, like bees in a hive. That is what her father did. Worked. He did not talk, because his language was no longer spoken in the world he inhabited, and besides he had chosen a wife who could do all the talking for him. And he did not write poems or stories. But he worked happily. That was his prayer, his mark on the world and his legacy to Marie.

He went to hospital on Thursday and that is the night Marie visited him, and had the long chat. On Friday she had a visitor to dinner, Gail Murphy, an American woman who was visiting Ireland for a few weeks to do some research on Irish artists. She was a small, chatty, kind woman, an excellent guest. She presented Marie with a bunch of yellow freesias, her favourite flowers, the flowers which smell of damp green meadows, of spring rain and of ethereal perfumes. They talked happily about the latest exhibitions, and the latest scandals. They ate something light and good, and Marie was complimented on her cooking, as she usually was, as she expected to be.

The conversation was so lively that they all forgot about the last train, so Marie and Karl drove Gail home to her hotel in town. The snow was falling lightly again, in the dark blue streets, but the roads were not dangerous. On a whim Marie decided to drop into the hospital. To her surprise, Karl did not object, although it was not exactly visiting hour, being past midnight.

They had to go in through the casualty department, and traverse many silent corridors, lighted and warm, but empty, to reach the ward. Daddy had been transferred to the coronary unit. The nurse there was friendly and spoke in a low, kind voice. There was nothing wrong with his heart, she said. Don't be alarmed. They merely wanted to monitor it while he underwent some treatment for his kidneys. His kidneys? Yes. The medication for his lungs had affected his kidneys in some way, so they were not working properly.

Daddy was sitting up in bed, delighted to see Marie and Karl.

'I'm grand!' he said. 'You didn't come all the way from Killiney to see me, did you?'

'We had to leave someone to town anyway,' said Marie. 'So we dropped in.'

'I'll be here until tomorrow, I think. Will yez be in tomorrow?'

'I will, probably. I might bring David.'

'Yeah. Bring David. I'd like to see him. How is he?'

'Fine. Your breathing is better?'

'Much better! They're great in here, they couldn't be nicer.'

His eyes twinkled, and his face was merry. The light in the ward was soft and yellow, and the room soothed with the familiar sounds of patients snoring, the regular comforting bleeps of machines which minded them, like watchful angels, as they slept.

The next day Marie put Gail's freesias in a small green jug and brought them to the hospital. She thought their spring colours would appeal to Daddy, who was fond of flowers. She thought he could lie in bed and look at them, when he was too tired to read or think.

But when she arrived in the ward, Daddy was lying on his back, his face crumpled, his eyes almost closed. His breathing was heavy again, gnarled, clotted, tangled. He looked cross.

'He's not responding to the treatment,' said the nurse. She motioned Marie and David outside to the corridor. 'The doctor will talk to you soon. Are you the closest relatives?'

Marie knew then.

'Yes,' she said. Her mother was still at home, sick with the 'flu.

'It could be a few hours, a day,' said the doctor, a tiny Oriental woman with skin as smooth as the lining of a nut. 'We don't know. We don't know why his kidneys have failed and we're trying to find that out.'

But it was clear from her tone that they would not find out.

'Oh.'

'He could have dialysis,' she said. 'But he is not a good patient for dialysis. His heart is weak and then he has the lung disease.'

'What chance does he have, if he gets dialysis?'

'I think if he goes on the machine he would not be able to take it. He'd go.'

Marie thought of dialysis as something painful, like chemotherapy. She thought of her father spending his last hours hooked up to a machine, in pain. She reiterated the doctor's comment that dialysis was not a sensible option and the doctor nodded eagerly.

'We can try to make him comfortable,' said the doctor. 'I think that is the best thing now.'

Comfortable. Marie had thought of dying as a quiet and simple task. She had thought people lie calmly in bed, breathing softly, and that one breath is weaker than the others, and that is the last. She had read of final words, of *bloscadh roimh báis*, where the dying person wakes up as bright as a bird and says goodbye to the family gathered around the bed. When the doctor said 'comfortable' that is what she imagined: they would make it peaceful for him. They would create a state of quiet and ease and painlessness to move him gently from life to death.

But that is not what 'comfortable' meant at all.

Daddy died after three days of struggle. 'He's not in pain,' the nurses said. How did they know? After the first day he was dumb; he could not talk and tell them. But he looked pained. His breathing was loud and noisy like a damp engine, his skin looked sore and tender. His eyes sometimes half opened, and what you could see in them was torture.

Sometimes the nurses gave him sedatives, and he had some peace. At other times, they gave him treatments – changed the tubes which failed to draw water from his kidneys, put other tubes down to his lungs to extricate the excess liquid which clogged them. After these treatments, he breathed easily for a half an hour or so. Marie did not witness the insertion of the tube, the suction of the lungs, but she felt it in her own body. She felt the intrusion and the pain. She thought of her father as a hapless victim, lying speechless, dying, on a high bed, while nurses circled, saying, 'He feels no pain,' inserting tubes into the centre of his body, inserting needles into his skin, needling him and turning him and twisting him. On the first day, when he could still talk, he said, his profound patience at last exhausted, 'Leave me alone.' But they could not leave him alone.

Marie's heartbroken mother and the other members of the family said it was for the best, that they knew what they were doing. Marie said nothing. She noticed that the treatments varied. On the day shifts, the nurses attended to him every half hour, and what they did seemed to depend on the personality of the nurse on duty. Some were brisk and sharp, and worked hard, helping or annoying Daddy. Others were soft and gentle, and gave him sedatives to help him sleep. The night nurses were the best. They left him alone, administering morphine, often at Marie's request. The nights, Daddy's last nights, were closer to her idea of what death should be than the days. The days belonged to someone else. To the hospitals, the nurses, the doctors. They had to be filled with activity. For Daddy, night cannot have been different from day except in this, that during the day he was constantly bothered by the hospital staff, and during the night he had peace. Marie sat by his bed and held his hand and asked for morphine, and sometimes he even slept, and his face was at least calm, not twisted with pain and despair, as during the day.

Three days. It was like labour. A long labour, leading not to a new life but to the opposite.

He died after the nurse had inserted the tube into his lungs for one last time. That was his last experience of life on this earth: three strangers in white sticking a plastic tube into the centre of his old, wise body, and sucking water from his lungs.

He had been born in a small country house, in a room with his mother and a midwife. He might have heard, soon after his birth, a seagull screaming. Or, more likely, the cranky squawking of hens, or the sombre lowing of the cow in the byre across the street. The medical equipment in the room where he was born might have stretched to a pair of scissors, a bowl of hot water. The light would have been dim: the shadowy amber of an oil lamp, if it was night; a slender ray of misty sunlight if it was not, because the window in the room would have been tiny. And he died in a room blazing with electricity, with wires attached to many parts of his body. He died with a plastic tube scratching his lungs, the centre of him, where the first, the simplest, the most natural function, had happened.

In the paper the notice said 'Peacefully'. And Marie, Marie's mother, everyone said he was lucky. Daddy was one of the lucky ones.

Marie has always wanted to work and produce, and if she is not doing that she feels unhappy, anxious, even guilty. But now there is a change. What she wants to do is nothing. She would like to lie in bed, with her cat, and like her cat, for days and days and days. She would like to spend her time sleeping and dreaming the long, lazy dreams she loves. Instead of wrenching from them abruptly in the mornings, losing them, she would like to stay in them until they fade away of their own accord. Then, if she must get up, she wants to sit and stare at the garden, to move through the house from room to room, silently and quietly. That is what she would like, for a while, until she has sloughed off her skin, until she has turned inside out and started again, until she has dreamt her fill.

David comes into the bedroom. She opens her eyes.

'Look what I made, mammy!'

He hasn't been doing his homework, it seems. He shows her a robot, a robot that moves with the aid of a small engine and can carry a tray from one side of the room to the other.

'Do you like it?'

David is small for his age, still very childish for ten. His hands are soft and tiny like starfish. But his eyes are wide and sky blue and they twinkle when he is happy. And with his little starfish hands he is always busy, building and moulding and making all kinds of things. The house is full of his productions.

'It's lovely.'

He pushes his petals of hair from his eyes.

'Did you ring the hairdresser again?' he asks suspiciously.

'I'll ring him right now.'

He smiles, points bossily at the telephone, and readjusts his robot. Marie starts to dial.

Inside Out

No, because he's always doing things like that. My father, I
mean. He gets the car loaded up with the lot of us, and then
decides to go off and change his clothes, this time into something more casual. Meanwhile, we're left sitting here in the
sweltering heat for a quarter of an hour or more, and he's off
making himself beautiful. Not that he'd express it that way
himself, of course. He'd be embarrassed by the feminine phrase.

We're heading for this Christian convention in the Royal
Dublin Society called 'A World Born Again', with guest speakers from America and elsewhere. Our family live as part of a
religious community, along with other Christian families on the
same housing estate, and some single people as well who live in
a 'Men's House' and a 'Women's House'. It's all part of the
Charismatic Renewal thing, which I'm sure you've heard of. It's
not exclusively Catholic, even though it's in Ireland. Ecumen-
ical is the word they use.

In my family there's me, Emily (Milly for short) and my two
brothers, Leo and Stephen. I'm sixteen (going on seventeen, as
the old song says) and the eldest, the others are fourteen and
eleven. Then there's my mother, waiting patiently in the front
passenger seat, fanning herself. She's pregnant again now, and
I can tell the weather's getting her down. The gift of a late child,
as they say.

At long last here's my father again, comfortable in his check
shirt and chinos, looking like an all-round regular guy. He
doesn't apologise for delaying us. He probably feels that, as lord
and master of his household, he can do what he likes.

I'm not really into the old religion trip any more, although I haven't mentioned my doubts, or indeed my certainties, to my parents. They'd probably send me off to talk to a priest, or to the head of the community, or something. I used to be quite religious, you know. As a kid I couldn't be stopped praying. It was the sound of the words of the prayers that I loved, and their arrangement in the lines. 'Blessed art thou among women/And blessed is the fruit of thy womb'. I also liked the way religion seemed to explain the world, or I thought it explained it. It was a way of looking at, and seeing things. The folks told me about God, who apparently loved me, but expected some things in return. They told me I had a soul, which was apparently immortal, and had to be saved. But they also did some things I felt were distinctly odd. Like they said that the teenage boys in the community shouldn't wear muscle T-shirts, heaven knows why. It's only recently that I copped on that they must have thought that girls in the community might have found them attractive, or even provocative, so they had to go. Then they confiscated a copy of *The Catcher in the Rye* that Leo had, to censor it and see if it was the kind of thing someone his age should be reading. All this made me think twice. Then what happened was the nuns in school decided I was a clever clogs, and took me and the other bright kids aside and instructed us in the proofs of the existence of God, all of which are nonsense if you think about them, and I stopped being such a fervent believer. Now I just think religion is silly. It keeps idiots happy, so I suppose it has its uses. But, as I said, mum's the word when it comes to Mum and Dad.

Just as I hold my own counsel at home, I do the same thing at school. Teachers like me, I suppose because I listen. Maths is a sore trial, but I'm good at English and History and French. But I'm not a swot. I have my circle of friends, and like a laugh as much as the next girl. 'We use our fathers' shirts/As mini-skirts/We neither smoke nor drink/That's what the teachers think'. Some other girls have boyfriends, some other girls write poetry. I don't have a regular boyfriend, and I know I'm a prose girl at heart. I keep a diary, and I write stories like this, with myself as the heroine. One day our English teacher complained about the punctuation in an essay I'd written for her.

'I will teach you to use commas and full stops and paragraphs if it's the last thing I do,' she'd said.

'What about Molly Bloom's soliloquy?' I'd replied. She wasn't too pleased with my precociousness. Of course, most sixteen-year-olds aren't supposed to have attempted Molly Bloom.

'You have to know the rules before you break them,' she'd cautioned me, which is true, I suppose. Teachers think we're eejits, using run-on lines, as though we can't write grammatically, as though we can't think logically. So that's why, just to show them, this piece has all the dots and spaces it should have. At least I think it has.

We've arrived at the car park in the RDS, and are getting ourselves and our things out of the car. The roads were quiet this morning, it being Sunday. All the other Christian families are getting out of their cars, and people are streaming into the hall. I wonder will Peter be here. I'm sure he will. His family are in the same community as us, and his parents and my parents are friends. I know I said I didn't have a regular boyfriend, but I've been out with Peter a few times. Our parents encourage our association, so there isn't much hassle. Peter's clever. He has no interest in literature or art, but he's a whiz at Biology and Chemistry and Physics and Maths. At least he isn't a pint swiller with the lads in the local under-age drinking oasis. He says I'm crazy, but he's not exactly a solid citizen himself. That boy has some strange ideas. He has secrets too, which may be why we get on so well, sometimes. He also doesn't buy the whole religion bit any more either. So I'm into him. Well, kind of. I'm very confused about this boys business actually, if you want to know the truth.

Like, a few weeks ago I was at this disco, and this guy asked me up to dance, and then after knowing me for the lengthy period of five minutes proceeds to stick his tongue down my throat. All I wanted to do that night was dance my legs down to my knees, but no, some moron had to start groping me. I think he must have been ecstatic, if you know what I mean. But I want to be wooed. Is it wrong to want to be wooed? It's not like I'm still a bloody virgin, or anything. Okay, I've only 'done it' once, but technically I have had that hard outside thing in my soft inside thing. It happened two or three months ago, at the start of the summer holidays, which are ending now, with this boy I know from hanging around a beach where I go to swim. It wasn't much to write home about, after all. In fact, it felt more like inserting a tampon than anything else. We went off to a secluded spot near the sea, and fooled around and then went all the way. I don't think he could believe his luck. Afterwards I was very disappointed. I didn't have an orgasm, whatever that's supposed to feel like. I went home and, out of sheer frustration, burned my left thigh with a cigarette, just to feel something from outside that would make me feel something inside. Pain and pleasure, maybe they're the same release. I still see the guy from time to time, but we never speak about what happened.

Why did I decide to 'lose it', as the saying goes? I was tired of being a virgin, and wanted to see what all the fuss was about. I'm still waiting to find out. Virgin on the verge: verging on the ridiculous, more like. I figured that something the other girls go on about and something the nuns want to keep from us must be worth investigating. 'The Loss of Innocence' it's called. I don't feel any less innocent now, or any more guilty, than before. Innocence isn't something you lose in ten minutes on a sunny afternoon, it's something you either have or haven't all your life. But is my body my self or is my self inside my body? My body is the unstable tissue between my self and the not self, between me and what's not me, the other, the world. My hymen is the most unstable tissue of all, it must be broken from outside for anyone to come inside, to penetrate and fill me. Does it matter who I sleep with? They tell me it does, the other girls, the nuns. But if my self is not my body then it doesn't. In religion class they told us about having a body and a soul. Maybe that's what they mean when they talk about a soul: they mean a self. I'm not feeling myself today. Actually I do feel myself, that is, my body, regularly. I prefer it to being felt by boys. Or maybe that depends on the boy. I'm distressed and oppressed by my body. It does things I can't control, wants things I don't understand. So it mustn't be my self. I wish I wasn't subject to this menstrual flow. Could you imagine me having babies? Having your breasts fill up with milk like a cow's udder. Yeuch! I wish I didn't have these desires. But maybe I'll learn to live with them. Yum!

Guys: you can't live with them, you can't shoot them. I talk like I know what I'm talking about. Apart from my adventure at the beach, I've only French kissed and been felt up by a couple of others. I haven't been too impressed. I'm not too impressed in general. Boys are such idiots. They judge everything from the outside. Maybe both boys and girls do, at our age. Maybe everybody does, at every age. Except those who grow up, and so few people grow up. Maybe there is no inside, or at least it can't be seen, so how can we know it's there? What's wrong with judging by appearances anyway? Like at that disco I told you about, I knew I was being assessed by how I looked rather than how I talked. He was more interested in my pose than my prose. Which do I prefer? I'm not entirely sure. What do I look like? Well, I'm not exactly a traffic stopper, but I can make boys like me without having to try very hard. Like I said, boys are such idiots. I have long dark hair, and a face that wouldn't stand out in a crowd for being either very beautiful or very ugly, but can be made to pass muster. How do I dress? I change daily, sometimes elegant, sometimes sloppy. Today I'm wearing a white blouse and a wide floral skirt, because it's hot, and it's down-homey looking enough to appeal to and blend in with all these Christians. But tomorrow it could be jeans and a sweat shirt. I'm more verbal than visual.

I notice I'm defining myself by how I perceive myself, rather than how others perceive me. But how can I know what others perceive? I could ask them, but they may not tell me the truth. It is not given to us to see ourselves as others see us. It is not given to us to see ourselves.

What I'm saying is that how I look and how I dress depends mostly on what kind of mood I'm in. Mood rules so much. Like at that disco, another night I might have gone off with yer man. Sometimes you feel like sex, sometimes you just feel like a cuddle, sometimes you don't feel like anything, or feel nothing. How do I feel today? But boys never know what you feel. Show them some attention and they treat you like dirt. Women are more sensible, in my humble opinion. Some women. It's funny the way boys' genitals just hang outside their bodies, as though they couldn't give a shit who they fuck, as though sex isn't that important to them. My genitals are inside my body. I have to open myself and be opened, before I can feel sexual pleasure, or have sex at all. Still sometimes I think I should have been a man. Then I wouldn't have to bleed from between my legs. I wouldn't have to carry babies inside me.

I notice that now I'm defining myself by my reactions to others, but those reactions vary; I could define myself by how others react to me, but those reactions also vary, depending on my actions, or not, which depend on my moods, or not. Maybe it's wrong to act on your moods, maybe you should act on principles. But my moods are my principles, my principles are my moods. These thoughts are too big for me just now. Then there's the words guys use about us: slag, slapper, slut. They make up and use these words, as though they had a definite meaning. Did my beau at the beach use them about me? I don't think so. I hope not. Although that would explain that fool being so forward at the disco. Boys use words like they have only one meaning. Girls do too, I suppose. I feel very different from most boys. From most girls too, I suppose. Words have one meaning for them, but they have many for me. Words are a single thing for them, but they have a doubleness for me. They mean both too much and not enough, at the same time. I don't know the words to explain this thing about words properly. Like I don't have all the words for this piece I'm writing. But I'm only sixteen.

We've taken our seats in the hall, and looking around I spot

Peter talking with a group of friends at the back. I tell my parents I'm going to say hello to him. Peter is tall and blond, and is wearing a white shirt and jeans. Unlike most adolescent boys, Peter is not an idiot, and I have a rare respect for him. Plus, he could pose for the cover of *Just Seventeen* magazine, with those cheekbones and lips. He's a year and a bit older than me, in his last year in school. He's only here because of his parents, like me. We chat about some CDs he lent me a couple of weeks ago. Then there's a call for silence and for people to sit down, as the conference is about to start. I tell him I'll see him later, and go back to where my family is.

The speeches get under way, talks with titles like 'Christ's Message in Today's World' and 'Ecumenism: The Way Forward' and 'The Enemy Within: Radical Feminism in the Christian Churches'. I get bored and restless, but do my best not to let it show. It seems like lunch time will never come, but when it does I go off and sit on the grass with Peter and his friends, and eat hot dogs and sandwiches, and exchange views on the speakers and what they said. Peter is noticeably reticent in expressing his opinions, as am I. Better to keep a clean nose.

After lunch I ask my parents if I can stay with the young people, and they agree. We're all Christians here after all, aren't we? Peter is aware of my uninterestedness in the general proceedings. He leans over and whispers in my ear to meet him at the entrance to the toilets in five minutes. He knows I'll be there. When we come together again he tells me he's discovered a place where we can be alone, if I'd like that. What the hell, I think, and agree. Anything's better than sitting listening to these old fogies. As we sneak behind the loudspeakers beside the stage, making sure no one sees us, a preacher starts to lead the whole congregation in prayer. He makes it up as he goes along, petitioning the Lord for all kinds of favours. We climb down under the stage, to a dark niche where nobody can find us, but we can hear everything that's going on. Peter puts his arm around me and leans over and kisses me, like I knew he would. Why else was I here? We've kissed a few times before, but this feels more like the real thing. Our tongues swim around in each other's mouths, then he presses his lips to my eyelids one after the other, then pecks the tip of my nose, then nibbles my earlobes, then back to my mouth. He starts to undo the buttons of my blouse, delicately and skilfully, and then feels my breasts, all perfume, first outside my bra, then he reaches back and undoes the strap, and drags his fingertips over my nipples. He's done this before. But then, so have I. It's better this time, though. Just then the preacher starts shouting about God loving the world and all His people, and how we must love Him back in return. I feel him stroking my thighs under my skirt, and I adjust my position so he can get at me more easily. I hear the crowd outside start to speak in tongues, and Peter stretches his hands up and slips his fingers inside the elastic of my pants and slides them down my legs. Then he leans down and starts licking me down there, and it's the first time I've had this and it feels so good. The preacher thanks the Lord for bestowing the gift of tongues. So do I.

Just as I'm beginning to come Peter stops, and so does the preacher, to be replaced by a new speaker, a pastor from a church in Oregon, who is going to talk on what is billed as 'the most important social issue of our day'. What could that be? Peter surfaces for air and kisses my lips again, and produces a piece of plastic which he places over himself, and then I feel him slowly come inside me.

'Today, millions of innocent babies are sacrificed, by official sanction. It is done in the name of secular humanism's *causes célèbres*: "the right of a woman to her own body", "every child should be wanted", "the viability of the foetus", or "the right to choose".'

He keeps kissing my face, and moves in and out leisurely, and I pick up from where I left off before.

'Pre-abortionists play with words. Terms like "pre-viable embryo", a classic example, are common now when abortion-ists are referring to unborn babies. Through semantics, they are attempting to dehumanise the tiny life. Common terms include "embryo", "tissue", "clump of cells", "it" and "product of conception".'

This is better than my finger, better than other fingers, much much better than the boy at the beach.

'Such issues as pro-choice, right of a woman to her own body, viability, wantedness, et cetera, are man-made arenas of discussion. Each of these issues has been conceived in our culture's God-ignoring, humanistic mindset, and then presented to us as if they were the proper points for the public debate.'

He's making me feel wonderful, and it's wonderful to know that he's feeling it too.

'As to the right of a woman to her own body, the Word of God would emphasise that we are created in the image of God and that our life, our bodies, are gifts from Him. Our first consideration is not our rights; it is the responsible use and behaviour of our bodies. Such a responsibility is first concerned that our bodies bring glory to God. It's a responsibility, for instance, that concerns itself with wholesome and beautiful attitudes toward sexual love. It accepts responsibility for God-given sexuality and fertility.'

I feel like screaming out with pleasure I'm getting so near to the moment, but I restrain myself in case someone hears me and we're discovered.

'Look at television and the movies. Where is God's hand in the programming and entertainment? Sexual promiscuity, homosexuality, adultery, and all of God's prohibitions are flaunted and touted as socially acceptable on television and in films.'

I'm just there, it's terrific, his name is Peter, and on this rock I will build my church, the church of carnal knowledge and love.

'Without God, man is the measure of all things, and man's laws are his only moral determinants. But man is not truly the measure of all things. God is. And God's laws are absolutes which cannot be legislated away.'

Yes I'm just there yes I'm there yes.

The congregation are cheering and clapping, and I'm lying in Peter's arms, kissing him gratefully. He seems pretty happy too. He withdraws, from inside me to outside me again, and takes off the rubber full of his seed which came from inside him to outside him, but which he doesn't let me see. Now I know what all the fuss is about. I am 'A Girl Born Again', a woman. There's a virginity of the body, but maybe there's a virginity of the self as well, that part that used to be called the soul. My soul is my self. I'd already lost the virginity of my body, but today I've lost the virginity of my self, my soul. My body did something I couldn't control, again, but this time I liked it, or my soul did.

We get ourselves together and make ourselves presentable, and climb out of our hiding place and slink back around the loudspeakers, taking care no one notices us, and rejoin the other youngsters.

'That talk on abortion was great, wasn't it?' says a girl from a neighbouring family, and I agree.

'I don't know how any woman could ever have an abortion,' she continues, and I say I don't know either.

'It just shows you how careful we have to be with boys,' she goes on, and I hold my peace, and don't say my piece. Inside my mind I think thank God for johnnies. Of course, this mob will tell you that they're not reliable, but they're better than nothing.

'Where did you get to?' enquires this guardian of traditional values, and I tell her we went up the front to see and hear better.

'I can understand that,' she tells me.

I glance over at Peter and see that he's being assailed with questions, just like me. He's so cute. Will he stay with me? I don't know. I hope so. But only if he treats me right. Otherwise, it's fly away Peter.

Just then my father approaches and asks where I was.

'We've been looking for you everywhere.' I tell him I was up the front, where I could pay attention more closely.

'Well, I didn't see you. I hope you were listening. Your mother's not feeling very well, so we're going home. You can stay and get a lift home with some of our friends, or you can come home now.' Much as I'd like to be with Peter, I can't stomach the others and want to get out of this place. So I wish my new-found lover goodbye, for the time being, disguised under a general goodbye.

My poor mother, she looks so haggard and pale. She had sex to get the way she is now. But she wouldn't think of aborting, ever. I would, if I had to. Whether through birth or abortion, what's inside comes outside. Unlike her, I'm more interested in having sex when it's considered odd or downright wrong to be having it than when it's considered odd or downright wrong not to be having it. So what'll I do when I'm older and it's expected that I'll get married? I don't know. Become a nun.

She asks did I like the man from Oregon, and I say yes, although I'm beginning to seethe inside. That pastor is spoiling my special day, even though he may have added to the thrill. Why am I so angry? I am a girl, a woman. I am unknowable, even to myself. Now there'd be Holy War if a man said that about a woman. Because I'm sixteen, and I've got the growing-up blues. But maybe the blues are going to be broken. Because sixteen is shit, ask anyone. But maybe things are going to get better. My insides are on the outside in these words I'm writing. Look at my mother. Soon something inside her will be outside her too, like I was once inside her and am outside her now. She has no choice, had no choice. Look at my father. Fussing around our car, making sure we have everything we came with. He doesn't know about being inside out, about choosing. Yes is what boys always want girls to say. Yes is what the church wants women to say. I may have said yes today, but that doesn't mean I always will. Only when I feel like it and it suits me. Otherwise, no I said no I won't No.

The Outfielder, the Indian-Giver

A s they touched down at O'Hare, Fergal wondered how he'd gotten himself into this. Okay, Martin was charming and clever, and as persuasive as an upper-class rat with a gold tooth, but Fergal had only known him a month and now he was going to be spending the next week covering swathes of a country Fergal knew nothing about with this middle-aged man who was completely drunk two hours after take-off, and whose seduction technique involved roaring at a stewardess that 'Kafka was in fact, sweetheart, a fucking *comedian*!'

They had met at a dinner party in Dublin. Martin was a sportswriter for the *Telegraph*. Cricket commentator mainly. Fergal was a research assistant to the Politics professor at Trinity College. He knew nothing about cricket, so when, in the middle of Martin's unintelligible gabble about front foot and middle stumps, cover point and deep mid-wicket, he quietly mentioned that he was going to America for a week or so, he didn't expect him to be interested. He was wrong. Martin pounced, grabbing his hand and spilling gin on his lapel.

'America! *Really?* Why?'

'Well, ah, I'm just going to have a look at the original homelands of the, um, the Choctaw . . . in Mississippi . . .'

'The what?'

'The Choctaw.' Fergal felt a little embarrassed. He wasn't sure if that was the real reason he was going, but he needed an excuse to get away, and if he could do some research on the relocation of native Americans in the 1830s, then that was as good an excuse as any. Research, hell – he just wanted to find himself driving through somewhere different. Martin was bewildered.

'So what's the Choctaw, then?' he demanded.

Fergal sighed, then sat him down and explained all about the Choctaw tribe and their $710.

In 1847, sixteen years after their forcible removal to Oklahoma, their Trail of Tears, news reached the Choctaw of Skullyville about the Irish Famine. So they took up a collection. And in the midst of their own poverty and the memory of their fourteen thousand dead, they raised $710. A fortune. Two years later, six hundred people died as they struggled across the Mayo mountains from Doolough to Louisburgh in search of food. The parallels made Fergal shiver, so he'd taken it upon himself to find out a little more about the Choctaw and the other Mid-West tribes, about where and how they lived before they were squeezed out west of the Mississippi River. He was planning to start in Chicago and work his way south to New Orleans.

'Chicago!' spluttered Martin. 'That's where they're sending me! Well, to start with anyway . . . they're sending me to cover the first couple of weeks of the baseball season. My editor thinks it's a cute idea.'

He spat out the word 'baseball' as if it were the most vulgar concept he'd ever encountered.

'The first game is on the first of April. Chicago Cubs versus the Anaheim Angels. If I screw this up, that's it – I'm out on my arse. This is my last chance, I think,' he said mournfully, staring at his gin.

Fergal looked at him for a while. He was pretty drunk. And he seemed to be in trouble, lost somehow. Then he suddenly clapped a heavy hand on Fergal's shoulder and almost shouted, 'Come with me! Really! I can cover games anywhere along your route. We can travel together – and the paper will pay,' he added conspiratorially. 'The car hire, the expenses – the lot! Come on – it'll be great!'

When he thought about it afterwards, Fergal didn't

remember actually agreeing to anything, but he didn't remember saying no with any great conviction either. And Martin was a great talker. Before the evening was out he'd had the whole thing organised. Fergal remembered vaguely thinking, 'This is insane. I don't even know this guy. This is insane.' But he was pretty skint. And he had to get away. So he let Martin talk, and plan, and nodded dumbly in all the right places. When Martin showed up on his doorstep a week later with a plane ticket and an itinerary, he didn't even bother to argue. What the hell, he thought, it might be good. It might be fun. Besides, this clown needed looking after.

As the plane taxied to a halt, Fergal glanced at Martin's sleeping form, and thought about Siofradh. If this trip stopped him from thinking about the past, about her, then that would be something, and maybe he wouldn't feel like a bully any more. Maybe he could discover something new and breezy, a small thing to make him feel lightweight and glamorous once again. As they left the airport to pick up their hired Pontiac, Fergal noticed a *Sun-Times* headline outside the newspaper stall – '*Appeal Rejected: La Salle to Die.*' After half an hour Fergal gradually got the hang of driving the Pontiac and headed, very slowly, into town.

In their hotel Fergal tried to phone home. Martin cleaned out the mini-bar and then started on his duty-free. He hated America and made no secret of it. He knew little about baseball and this assignment scared the hell out of him. He would much rather have been at home, covering the cricket, and the drunker he became, the more sour his rant.

'Multi-ethnicity, my arse! These people can't stand the thought that they're surrounded by shite, so they call it something else. Their theatre is vaudeville, their psychiatry is babble, their art is self-conscious tat and their whole fucking culture consists of giving enormous amounts of money to manicured gits who tell them it's okay to have the attention span of a fucking gnat!'

On his sixth whiskey, he was getting into his stride.

'Huxley was right,' he growled. 'We won't be corralled off and marched into oblivion – we will quite cheerfully dream and *dance* our way into it. Silence is mistaken for profundity, incompetent nonsense becomes "artful" kitsch and *Mr Ed* is hailed as seminal television!' He ranted on, becoming drunker all the while, not caring if Fergal was listening or not.

'This guy's off his rocker,' thought Fergal, as he tried Siofradh's number again. And again there was no answer. She'd told him not to call her. Ever. But somehow, he thought that the novelty of his calling her from another continent would make a difference. After a while he gave it up, and persuaded Martin to get some sleep. He was still rambling angrily to himself when Fergal climbed into his own bed and turned out the light.

'And they're all so fucking cheerful too . .. my God, you could probably get arrested for having a depressing thought . . . they wouldn't recognise a thing of wit or grace if it jumped up screaming and bit them in the arse . . . well, I don't care what the revisionists say – *The Beverly Hillbillies* was talentless shite then, and it's talentless shite now . . . baseball . . . Jesus H. Christ on a crutch.'

He fell asleep on his bed, still fully clothed.

In the dark, Fergal cursed silently. This was going to be a long trip. He knew little of America, but he liked the idea of it. And he'd come to be fascinated by its first inhabitants, the first true Americans. He thought about Sears Tower, built by the Mohawks, the Genawoggi to be specific, the legendary tribe with absolutely no fear of heights and therefore a talent for building skyscrapers, who would dance and shimmy on its steel skeleton at 1,400 feet, and do two hundred sit-ups before breakfast, their torsos dangling over the abyss. As he drifted off to sleep, it occurred to Fergal that if a thing *belonged* to the man who worked on it, who built it, then London belonged to the Irish, America's railways belonged to the Chinese, and all the grand, soaring towers belonged to the Mohawk.

'How long will the noblest of God's creatures, honest men, be

doomed to want food and to famish in the midst of plenty in their own
nature-blessed but misruled country?'
                              The Waterford Freeman, 9 June 1846

'You ask me to plough the ground. Shall I take a knife and tear my
mother's breast? Then when I die, she will not take me to her bosom
to rest. You ask me to cut grass and make hay and sell it and be rich
like a white man. But how shall I dare cut off my mother's hair?'
                              Smohalla, of the Sokulk (Nez Perce) tribe, 1850

The next morning, Martin awoke, groaning and clutching his
head.

'Oh, Christ, I feel like a pigeon caught in a badminton match
– what the hell did I drink last night?'

Fergal laughed and pointed at the empty bottles on the floor.

'C'mon kid – you've got copy to file – up and at 'em!'

Martin's first game coverage was over at Wrigley Field, home
of the Cubs, and he had to e-mail his report from his laptop to
London by 8 o'clock at the very latest. Still groaning, he headed
for the bathroom while Fergal called Reception and asked them
to arrange a hire car for him, just for the day. Preferably
European. He was going for a drive. He just hoped Martin's
expenses weren't going to be examined too closely when they
got home. He was poring over a map of Illinois when Martin
emerged from the bathroom.

Fergal said, 'So, Theresa's Lounge, nine o'clock, okay? It's on
the south side, near the – '

'Hey!' Martin threw him a withering look. 'I've never failed to
find a pub in my life, and I'm not about to start now,' he said.
'See you later.'

Fergal tooled the Volkswagen down East Wacker Drive into
Adams Street, then left into Franklin. The traffic was sur-
prisingly civilised. He drove slowly out of town in what he
hoped was a vaguely west/north-westerly direction, found
Highway 20, and headed for what two hundred years ago was
the Peoria homeland. He wasn't sightseeing, he was just

driving through. He drove for a couple of hours through Elgin, Cherry Valley, Pecatonica, before hitting Dubuque, almost on the Wisconsin border. There was no real countryside, just flat expanses dotted with gas stations, motels, diners and sub- urbia's identikit presence, again and again. There was nothing much to look at, but Fergal enjoyed the simple fact that he was moving through it, simply travelling.

He turned north on to Highway 151, past Cuba City, on to Platteville and east on to Highway 18. He was enjoying himself. He loved the bizarre names – Mt Horeb, Verona, New Glarus – but after two hundred miles of driving in a wide circle, he decided to head back to town. He was in another State, for God's sake, and the sheer hugeness of the place was beginning to scare him. He skirted Madison and, as the light began to fade, headed south on I-51 towards Chicago. He enjoyed his jaunt and was feeling quite brave at having negotiated these alien roads. But there was no trace left of what the Peoria had been, nor of their lives before the whites came. He hadn't expected any. He just found it interesting to wonder, to guess about the intricacies of their daily existence in this giant parish where once had been only prairie, timber, buffalo, and greenness as far as the eye could see. This part of Illinois had been home not just to the Peorias but also the Kickapoos, the Cahokia, the Sauk and Fox, the Kas-Kas-Ki-As, the Illinois themselves. Sophisticated farmers and vintners, they also cultivated square miles of plum trees, gooseberries, wild currants, prickly pears and, for the love of it, wild roses. Whiskey and smallpox did for the Kickapoos and the Kas-Kas-Ki-As, and by 1830 the kind and inoffensive Peorias were down to two hundred civilised members, under contract to move west of the Mississippi. Just like everybody else.

He dropped the keys at Reception and, outside, hailed a cab. When he got to Theresa's, Martin was already there. He'd filed his copy an hour ago and was sitting in a dim booth at the back, rewarding himself with a bottle of Black Bush.

'So, how was the game?' said Fergal as he sat down.

'Three hours of boredom, topped off with fifteen minutes of mild excitement, I'd say. What did you do, anyway?'

'Oh, I just went for a spin around the county.'

He knew that Martin wasn't remotely interested in either the landscape or the Indians.

'Really, though – tell me about the game.'

If I can keep him talking, thought Fergal, he might not get completely rat-arsed.

Martin looked at him for a moment. He smiled slightly.

'Well, the Cubs have got Brant Brown, a fine defensive first baseman, who hits for a high average but without much power. Against that is the Angels' Rob Jennings, the front runner in what is, admittedly, a pretty crowded left field. Okay, he doesn't have the highest ceiling of his group, but he's a .293 hitter over his career, a utility player and heir apparent to second base. Now, the first six innings were low scoring. The Cubs kept trying to steal second base before the pitcher got to the plate, and Doug Abbott just picked 'em off one by one. Sloppy running as well, I noticed – too many fade-away slides; okay, it's effective because it gives the fielder nothing to tag, but not very interesting to watch, you know? Now in the bottom of the ninth, it actually became quite exciting. Two bases were loaded, the score was close, Castillo batted to the infield after a couple of sacrifice bunks, Garvie the catcher bounced up as first baseman, and shortstop Pemberton covered second. Cameron on third didn't stand a chance. Ball came back in from fair territory, he broke too early, catcher tagged his arse. Castillo should've bunted, given him a sacrifice fly. But there were less than two outs, and it was a classic suicide squeeze. Hajek's split-finger knuckleball, that's some asset, believe me . . .'

Martin winked at him and sipped from his glass, pinky in the air.

Fergal stared at him. He'd barely understood a word.

'So who won?' he said through gritted teeth.

'The Cubs,' replied Martin, smiling sweetly.

'How did you get to be so knowledgeable about baseball?'

'I didn't. I lifted it straight from this afternoon's radio coverage. Why do you think I brought a tape recorder?'

And then he began to laugh.

'You think my editor knows the first damn thing about baseball? You think he's going to know the difference? Of course not. All he wants is jargon, a spiel, something that makes everybody feel as if they know what they're talking about. When they don't. To tell you the truth, it's not so different from my early cricket days. All I have to do is walk the walk, talk the talk, throw in some fancy verbiage and spell the fucking players' names correctly! Besides, when I get home, he's probably going to fire me anyway. Bastard. The man is not a writer. He doesn't know good coverage when he sees it, so how's he going to recognise a straight lift? Good writing? That swine couldn't write the word "FUCK" on a dusty Venetian blind. So why should I bother . . .? Hey! Just call me the Bubonic Plagiarist.'

He laughed again and drained his glass. This is not a happy man, thought Fergal. But even so, it was pretty funny.

'Fair play to you,' he said, smiling. 'Why not? It's a good plot.'

He wanted to talk about the Peorias, but he knew there was no point. As he went to the bar for another bottle of Bush, he glanced up at the television. The news report was about James La Salle, the convicted killer on Death Row in Jackson, Georgia. He was due to go to the chair in six days. Behind him, Martin was staring intently at the screen. La Salle was convicted eight years ago of murdering a gas station cashier. He had been as high as a kite. But he did it. No question. The location TV reporter, a pretty brunette, was standing outside Georgia's Diagnostic and Classification Center, where La Salle and a hundred other Death Row inmates were being kept, most of them in H-5 block. The camera panned across the dozens of pro-capital punishment groupies as they waved banners and drank from their thermos flasks and hollered for blood in the chilly night. Further along was a small group of La Salle's supporters, with candles and prayerful songs and no banners. They looked pretty pathetic. When it was announced that La Salle's latest application for a stay of execution had been turned down, there was a low murmur of approval from the other patrons, but apart from that no one was really interested. Except Martin. As the night wore on, he became increasingly vocal in his disapproval.

'Fucking savages,' he snarled, loudly.

'Please Martin, shut up,' pleaded Fergal.

A few people looked around.

'No, I won't shut up! It's barbaric and it makes me sick. And they call themselves civilised? Fucking Americans . . .'

At this, a large man stepped out of the next booth and, looming over their table, said, 'Well, I think the scumbag should fry, and the sooner the better. I ain't got no problem with that, not one bit.'

He stared menacingly at Martin, who merely arched one snobby eyebrow.

'Well, sir,' he said pompously, 'as a guest in your fine country, my position does not permit me to argue with you. However,' he hissed, narrowing his eyes, 'if it ever did come to a choice of weapons, mine would be *grammar*.'

For a long moment there was silence.

He didn't even see the punch coming and he was probably too drunk to feel it. Fergal spent the next ten minutes apologising for his friend's rudeness and, when Martin had managed to haul himself off the floor and was steady enough to walk, they headed outside for a taxi. Fergal was furious.

'What's the matter with you? Why are you always looking for a fight? Jesus Christ, man – you want to get yourself killed – fine, but just don't drag me into it, okay?'

'I'm sorry,' Martin said thickly, holding a hanky to his nose. 'I'm just fed up with people dying all over the shop. Ah, fuck it, I need some kip. Let's go back to the hotel.'

This time, despite another whisky, he actually managed to get his jacket and shoes off, before collapsing face down on his bed, mumbling to himself about fat comedians.

'What's that all about then, eh?' he drawled, his voice muffled. 'Oliver Hardy, Jackie Gleason, Zero Mostel, Jonathan Winters – '

'Martin, please be quiet. Go to sleep.'

'Alexei Sayle, Fatty Arbuckle, George Wendt, Mike McShane – what is it about big blokes and jokes? And why is it – '

'Martin, *please.*'

'– why is it that we got the best tragedy when times were good, y'know, like ancient Greece and Elizabethan England, and the best comedy – '

'I'm going to kill you in a minute.'

'– and the best comedy when times were tough – the thirties, y'know, the Marx Brothers and that, eh? I wonder if Shakespeare could've come up with a decent comedy if he'd been writing in the 1980s, eh?'

Yeah, thought Fergal, he'd have written a blistering comedy about sleep deprivation and dead sportswriters . . .

'And another thing – '

'Martin, SHUT UP!'

People dying all over the shop. What had he meant by that? Something was eating this guy up, but Fergal was too tired to figure it out.

In the dark he wondered if she would ever speak to him again. God, Siofradh was so lovely. A placid, delicate woman with a breezy intelligence who was too nice to deny his anxiety, his fears for the future, a woman who had caved in so quietly he'd barely noticed. His decorative common sense had been too much for her; when she found she was pregnant, the whiplash dynamic of his logic, his financial nous, simply left her with nowhere to go, no space to stroll. The fresh, scrappy enchantment she'd felt in those first few days didn't stand a chance against him and his list of effortlessly worrying formulae, and gradually he whittled her precarious joy into a gloomy little problem that had to be solved. With his pessimistically steely chatter, he just wore her down until he had turned it into little more than a day trip without privileges. He never knew he

could do that. He had never realised that fear could turn a good
man into a kindly and nerveless lout. In the dark Martin's
phrase made a little more vile sense, and Fergal forced himself
to think of other things.

*'Fellow countrymen – surely God is angry with this land. The
potatoes would not have rotted unless He sent the rot into them; God
can never be taken unawares; nothing can happen but as He orders it.
God is good, and because He is, He never sends a scourge upon His
creatures unless they deserve it – but He is so good that He often
punishes people in mercy . . .'*

Rev. Edward Nagle, Achill Island, *Missionary Herald*,
24 February 1847

*'When he first came over the wide waters, he was but a little man,
very little . . . But when the white man had warmed himself at the
Indians' fire, he became very large. With a step he bestrode the
mountains and his feet covered the plains and the valleys. His hand
grasped the eastern and western sea, and his head rested on the
moon. Then he became our Great Father. He loved his red children,
and he said, "Get a little further, lest I tread on thee . . ." Brothers, I
have listened to a great many talks from our Great Father. But they
always began and ended in this – "Get a little further; you are too
near me . . ."'*

Speckled Snake, Creek Indian, 1829

They paid up and set off very early the following morning for
Indianapolis. And despite feeling about as lively as a galvanised
corpse, Martin actually volunteered to do some of the driving.
After a couple of hours and 150 miles, they stopped off in
Peoria, Illinois. In a shiny café that seemed to be constructed
from plastic, Martin sucked on a beer and studied his new-
found bible, USA TODAY's *Baseball Weekly*. The Seattle Mariners
were taking on the Milwaukee Brewers. In Peoria. Peoria,
Arizona, that is. He sighed and looked at Fergal across the table.

'God knows how many Peorias there are. Jesus, sometimes the *size* of this place just does my head in.'

He went back to his paper, concentrating hard. He looked like a one-man slum. Talk about a fish out of water, thought Fergal. He studied Martin's furrowed brow.

'"Ken Cameron",' said Martin, reading from the paper, '"the best, and most underrated five-tool prospect around", it says here.'

He looked up and winked at Fergal, smiling evilly.

'"This right-fielder's prospect ceiling is sky high; he flirted with a 30–30 season at Double-A Birmingham, falling two short in the homer department, but still leading the Southern League with 39 steals, a great vertical leap and a good, solid work ethic."'

Fergal laughed gently.

'So a few more paragraphs nicked and that's today's copy sorted, is it?'

'Pretty much, yeah,' said Martin. 'Mind you,' he said, his nose still buried in the paper, 'This game's beginning to make a bit more sense . . .'

He read in silence for an hour, while Fergal stared out the window at the people going by in the town plaza. Everything outside shone in the bright early afternoon sun. Over to the left of the square there was a space in the throng, a gap around the edges of which shoppers veered, as if quietly avoiding something, and yet not avoiding, just subconsciously veering, smoothly. And in the middle was a man, a preacher of sorts. Fergal shielded his eyes against the sun to have a better look at his livid mime. The man wore an ill-fitting suit and thrashed in circles, pointing accusingly at passers-by. Some smiled nervously, but most shied away from his mad eyes and windmill arms and his yawning threnody, a silent rant of doom and condemnation. Fergal was mesmerised. The man was actually frothing, his pet faith, whatever it was, insanity's party line. On-lookers were scared and yet not scared, veering yet laughing, and shaking their heads at this duff casualty. And the longer he sloshed around in his well-defined circle, the surer Fergal became that what he was screaming about was retribution and death and days to come. He watched that mad, miserable flamenco until he realised that Martin was watching it too, and that he also was dumbly hypnotised. His cigarette had burned through his bible's 'White Sox Spring Training Review', and he had noticed neither the smell of scorched paper nor his own trembling fingers.

Fergal took over the driving, south then east on to Interstate 36 through Normal, Bloomington, Decature and Tuscola. At last, he thought, some of the open space he'd read about. Out here, at last, there existed a fine, big sky with ball-point streaks of dirty cloud, and all around a montage of sheer, spring fields, growing little yet, but green and promising. An immense and orbiting version of home. He gathered speed, enjoying the Pontiac's power and the space he found himself in, and aimed the wheel at the goalposts of the road's distance horizon. Whatever had happened in the past, at that moment he felt better than he had in two years, and neither this place's metallic cities nor Martin's sulphuric, cavalier piffle could drag him down. He was tired of being held a twitching hostage to thoughts that mugged him in the night. He was just bloody fed up with it.

After 250 miles, Martin hadn't said a word. In Indianapolis they checked into the Regal 8 Inn around 7 o'clock. Martin headed for the nearest pub and Fergal settled on his bed with his books. This could get to be a routine.

Indiana. Shawnee territory. This once powerful tribe had occupied grand tracts of Pennsylvania and New Jersey, and the Delaware and Chesapeake Bays, before being shunted west into Ohio and Indiana on a long and disastrous pilgrimage which reduced them to 1,200 in number, poor, miserably dependent, and without the nerve either to work or hunt. Even Tecumseh, Shooting Star, their greatest orator and celebrated war chief, could not rescind the 1809 Treaty whereby the Shawnee ceded most of the land others regarded as theirs to the government. They sold it because quite possibly they had never regarded themselves as its owners. Whatever prospects Tecumseh's great Indian Confederacy ever had, died with him. There would be no Red uprising from Mexico to the Great Lakes, no mystery fire nor schemes of sacredness, nor battle frenzy to drive back the Whites. Placid agriculturists, raising corn and beans, potatoes and hogs. A small piece of land in promised perpetuity was, by 1850, all that remained.

Fergal threw the book aside, irritated. He was getting tired of sad stories about loss and plunder, true or otherwise. His earlier, buoyant mood had disappeared and offensive sorrow was crowding in on him. This trip was to have taken him out of himself, to banish the past, yet that was all he could think about. Whole peoples shrinking and shivering into nothingness, his own vicious heart, and a fellow traveller whose dedicated mockery spoke of something Fergal could not read. Christ, he needed a drink.

When Martin said 'the nearest pub' he'd obviously meant just that. Twenty yards from the hotel, Fergal found him perched precariously on a bar stool in a place called Gerry's. Unsurprisingly he was pissed, but that didn't stop him talking. As Fergal approached, he was expounding to a recently acquired coterie of bemused locals his theory on Heaven and Hell. His accent had acquired an almost cartoonish Englishness. He sounded like Prince Charles stoned. The locals loved it. Nothing better than a drunk, talkative tourist. Cheaper than the juke box. Fergal parked himself with a lager at the far end of the bar, head down.

'You think Heaven is some out-of-body experience, where everybody finds their own little psychic niche?' shouted Martin. 'Where everybody's happy and redeemed, and floats about like a fart in a blizzard in a place of great and infinite height? The ethereal, vaulted abode of God? Well, that's bullshit, okay?' Oh, this was going down well. A couple of drunk girls asked to check his wallet, just to see if he was for real; Martin handed it over. He didn't give a shit. Fergal swerved quietly into the noise and the giggles and, smiling the smile of the apologetic friend, retrieved the wallet, while Martin just carried right on. People were starting to laugh at him, but kindly so. He kept swigging and he kept blathering.

'The Heaven we imagine, right? It's shite. The true Heaven is the Heaven we were taught when we were six years old. Heaven really *is* the pearly gates, choirs of angels, gleaming spires and an old, white-haired bloke who's been in a bad mood *forever*. Except his son's a cripple. And it's the most boring place imaginable. Marginally worse than Hell, which, I might add, is also *exactly* how you remember it – fire, brimstone, screaming souls, guys with horns and pitchforks. The works.'

'Great stuff,' he added happily, and polished off another drink.

One of the girls draped an arm across his shoulder and said, 'Guys with horns, eh?'

Martin cocked a baleful eyebrow at her.

'You can buy me a drink if you like, sweetheart,' she cooed.

'Madam,' snapped Martin, recoiling, 'I strongly suspect that if *you* were in Hell, Dante himself wouldn't piss on you.'

Her smile slipped.

'But being American, I imagine you already know what Hell is like,' he added spitefully.

That did it. After she'd slapped him across the face and kicked him in the kneecaps a couple of times, Fergal was obliged to bundle him out the door before her burly friends did it for him, probably breaking a few bones in the process. You just don't go around insulting women, that's all. Or America, for that matter. As Fergal dragged him outside, Martin was still shouting over his shoulder.

'And if this place is so fucking great, how come the bald eagle, your national symbol for God's sake, is practically fucking *extinct*, eh? Answer that and stay fashionable, you bastards!'

I should've let them have his bloody wallet, thought Fergal, as he dragged Martin down the street by the scruff, still mouthing to himself. He suddenly pulled up short and looked blearily at Fergal.

'I did it again, didn't I?' he said miserably.

'Yep. Martin – what exactly is your problem? These people haven't done you any harm. This place is okay. Why are you always trying to get yourself hurt?'

'That's what my wife used to ask. All the time,' Martin said, looking at the ground.

'Your wife? You never mentioned a wife.' Fergal was surprised.

'Ex-wife.'

'Ah.' Hardly surprising, really.

'Can't blame the girl, I must admit. When she found out what I was like, she went through with the divorce faster than a dose of salts through a short grandmother.'

'Nice girl,' he added sadly, swaying and rubbing his eyes. 'A very, very nice girl. Mind you, when she was annoyed about something, she could have a tongue on her like a bee's bum . . . Poor cow.'

Fergal looked at him for a moment. He was too tired to be angry for long.

'Come on,' he sighed, 'bedtime,' and took him by the elbow.

Martin fell asleep sprawled on his bed, so Fergal took off his shoes and tie and made an effort to cover him up and tuck him in. Those guys would've killed him if I hadn't been there, he thought, and that thought made him, in an odd way, feel good.

At some point during the night he heard Martin's voice in the dark, a small child's voice, saying his name and asking him a question. Fergal struggled to waken properly.

'What?'

'I said, do you know how many US soldiers died in Vietnam?'

'For God's sake – no, I don't know. I don't know. How many?' he asked wearily, blinking into the blackness.

'Just under sixty thousand.'

'So?' This was ridiculous.

'Almost eighty thousand veterans have committed suicide since then.'

'Martin,' Fergal hissed, 'it's the middle of the night. Is there a point to this?'

'No. I'm sorry. It's just that some figures stick in the mind, that's all. Sorry.' His voice was barely more than a thin, grieving whisper.

'Sorry. Go back to sleep . . .'

'The Public Works have been a costly failure . . . the tide of Irish distress appears now to have completely overflowed the barriers we opposed to it. This is a real famine in which thousands and thousands of people are likely to die; none the less, if the Irish once find out there are any circumstances in which they can get free Government grants . . . we shall have a system of mendicancy such as the world never saw.'

Lord Trevelyan, 1 February 1847

'I can remember when the bison were so many that they could not be counted, but more and more Wasichus came to kill them until there was only heaps of bones scattered where they used to be. The Wasichus did not kill them to eat; they killed them for the metal that makes them crazy, and they took only the hides to sell. Sometimes they did not even take the hides, only the tongues . . . Sometimes they did not take the tongues; they just killed and killed because they liked to do that. When we hunted bison, we killed only what we needed.'

Hehaka Sapa (Black Elk), Sioux Chief, 1890

In the morning Fergal agreed to detour to St Louis so that Martin could take in the game between the Cardinals and the Minnesota Twins. Martin found it strange that a lot of teams weren't even based in their home town. The Cardinals lived in Phoenix, Arizona; this was just a visit home.

'And the Atlanta Braves are based in Palm Beach, for God's sake – next year, they're moving to Walt Disney World! And some of the best players are Cuban, or Puerto Rican or, these days, Japanese. It's strange,' he murmured, as he looked out the car window. 'It doesn't seem to matter where they call home.'

He'd been reading more about the game. That morning before they set off he'd nipped out and bought a couple of books about the history and strategy of baseball, and buried his nose in them as Fergal eventually found Interstate 40 and headed south-west. They passed through a couple of medium-sized, compact towns – Brazil, Casey, Vandalia – before it started to rain. Sure, they all had the iconic pinnacles of MacDonald arches and out-of-town small malls, but Fergal loved each of them. He had trouble keeping his eyes on the road, he was so busy watching the kids and the late-afternoon matrons, the shops and the generally flat, two-storey, unambitious skylines. He'd seen this populated, concrete landscape a million times on TV and in the movies. It was ordinary and familiar to him and yet, because he was now in it, screamingly different. The rain kept up until they reached town, then lightened and stopped. The 630 ft steel Gateway Arch gleamed in the sudden early afternoon sunshine; Martin swapped his books for a city map and they headed for the stadium. Flicking around the radio stations, Fergal alighted on a brief news report. La Salle had been granted a stay of execution. Martin stopped wrestling with the map for a moment and glanced at the radio, but he didn't say anything.

In the car park outside the stadium they agreed to meet back at the Ramada after the game. The Pontiac could stay there all night and to hell with the expense.

'Why don't you come on in and watch the game?' said Martin suddenly. A dull cheer went up from inside the grounds.

'No thanks,' said Fergal, 'I'm not really interested. I think I'll just go for a wander, have a beer, do some reading . . .'

'Well, okay, but to be honest, I could get quite fond of baseball. Once you understand the rules, it's pretty interesting . . . well, anyway. See you later.' Martin looked disappointed.

'Yeah.'

A thought occurred to Fergal as he walked away.

'The Choctaw played ball, you know,' he called. 'A hundred years ago. Great ball players. Nothing like baseball. Or cricket, either. But they played a massive, big bloody game of ball.'

Martin looked at him, baffled.

Fergal laughed. 'I'll tell you about it another time.'

He walked around the city for a couple of hours, poking around in second-hand bookshops and coffee houses, visiting the Old Cathedral Museum, learning about the fur trade and the tobacco trade and the cotton trade, the selling and the buying, the loading and the shifting and the unloading, the slaves and the free men, the lives lost and the fortunes won. He learned a lot in one afternoon but, after a while, his head began to spin and he needed to sit down somewhere quiet with a cold beer and no one for company. In a small, graceful bar on Chestnut Street he flicked through the books he'd bought – local history mainly – and sipped his Miller. He hadn't attempted to phone her in two days. There was no point. And there was no point in wittering on internally about the possibility of getting her back. At the bar no one bothered him. No one spoke to him. Fergal had always liked that. In public places he had a knack for creating around him an impenetrable shield which, while not making him appear remotely unfriendly or odd, simply put people off. But if he did feel like talking, he just had to smile or raise an eyebrow, the invisible barrier dissolved, and after ten minutes most people thought he was a pretty nice guy. Maybe it wasn't a knack. Maybe it was dumb strategy. But he had never done that with Siofradh. No, she had marched right in like some fearsome pixie and nibbled on his heart until he felt bright and chuffed and madly in love. He could not understand why he had been so afraid, so anxious, why this announced little snippet, barely a life, had sent him into that bullying freefall. She went to the clinic by herself and, after that, he wasn't brilliant any more. After that he was a care-beaten chicken who'd won his

argument. He was the clever, steroidal boy whose touch she
could no longer bear. He was the man with all the wrong jokes.
A month later she'd packed and moved out, crying and empty
still.

Martin showed up in the Ramada bar around 10 o'clock,
looking flushed and pleased with himself. He'd finished his
report earlier in another bar; the owner, an ex-pat Brummie,
had let him plug in his laptop and send it there and then.

'And it's good stuff too – you missed a really good game!
Wanna hear about it?'

'Oh sure,' said Fergal drily. 'Do I have time to run out and get
hit by a bus first?'

Martin laughed and talked enthusiastically for ten minutes
about the outfielders' balleticism, about Mark Wellington's
miraculous south-paw hitting (in spite of a shoulder injury),
about how the Cardinals' second and third base runners almost
accidentally flattened each other, about the Twins' three
homers from Hideki Hirasatu, about how the crowd went crazy,
and did the cleanest Mexican wave ever . . . Martin stopped and
looked at Fergal. He laughed, almost sheepishly.

'I think it's that thing about the rules. Once you understand
the rules, everything else just automatically makes sense. Sort
of. And I didn't even swipe the copy. Wrote it myself.'

'I understand that, I think,' said Fergal.

They talked for a while about St Louis and tried to ignore the
TV report on La Salle. The flickering background candles,
people in thick jackets, the pseudo-urgency of the reporter's
voice, mike in hand – it was becoming as familiar as *Panorama*.
La Salle's stay of execution had been withdrawn and a few
banner-waving rednecks were having a satisfying whoop.
Martin poured himself another Scotch, downed it in one and
covered his ears with his hands. This case was getting on his
nerves. Fergal didn't mind it so much. He patted him briefly on
the head. Poor Martin. It was sad, but what can you do? Why,
scientists in Moscow and Atlanta were currently arguing the

toss about whether or not to kill off the world's last two remaining stocks of the smallpox virus, kept in secure laboratories. Kill it and keep us all safe in our beds, or let it live and study it? Fergal didn't fancy the idea of a life without risk, or even the desire for a life without risk; otherwise we'd all end up like the moron who got half-fried in Yellowstone Park and sued the authorities for not advising her on where lightning was likely to strike. And won. As for risk – well, thought Fergal, if Martin was too tired to start another fight, then he'd be happy enough with that particular result. Martin had uncovered his ears and was listening to the news. The way they mangled the English language seemed to hold for him a kind of horrified fascination.

'My God,' he said at last, 'it's like watching a monkey with a Ming vase . . . Christ, I need some kip.'

As he drifted off he was mumbling about TV shows and their 'chickenshit 5-5-5. You don't get that at home, I'll tell you. I bet our lot give out *real* phone numbers. I'll bet we've got thousands of little old ladies being tormented twenty-four hours a day, up and down the country . . .'

There was no real venom in it though; he was simply talking for the quiet joy of hearing the sound of his own voice. It was his own sweet personal lullaby, a thing to keep a man company when nothing else seemed to work any more.

In the dark Fergal found his thoughts drawn to La Salle and his three days of life left. What a thing that must be. To know. I'd rather be sitting in a Chinese restaurant with my friends, he thought, after a good meal, plenty of wine and beer, and just have some total stranger sneak up behind me with a double-barrelled shotgun. I wouldn't know a thing. Perfect. The chair. Jesus, that must be like some modern equivalent of being burnt at the stake. Fergal had read stories of prisoners' eyeballs popping out and their hair catching fire, of how the brain reaches 60°C, about how, when the autopsy is performed, the liver is still so hot it cannot be touched by human hands, about how one guy took six jolts and forty minutes to finally die, whimpering for his life most of the way.

Fergal shuddered and turned over in his bed. He didn't want to feel sympathy for La Salle. What he did feel wasn't sympathy, exactly. It was more like what a soft, shrinking child feels when scolded. The feeling that rebounds, antiquely, saying 'You should have known better'. La Salle should've known better. Fergal should've known better. Better than to have trusted the interior colony of his own scared common sense. Martin's distressedly quiet snoring drifted across the room, a trademark of wincing bliss. Wondrous affliction.

'The general feeling is one of despair. The subjection of the masses in Westport is extraordinary. A large crowd marched to Westport House and asked to see Lord Sligo. When his lordship appeared, someone cried "kneel, kneel," and the crowd dropped on its knees before him.'

Commissariat Officer, Westport, October 1846

'In the life of the Indian there was only one inevitable duty – the duty of prayer – the daily recognition of the Unseen and Eternal . . . His mate may precede him or follow him in his devotions, but never accompanies him. Each soul must meet the morning sun, the new sweet earth and the Great Silence, alone . . . He sees no need for setting apart one day in seven as a holy day, since to him all days are God's.'

Ohiyesa, Santee Dakota physician, 1911

Martin, despite his hangover, drove most of the three hundred miles from St Louis to Memphis, where he wanted to drop in on a small game between the Knoxville Smokies and the Memphis Chicks. Neither team was major league, but that was okay. Besides, Fergal wanted to be able to say he'd at least driven past Graceland. In filthy hail, they caught Highway 45, east through Cairo, Clinton and Greenfield. After stopping off for a quick beer in Milan – Martin wanted to commemorate the fact that he'd just driven through a town called Martin, and Fergal had just about persuaded him that pissing on the town's namepost was neither a grand nor a wise gesture – they headed south-west on 70 through Humboldt and Bells. Flicking through his reference books, Fergal realised vaguely that this had once been Chickasaw country, along with the Quapaw slightly to the north-west, and their eastern neighbours, the Koasati. The Chickasaws and Choctaws were amiable enough neighbours, sharing cultural idiosyncrasies such as head-flattening, which they seemed to have borrowed from the Chinooks. According to Fergal's reference book, from which he read aloud, 'This process was done in earliest infancy, with an inclined piece of wood strapped against the child's forehead, and drawn down a little more tightly each day. Whilst seem-ingly cruel, it probably caused little pain since, at that age, the bones of the skull are soft and cartilaginous, and easily pressed into that distorted shape. By this process, the brain was chan-ged from its natural dimensions, but not in the least diminished or injured in its natural functions.'

'They probably ended up looking like some of the guys I went to public school with,' snorted Martin. 'Flatheads, to a man.'

Despite the dirty noon weather, Martin was determined to catch at least some of the game. He dropped Fergal off near Elvis Presley Boulevard, agreeing to meet at the same spot at 5 o'clock. They had to get to Atlanta, over four hundred miles away, before their hotel gave the room away. Fergal thought he might go for a wander around town, see a few things.

In the end he saw nothing of Memphis and nothing of Graceland. He spent all afternoon in the gift shop. It was the most mind-boggling shop he'd ever been in, and he wasn't even a fan. He pored over the velveteen paintings of the King in Heaven, the mugs, embossed with the lyrics to 'Love Me Tender', in the shape of Elvis's head, the 24-piece dinner sets emb-lazoned with images of the mansion. He was mesmerised by the sheer imagination required to come up with something like a white jump-suit teacosy. Who drank tea, anyway? Eventually, he caved in and, for $4.50, bought himself a small pouch of dirt in a special folder, officially certified to be taken from

Graceland's flowerbeds. It even came with a stamped gold seal of authenticity. A snip.

It was almost dark when Martin rolled up. He'd filled the tank so they made straight for I-78, and south-east. Just after New Albany, Fergal took over the driving.

'So, what was the game like?' he said.

'Oh, the Chicks got hammered, but it was good. Lots of families. Lots of kids. Guess what I did?'

'Punched a linesman?'

'Sod off. No. I had a hotdog. And a Coke.'

'Oh Jesus,' said Fergal, 'that's it. There's no hope for you now. You've gone the Way of all Flesh.'

'With mustard and onions.'

'Well, I might as well just take you out and shoot you right now, eh?'

Martin smiled to himself and got out his copy of *Baseball Weekly*.

They drove through the evening gloom for a couple of hours in a silence that was almost comradely. Forty minutes after crossing the Alabama State Line, Martin shouted.

'Stop! I've got to see this!'

'What? Jesus . . .' said Fergal anxiously.

'Turn left here.'

'We can by-pass Birmingham.'

'No, I want to see it. It'll only take a minute.'

'See what?'

'The Stadium. Rickwood Field. It's the oldest baseball stadium in America, according to this,' Martin said, jabbing a finger at his paper. 'Come on, please. I want to see it.'

'Well, gee whiz . . .' muttered Fergal sarcastically as he found the next exit.

Outside the stadium Martin produced a bottle from his pocket, took a swig, replaced it, and began to climb over the fence. He rolled over the top and landed with an audible thump.

'Martin, this is fucking insane! We're gonna get arrested!'

'By whom, pray tell?' came Martin's voice, grunting, from the other side.

He had a point. There was no one around. It was dark.

'Oh, fuck it,' thought Fergal, and climbed over. Sitting smack in the centre of the pitcher's mound, in complete and frosty darkness, Martin took out his pen-torch and his bottle, and offered it to Fergal.

Fergal took it and sat down. This was surreal.

'18 August 1910,' said Martin, shining the light in Fergal's face.

'Don't do that.' Fergal took a large swig.

'Sorry. Ty Cobb, Babe Ruth, Satchel Paige, Josh Gibson, Frank Thomas, Walt Dropo, Cool Papa Bell. They say Papa Bell was so fast he could turn off the light switch and be in bed before it got dark.'

Martin laughed. He flopped on to his back and laughed gently to himself. Then he stopped laughing, grabbed the bottle and finished it off.

'The White Sox shouldn't have been crucified for taking the easy option,' he drawled. 'That wasn't right. Nobody should be crucified for doing the only thing they can do. For just looking after themselves. Everybody would go crazy otherwise, wouldn't they? That's why I left. I left and *then* she divorced me. And I don't blame her one bit. No sirree Bob – hey, I'm even picking up the language!'

And he started to laugh again, and a crusty, bitter sound it was. Fergal shone the torch at him for a long time.

'Why did you leave?'

The Stadium seemed to him like a giant grave. The blackness and the deserted space were tangible things, swallowing up Martin's cracked laughter, dissolving blackly the torchlight, the feel of cold grass, sucking their very breathing into funky silence. They lay on their backs for a while, freezing and thinking about people who leave and people who are driven away, freezing and staring at the stars, the only light, cold and considering their options.

Martin didn't answer.

Eventually, Fergal decided he was still sober enough to drive, so he hauled Martin off the grass and they searched blindly for an exit. With the thin torch, they found a tunnel leading out on to the street. The place wasn't even locked . . .

Fergal drove through the chilly night, through Leeds and Bremen and Tallapoosa, while Martin slept on the back seat, and he remembered that this was Cherokee country. He couldn't get out his books, but he remembered, as cars thundered past him in the dark, that in the 1830s they comprised about 22,000 members. Skilled agriculturists and well advanced in the arts. Their chief, John Ross, was a man known for the 'rigid temperance of his habits and the purity of his language', a man who opposed the treaty obliging the Cherokee to move. Again, west of the Mississippi. The river seemed to be a totemic benchmark, the watery line of banishment. Even Ross couldn't fight it, and they moved. West of the Mississippi. Fergal looked out the side window into the dark at the orange, distant chimera of towns he had no wish to visit, and tried to imagine their obliteration and a green ancient daylight, filled with quiet colour and underpopulated industry, without exotic Whites, shorn of grimly flashy incomers. They never stood a chance. Neither the Cherokee nor their good North Carolina neighbours, the gentle Yuchi, nor any of the rest ever stood a chance. To move west was the ultimate, unbeatable virtue. For Fergal, to try to imagine a flipside history, with eternal stasis and no one having to leave, simply made his head hurt. And besides, the notorious Atlanta By-pass was coming up. He had to concentrate on what he was doing if he wasn't going to get blown away by the Indy-500 boy racers. Even at 10.30 p.m. it was packed and furious. Once in town, Fergal stopped dead in a sidestreet and asked for directions to the Red Roof Inn. In the back Martin began to talk softly to himself.

In the hotel room neither of them wanted to turn on the radio. Martin laid his clothes out neatly. He didn't touch the mini-bar. He sat silently for an hour, typing out his copy on the small, unimportant game between the Chicks and the Smokies. It was going to be late, but he wanted to take his time with it. He wanted it to be good. He wanted it to be poetic. Fergal swiped a min-gin, read his book and said nothing. Just after they turned out the light, Martin slotted a tape into his cassette, pressed 'play' and turned the volume almost completely down. Fergal could just barely hear it, a sweet, forlorn horn, so familiar yet now a strange, fine sound. He smiled to himself as he drifted off. The tune played all night on a soft and low continuous loop. It was the theme from *Coronation Street*.

'I often think of betaking myself to some other country, rather than see with my eyes and hear with my ears the melancholy spectacle and dismal wailing of the gaunt spectres that persecute and crowd about me from morning until night, imploring for some assistance.'
Archdeacon John O'Sullivan, Kenmore, Co. Kerry,
January 1847

'Had our forefathers spurned you when the French were thundering . . . to drive you into the sea, whatever has been the fate of other Indians, the Iroquois might still have been a nation; and I – instead of pleading for the privilege of living within your borders – I might have had a country!
Wa-owo-wa-no-onk, Cayuga Chief, May 1847

In the late morning, Martin sat in the lobby, boning up on the Braves who that afternoon were making an infrequent trip home to take on the New York Yankees. He was actually pretty excited about this game. He'd learned a lot in less than a week.

Fergal took himself off for a wander and some lunch. He mooched around the art gallery, or rather the High Museum of Art, on Peachtree, with its great Le Witt and Stella rooms, and then decided to try out some southern cooking in a nearby restaurant. After an astonishing plateful of fried chicken, baked squash, turnip greens and corn muffins, he settled back in his chair with his books. The waitress didn't seem to mind. The sun streamed in the window. There were only three other diners. It was very quiet. He skimmed over the pages and wondered if Martin was okay. In the last five days Fergal had spoken to virtually no one else; he wasn't a great one for getting in with the locals. Hotel receptionists, gas station attendants, waiters, dog-walkers – with fingers pointing vaguely and garbled directions – that was it. That suited him. His books spoke of authentic tongues, of Mak-pi-ha Lu-ta, and of Tatanka Yotanka – Red Cloud and Sitting Bull – but Fergal felt too full and sleepy and warmed by the sunshine to think about anything very deeply. He knew he wasn't adventurous or a great and good talker. He could do it, but he preferred to watch and to indulge himself in the wisdom of idleness and observation. Well, that's how he liked to think of it. If he was honest, it was probably laziness as much as anything. He leaned further back in his chair and closed his eyes and hoped Martin was getting a good take on the game. He kept his eyes closed and allowed the sun to warm his face and decided that he might make a phone call home. And then he decided that he wouldn't. He could not compete with the ferocious niceties of justified hatred. And that's what it was. No getting away from it. She hated him. It was a hatred so tangible, distantly, it felt like reassurance. He could hang on to that. There were to be neither sophisticated pleas, nor hot sympathy, only a taut acceptance. His stomach heaved every time he thought about it. He couldn't help it, but no amount of haywire, hurtful gut-rumbling was going to make him pick up a phone. No point in being a sheer fool about it. Sometimes he wished for Martin's syncretic blather, a small turn at being aloof, at playing the bristling fancyman who could advise earn-estly and with real love. Instead of leaning with a cool and heavy kindness, and a fear that spoke of no love at all, a fear that spoke of solutions, of cares and of a grieving commonwealth. Fergal leaned further back in his chair, knowing, even with his eyes closed, that the waitress was watching him and waiting for him to fall over backwards. No chance. He teetered in the sun's rays for a long while, head back and filled with nothing very much.

'Let's go to Jackson!'

Fergal opened his eyes. It was Martin. The sun had begun to set.

'How did you know I was here?'

'I didn't,' said Martin. 'I was just looking for a drink. I walk in and here you are. Amazing eh? Anyway c'mon, let's go to Jackson.'

'Isn't that a song?'

'Yes. No. I don't know. Never mind. I want to go to the Centre.'

'La Salle?'

'Yeah. C'mon, let's go.'

'Why? I mean, *why?* Martin, you hate all this La Salle stuff. You *hate* it.'

'I know. That's why I have to go.'

Martin swiped him over the head with his *Baseball Weekly*.

'It's only thirty or forty miles south of here. I just want to see it. Please. I'm half-pissed. I can't drive. I have to see it. Come on, Fergal, be a good boy and do the driving. C'mon Fergal, we have to at least see it. To just stand outside for a while.'

That was the first time in a month and a week that Martin had used his name.

'What was the game like?' asked Fergal, trying to calm him down.

'Never mind that. It was wonderful. It was sublime. It was fantastic. Never mind. I'll tell you later. Never mind that now. C'mon. Now!'

The man seemed to be raving. But he wasn't. He wasn't even that drunk. Fergal decided – what the hell. They might as well. But if Martin started anything, Fergal was going to throttle him.

They found the prison easily. It glowed from a mile away in the late dusk, and the approaching roads were jammed with TV vans and parked cars and pedestrians all heading in the same direction. Fergal parked on the side of the road several hundred yards from the prison walls and walked towards the gathered crowd. It was like a quiet circus. On one side the eerie, almost blinding glow of the high prison lights picked up every shiny surface, reflecting them back until it seemed almost like daylight. Outside the walls, dozens of TV crews had rigged up their own lightshows; the place was a metallic jungle of cameras, cables, aerials, sound booms, and of the tinny, continuous babbling from the reporters, each more sincerely urgent than the next. The anti-death penalty protesters numbered a couple of dozen at most, separated from the other lot by a line of policemen. They stamped their feet and hugged themselves against the cold and tried in vain to keep candles lit against the slight, nippy breeze. There was no shouting from either side. It was all very placid. There were to be no more appeals. La Salle would fry either tomorrow or the day after. Fergal and Martin backed off a hundred yards or so, and sat down on a grassy patch, observing the scene. Martin produced a half-bottle and took a long, mean swig, never once taking his eyes off the prison walls.

'Martin, what are we doing here?'

'Same as everyone else,' replied Martin quietly. 'Nothing. We're just here to watch. We're just here for the sake of being here.'

Fergal studied the quiet, milling, glare-lit crowd outside the walls, all bundled up in their thick jackets, trailing wires around, pointing, patting their dogs, smoking. He felt strange. He scanned the building, wondering where La Salle was within, what he might be doing, thinking, eating. His dull, mean-featured face popped up periodically on the TV crews' monitors, an ugly cathode poltergeist, accompanied by the familiar drone of his crime recounted. Oh, he was a brutal bastard all right, a plundering, vicious life-grabber. The steam from thermos flasks rose through the cold air like a sugar-spun, thin textile. Fergal couldn't take his eyes off it. He felt as if he would not be able to haul himself off the grass, to turn away, to stop looking at what was in front of him. He felt calm and transfixed at the same time. Marooned in the strangest place, with a man whose inexplicable and drunken concern made no sense. He looked at Martin. He had finished the bottle, still staring beyond, then dropped his head into his hands. He sighed a hard, jittery sigh.

'It was such a beautiful game today,' he said softly. 'All that energy. All that skill. The Braves were so good. It was almost like being at Headingley. Lopez pitched like some kind of lovely, short-arsed android. The Yankees couldn't touch him. The last time I saw a thrower as saucy as that was Patterson in the '86 One-Day International in Jamaica.'

Martin kept his eyes closed tightly and his head bowed, as if he was praying for a miracle, or a refuge from disaster.

'Martin, are you okay?' Fergal was beginning to feel a little worried.

'And Jones, my God, that youngster's a bloody marvel. He hit three homers in twenty minutes. Big, soaring bastards, too. He still needs to work on his switch-hitting, but maybe he should forget that and concentrate on his fastball – he can hit the low 90s on a good day, y'know, and today could've been a good day. Today could've been such a good day. Now Perry, he could've shown us the shiftiest, most subterranean pitches you've ever seen; I know all about *his* plays. After *that* trade, the Braves couldn't find room for him on the forty-man roster. So they've gotta trade or release, trade or release – '

Martin's eyes were still screwed shut and he was balling his fists spasmodically.

'Martin, come on, let's go.' This babble was beginning to unnerve Fergal.

'– trade or release, or send to the Minors. Trade or release. Trade or release . . .'

'Martin. Stop it. Come on. Let's go back.'

Suddenly Martin opened his eyes and looked at the crowd. He could barely focus. He was breathing in soft ragged gulps.

'It was so beautiful.'

Fergal laid a tentative hand on his shoulder.

'Come on. Let's go.' He couldn't think of anything else to say.

Martin stood up, wobbling slightly.

'I'm just fed up with bastards dying everywhere,' he said, and weaved away towards the car.

Fergal stared after him. He suddenly felt very tired. The

candle-wavers had started to sing an anthemic song, but softly so, marred by a yelping dog and the damn lights. Fergal looked at the ruined skyline, at the devout cameras and the steamy, well-behaved people, and for a moment he felt that he might never be able to walk away. The sound of Martin falling over in the dark twenty yards away brought him up short. He turned his back and walked.

In the middle of the night a noise wakened him. It was a near-inaudible crying, the kind of shuddering, silent-type crying that tears out your heart and against which you must, for the sake of decency, turn your back.

'There should be no question of supporting a government that will not fling its wretched blighted theories to the winds when the people are starving – open the ports, establish depots for the sale of food to the poor at moderate prices, and employ the destitute.'
Father Bernard Duncan, Kilconduff, Co. Mayo, December 1846

'We did not think of the great open plains, the beautiful rolling hills and winding streams with tangled growth as "wild". Only to the white man was nature a wilderness . . . To us it was tame. When the hairy man from the east came and . . . the very animals of the forest began fleeing from his approach – then it was that for us the "Wild West" began.'

Chief Luther Standing Bear, Ogala Sioux

In the morning, Martin was listless and quiet.

'Where are we going now?' he asked, sitting on the edge of his bed like an obedient, debauched child. 'I've forgotten.'

'Jackson,' said Fergal, putting on his coat. It was 6 a.m. They had ground to cover.

'We've *been* to Jackson.'

'Jackson, Mississippi, you clown. It's almost five hundred miles west. We'd better get going.'

'And what's in Jackson, *Mississippi*, then?' He was still barely awake.

'My Choctaw turf. Your baseball game. Whatever. Let's go.'

He wasn't drinking but, nevertheless, Martin slept the sleep of
the dead in the back seat as they headed south-west on I-29
through La Grange and into Alabama. He woke up briefly,
struggled upright and stared gloomily out of the window at the
dainty, tidy towns of Opelika and Auburn, before falling asleep
again just as they reached Montgomery. Fergal pitched an
almost perfectly western route through Uniontown and Dem-
opolis, then after getting briefly lost looking for I-80 made
pretty good time across the Mississippi State Line, through
Meridian, Forest and Pelahatchie. He was dog-tired, and the
lowish, springtime, sidelong sun was baking the right side of his
face and making one eye water.

They got to Jackson around 2 o'clock in the afternoon. After
badgering a sleepy Martin out of the car, Fergal booked them
both into the Friendship Inn International. Budget, but at least
it was clean. Martin collapsed on to his bed and Fergal fresh-
ened up, as best he could. His back was beginning to ache
continuously from all this driving.

'Aren't you going to cover the game?' he said, emerging from
the bathroom.

Martin sat up slowly, rubbing his chin. He needed a shave.

'A *college* game? What's the point? Memphis State versus
South Alabama University? Jesus Christ, I doubt if either team
could pour piss out of a shoe if the instructions were written on
the heel. I've seen footage of this college crap. They're babies.
They're fat. And they're lazy. Lazy, lazy, *lazy*! Give 'em a
cocktail mixer and most of these fuckers would stand around
and wait for an earthquake. I don't want to see that game. I've
already seen the best game. I saw the best game I've ever seen in
my *life* and I'm too tired and too fucked up to describe it. I
couldn't type one word. Not a word. I'm not even going to try.
Because I'm fired already. He's got it in for me. I know it.'

He put his head in his hands.

'I'm dead meat. Where am I going to get another job? I'm
dead meat. I'm dead. She's dead. I'm dead.'

Fergal stared at him.

'What do you mean "She's dead"?' he said, as softly as he could.

Martin's head snapped back. He smiled warmly.

'Nothing. Nobody. Figure of speech,' he said and, without even taking off his coat, reclined gracefully back on his bed. Within a minute he was snoring.

Fergal sat by the window, looking out at a delirious sunset. He was 160 miles from New Orleans. Everything that happened to him seemed to be happening at dusk. That's early spring for you, he thought. At home everything would be growing, a fête of greasy particles and green things whose names he didn't even know. He looked at Martin's prone form, twisted up in his glossy overcoat. He was just hanging around for contrast's fun, a baseball tyro whose wet arrogance hid very little these days. If he doesn't watch himself, thought Fergal, this bossy dazzle-dragon is going to plug himself into the mains. He's going to skedaddle from one crisis to another until he's hobbled for good. And Fergal wasn't entirely certain what those crises were. Suddenly, and without knowing why, he was almost over-whelmed by a protective tenderness for this dodgy messer, this mournful jackass who genuinely needed looking after.

He stood up, walked over and kicked him on the shin.

'Come on, get up. If you're not going to the game, then we're going for a drive. I want to show you something.'

Martin snorted, grunted almost angelically, and pulled him-self off his cot.

'What? Show me what?' he demanded querulously, eyes still closed against the light.

'Nothing very much. In fact nothing at all, really. But let's go for a spin anyway. Better than sitting around here.'

They drove south for about thirty miles. There was still a good deal of light in the sky. Fergal wasn't looking for any-where. He was looking for nowhere; or more specifically, the middle of nowhere. Just past Crystal Springs he found it. An out-of-town, mall-free, open and empty field. Grass and nothing else. Some farmer's big fallow patch. He parked by the road, got out and looked around at the landscape. This had been Choctaw territory. Sainted Mississippi, virtually a third of it, had been their home since God knows when. Not because they owned it, but because they moved through it, up and down, following the food, north and south. Of course, he knew that two hundred years ago there had probably been forests and scabrous beasts, but just being in that place, looking at a modern, clean patch of grass, made it easier for him to close his eyes and grab some vicarious memory.

'Fergal, why am I standing in the middle of a field, in the middle of the night, in the middle of fucking Mississippi?' said Martin politely.

Fergal looked at him and laughed aloud, spreading his arms wide.

'I don't know. I just wanted to show you where the Choctaw used to live. Anyway, there's a little light left yet. It's not dark yet. Remember their ball game I told you about? Remember the $710?'

Martin leaned against the car, extracted his bottle, took a civilised nip, folded his arms and said, 'Yes. I remember. Carry on. Show me.'

Fergal should have felt self-conscious but he didn't. He wanted to teach Martin *something* about the Choctaw. He marched into the middle of the field and whirled around, arms outstretched. The light was fading fast.

'Well, for a start there would be two narrow goals and one ball. And anywhere between six hundred and a thousand players.'

Martin almost choked on his whisky.

'Yeah! And the whole tribe would gather and there would be five or six thousand people watching.'

Fergal's voice grew louder in the gloom.

'And the players were all naked, except for a breech-cloth with a beaded belt, and mane of dyed horsehair on their heads!'

'And then what happened?' called Martin across the field, as he leaned in and switched on the car's headlights. Fergal found himself bathed in light, centre-stage, and he felt like shouting and hollering.

'These games started at sunrise and ended at sundown, Martin! A thousand guys, all going *mad*!' He gesticulated wildly, trying to describe the beribboned, thronged sticks every player carried, the throw-up, the instant scrambles, the insane dust and the kicking, the jokes and the water-breaks, the tripping and throwing and howling, and the women gambling on the sidelines, gambling with pots and kettles, dogs and knives, blankets and guns.

'Can you imagine the noise, the *commotion*?' shouted Fergal. 'A thousand players, all going after one ball on a pitch the size of two acres? Mad! And when their ball-sticks were all broken, they used their hands, their feet, their heads, *anything* to keep the game going until new ones were brought on. And this went on for twelve hours without a break! Can you imagine it, Martin? Can you imagine it?'

He was getting hoarse and the headlights blinded him, but he didn't care. He whirled and whooped and ranted on about the Choctaw, imagining hysterically, until it felt as real as remembering.

'Sometimes, when the ball got to the ground, a hundred guys would pounce and for fifteen minutes there would be nothing but a man-high cloud of dust, with no one even able to *see* the damn ball! Sometimes it would be two hundred yards away, and these guys would still be whacking and scuffling and barking and eating dust like madmen! God, it must have been something to see ... And when the game was over, ten thousand people had a party, danced the Eagle Dance in their finery and drank for two days. Christ, it must have been something to see. A game of a thousand players ...'

His voice trailed off. He put his hands on top of his head and walked around in small circles, trying to imagine, in this quiet carlamp-lit field, a scene of such nourishing chaos. Such fun. He looked over at Martin's silhouette, black against the headlights. And he still wasn't embarrassed.

'Better than baseball any day, eh?' he called. His voice now seemed unbearably loud in the near-dark.

'Better than cricket, too.' Martin's voice was barely audible. The bombast seemed to have leaked out of his throat, and in Fergal's beam-wounded sights Martin's outline suddenly looked hunched and smallish.

'And on 27 September 1830, it all ended,' Martin whispered, and his words zoomed the distance between them. Fergal stared at his outline.

'The Treaty of Dancing Rabbit Creek. The Choctaw gave up their last acre in Mississippi, and twenty thousand of them moved west, in steamboats and wagons. The government paid for it. Sixteenth Article. The government pays. I've been reading some of your books.'

Fergal just stared at him. He couldn't even see his face, but when he looked up at the starry sky because he didn't know what else to do, Martin's voice carried on floating across to where Fergal stood and, against the washing cascade of stars, it was a shy and playpen sound, a sound of hardness abandoned and efforts made. His voice was that of a holy academic.

'But the Choctaw believed that spirits of the dead lived in a future state, that they had a great distance to travel after death, across a dreadful, high river. And that while they crossed, those spirits who had gone before separated the good from the bad by throwing rocks at them as they crossed over a slippery pine-log bridge. The bad people succumbed and drowned. But the good people walked on safely, to the good hunting grounds, where there is one continual day, where the trees are always green, where there are fine breezes and the sky has no clouds, where food is plentiful for ever, and where there is no pain or trouble and people never grow old but live, young, for ever, where . . .'

Martin's voice cracked in the dark. His silhouette shrank from the shoulders down and, as Fergal ran towards him, he sank to his knees and began to weep. Fergal grabbed him and looked directly into his eyes.

'What was her name?'

'Hannah. Her name is Hannah,' Martin croaked, head bent.

'You said she was dead. You said "She's dead". I heard you.'

'She's not dead yet. She will be. Three or four months. Tops. Cancer. Breast cancer. I have to go and see her. I have to. But I can't. I'm afraid. I haven't spoken to her in four years, for God's sake.' Martin covered his face and sobbed silently, his whole frame shuddering.

'All I ever did was hurt her,' he whispered wetly. 'When I found out, all I wanted to do was run. That's why I didn't tell them to stuff this bloody assignment.'

Fergal sat down heavily beside him in the dirt and leaned against a tyre, eyes closed. He patted Martin on the shoulder, and gently on the back of his clenched hand until he'd stopped crying and sniffing, and his breathing became more stable.

'Ah, Christ,' sighed Martin.

'Martin. Why did you leave? It wasn't just the booze, was it?'

Fergal was terrified of asking, but he had to.

'No, it wasn't just the booze. The booze was the least of it,' Martin said quietly. 'Let's just say I turned out not to be the man she married.'

There was a sardonic condescension in his voice that was not entirely unkind. And with that, he took Fergal's hand and looked into his eyes with the look of a man who was no longer scared of being crucified one more time, a man who had travelled the scant distance between fear and fearful fun, a man who had once tried to be brave and gotten it half-right.

He patted Fergal's frozen hand and said, 'Hell's teeth, pet, precisely how thick *are* you?'

Fergal stared at him. He didn't exactly recoil. He remembered how Martin's flinching disdain had exquisitely clobbered that poor cow in Indianapolis, and he felt like the stupidest man on the planet. Oh Christ, he thought, withdrawing his hand and covering his eyes – I've been *stripping* in front of this guy for a week . . . And for some reason the thought made him smile, and then laugh to himself. He was only embarrassed, and if he was honest about it, he wasn't really that surprised. He was just embarrassed and sorry.

'Don't panic,' said Martin almost brightly. 'And stop flattering yourself, for God's sake – you're not my type. Besides, haven't you heard? Celibacy is the new rock'n'roll . . . and I should know, believe me.'

Fergal stared at the ground and felt insulted. Almost. He was too tired to care, really. Slightly sheepish and couldn't-care-less. He felt just like that. And more.

'Nothing more tiresome than a cowardly old queen, eh kid?'

'You should go and see her,' said Fergal quietly. 'You really should. Listen, I know it's none of my business, but it would be . . . the gentlemanly thing to do.'

'I know. Oh God, I know. But that's me – every other inch a gentleman. Oh Christ, I hate hospitals . . .'

They sat on the grass at the field's edge for a while. The wind picked up a little and the cold began to set in. But neither of them felt like moving just yet. Martin blew his nose loudly, took a comforting swig and sighed a sigh that lasted for a frosty age. Fergal took the bottle and finished it in two swallows. The damp of the grass was beginning to soak the arse of his trousers. The night darkness was complete now and the blackish sky a hand-tinted thing so huge it could have been a terror. A few cars passed by on the main road, a hundred yards away, their noise and light scared into needle-thin redundancy by the darkness. Fergal thought of Siofradh and felt his gorge rise. But he knew for a fact that it was the whisky. He knew for a fact. Whatever twists of distress were going on in his gut were no longer for himself but for this poor, bereft bastard beside him, whose loss had happened once, and would happen soon again.

He looked out over the black field, whereof only a sliver existed in the narrow, jealous headlight. It was so quiet. Martin sat beside him, still with his head in his hands. So anxious. So quiet. Whatever hybrid sympathy Fergal felt was for him.

Fergal needed someone to take care of. He was filled with a need to rummage through the debris and find a one that he could look after, a one whom he could drag, priceless, from the mire and look after. He'd had his chance once. And he blew it. He had worn his common sense like a girdle of chastity and he had lost her because of it. The thought of his own foolishness made him clench his fists and fling away the bottle, and feel dressed in violence, but then Martin, head still down, coughed and sniffled like a sick baby, so Fergal again patted his head in the dark and made a soothing sound and thought, again, about the Choctaw and their $710. What a thing that was. What a thing that was. Wherever loss and the pain of banishment existed, he could still hang on to that. He leaned his head back against the car's cold metal and comforted himself with the ringing focus of that particular piece of generosity. The rest of us could fashionably slum, but there was no subtracting from that $710.

It was getting really cold now and he could feel Martin begin to shiver. Troublesome, muddy swine that he was, a dim and pained poor sod. Well, Siofradh was gone and Fergal didn't know where to put himself any more, so he stood up and took off his coat, and wrapped it around Martin's shoulders. He didn't get as much as thank-you, but that was okay. He looked around this now ridiculous patch of blacked-out green and wondered what the farmer grew in this place. Not spuds, anyway, that's for sure. Behind him Martin very slowly keeled over and curled up on the ground, drawing Fergal's coat around him with a polished smoothness that spoke of many, many nights on other people's sofas. Fergal looked up again at the sky. He couldn't help it. It was a fine and mesmerising sky. The kind of sky he could only see at home, with no light pollution, no streetlights to get in his way, no delta of spots or the becurtained, sneaky blue of TV sets. There was nothing out here, just one dilapidated set of headlights, his famished heart and a gently purring heap who called himself a sportswriter. Fergal sat down again and

wished he had another bottle, even though he felt pretty
drunk already. He thought of hunger, although he was not
himself hungry. He was very cold. He was beginning to freeze.
But the thought of hunger hit him in his gut like some rebel,
historical strand of DNA kicking in, and for a nanosecond he
felt starving and perished in the night, with pictures of gleaming and bony stretched skin thieving and shifting around his
head, and for a longer moment he felt the archivist's malice
creep upon him.

Fergal leaned across and, just the once, stroked Martin's
head. He was dead to the world and snoring still. Whatever
dented skill in denying the past Fergal had left dribbled away
from him just then; he kept patting Martin's sleeping head and,
looking upwards at the sheen and stranded sky, he was stunned
by a tiny vision of scrawny, needful hordes and a killer killed,
and a nice girl's hatred, and if he hadn't been flattering himself
on being tougher than that, he would've laid his head down
next to Martin's and wept. He was freezing and he wanted to go
home. He was hungry and he wanted to go home, and in this
difficult place he could find no compensation. No compensation
at all. He was tired and sick of being touched by memory and by
Martin's ailing warmth. He wanted some cool distance and he
knew that, if only he were selfish enough, he might, someday,
get it before he died. Even if she didn't take him back, and he
knew she wouldn't, he still might get that thing before he died.
So he hauled himself up, again in the frosty air, and struggled
with a limp and annoying Martin. And he bundled him exhausted into the car because he wanted to feel responsible, and to feel
good, and to feel like a man who had once known how to be
kind without thinking about it first.

*'We are told that we have a large number of our own poor and
destitute to take care of, that the charity we dispense should be
bestowed in this quarter, that the peculiar position of ourselves and
our co-religionists demands it at our hands, that justice is a higher
virtue than generosity, that self-preservation is a law and principle of*

our nature . . . It is true that there is but one connecting link between us and the sufferers . . . That link is humanity.'

Rabbi Jacques Judah Lyons, Famine Relief fund-raiser,
New York, February 1847

'Brother, my voice is become weak – you can scarcely hear me. It is not the shout of a warrior but the wail of an infant. I have lost it in mourning over the desolation and injuries of my people . . . Our warriors are nearly all gone to the West, but here are our dead. Will you compel us to go too, and give their bones to the wolves? Our people's tears fell like drops of rain, their lamentations were borne away by the passing winds. The palefaces heeded them not and our land was taken from us. Brother! You speak the words of a mighty nation. I am a shadow . . . my people are scattered and gone. When I shout, I hear my voice in the depths of the forest, but no answering voice comes back to me – all is silent around me. My words therefore must be few. I can now say no more.'

Colonel Cobb, Choctaw Chief, 1831

It was their last day. Their flight home from New Orleans airport was due to take off at 9.15 p.m. Fergal and Martin were sitting in a bar on Decatur Street, on the river front. They'd delivered the Pontiac to Hertz as soon as they'd arrived in the early afternoon and Martin, between beers, was sorting out his expenses. The table was covered with invoices, receipts and a hundred other scraps of paper rescued from various trouser pockets. When he'd totted it all up, after much head-scratching and mumbling, he winced.

'Jesus,' he said, 'if they believe this figure, I'll be getting away with it by the skin of my rosy, red, royal, English arse. Luckily, they never check. Well, hardly ever. To tell you the truth, I'm past caring. I don't care what they do to me.'

He looked pretty rough. But to Fergal he seemed calmer, as if he'd made a decision. Fergal decided not to bring up the subject; it would only upset him. And since he had never mentioned Siofradh, he wasn't going to bring up that subject either. He didn't really feel like talking much, so the pair of them just sleepily sat and looked out over the Mississippi. It was such a beautiful day, warm and comforting. Even the steamboat chugging along looked, not like something for the tourists, but like a real working craft, a boat with a heavy purpose and crucial cargo. The bar's background nattering was a nice watery sound, a quiet buzzsaw, and the waitress was under instructions just to keep the beers coming. Fergal reached into his pocket and took out an A4 page, ragged and crumpled. He'd been carrying it around for months.

'Martin. *Sa-ga-nosh.*'

Martin opened his eyes.

'I want to show you something. I made it myself. I'm thinking of getting it printed up and framed.' Now he felt embarrassed. Martin held out his hand, puzzled, and studied it. It was a calendar. A Lakota Moon Calendar, in which every fourteen days of all our months Fergal had translated into an Indian Moon. Martin stared at it.

'Where are we now?' he whispered.

'7 April.'

'7 April – "Big Leaf Moon".' He read out others – 'Silk Corn Moon, Flying Ants Moon, Moon of the Deer Pawing the Earth, Geese Going Moon, Moon of Popping Trees, Moon of the Snow-blind, Moon when Wolves Run Together, Moon of Making Fat . . .' He looked up.

'How long did this take you?'

'Oh – months of research!' laughed Fergal. It was closer to two years. 'I dunno – I kept reading all this stuff and it just struck me as a nice idea. Something to do.'

Martin trailed his finger along those Moons which represented June, and July, and August, and was struck by the optimism and beauty of how they sounded. July or August. Tops. No chance for her beyond that. Not seriously. Strawberry Moon, Ripe Cherries Moon, Moon of the Red Blooming Lilies, Hot Weather Begins Moon. He was miserable but he smiled to himself anyway, and Fergal studiously looked out the window.

To Martin this made it seem a tiny bit less painful somehow, as if by stepping outside our own notions of time, we could make the history to come bounce off us in a different way.

'What does *Sa-ga-nosh* mean, by the way?'

'"Englishman". Sounds like "*Sassenach*", doesn't it . . . ?'

'Oh – I thought it might have meant "faggot".' He smiled before Fergal could protest.

Behind the bar someone turned on the TV.

'Fergal?' said Martin.

Fergal turned to look at him. Martin had tears in his eyes, but looked less of a mess now. Stronger, more nailed down somehow.

'I just want to thank you for letting me tag along. It's been . . . interesting. And I'm sorry for being a pain in the arse sometimes.'

He really meant it.

Fergal smiled warmly. You silly sod, he thought.

'Hey – don't worry about it. Thanks for the car hire. And listen – when we get home, I'll come with you.'

Martin flinched slightly.

'I'll come with you. You won't have to go to the hospital by yourself. It'll be okay. It really will. I'll come with you. That kind of thing doesn't bother me at all.'

Martin looked at him seriously.

'Thank you. I'd like that.' He reached out his hand. Fergal took it and as they grasped each other's palms, the TV reporter's astringent voice pierced the cool and placid air.

'James La Salle, convicted killer, died today at fourteen minutes past two, in the electric chair at Georgia's Diagnostic and Classification Center. Officials at the Center report that it was a clean and standard execution. About twenty anti-death penalty advocates remained outside the prison right up to the end. At this stage, we do not yet know if La Salle had any last words, but it is rumored that –'

Behind the bar someone turned off the TV. A disinterested murmur moved around the lounge.

Fergal and Martin gripped each other's hands still, and

stared into each other's eyes. Martin was trembling. Fergal tried to transmit calmness through his pores. Martin looked quietly transfixed for a moment, and Fergal's knuckles were beginning to hurt. After a long moment, Martin took a deep breath, very slowly let go of Fergal's hand and sat back in his chair, staring at the table. Then he looked up and smiled the saddest smile Fergal ever saw.

'It's okay. Really.'

And then he poured himself another beer, got out his paper and began to read. It wasn't okay. But it might be. Good enough to be going on with.

Fergal gazed out again at the river. He felt calm. Misplaced tenderness. That was okay. Nourishment for the guilty. A slap on the wrist for the despairing. A little plundering mirth for the hungry. He glanced at the phone and glanced away again. Had La Salle asked for forgiveness in his last moments?

The sun began to go down west of the Mississippi and a piece of sweet and anxious blues leaked from the jukebox, like some eighth harmony of the rainbow. He lazily watched the bar staff moving around and the waitresses, the essence of caution, with their trays balanced, and balancing themselves over tables like shy apprentices. He watched Martin put down his paper and pick up a pen and take a piece of blank paper from his inside pocket and begin to write in careful longhand. He was writing his last piece of copy. He didn't even know if he had a job any more, but he was going to get the Braves down on paper if it killed him. Without asking, Fergal knew what he was writing, and he knew that it would be good. He was writing and oblivious, brow furrowed, tongue protruding, and it would be a wonderful story of guts and skill and the broken hearts of some players who have to lose because they are scared of winning. Fergal settled back in his chair. He had never felt so sleepily comfortable in his life. He looked again at the phone. He would go with him, and perhaps look after him a little, and he would try to be an impeccable friend. There was always hope. There must be. Because if there wasn't, then he and others would lie down and simply die. So there was always hope. It was common sense. He hoped that La Salle had asked for forgiveness. That would be a good and clean thing, if he had. A clean moment for all our charlatans' hearts. Charity from a wounded and disappearing wife, from a stunning and reasonable girl, forgiveness from a small life barely started. It was not a possibility. It was a necessity.

The sun went down and the bar filled up and Fergal spent the late, lazy afternoon simply watching. Watching, and glancing now and again at the phone, and listening to the jukebox and the muffled crinkle of pen on paper.

'What is life? It is the flash of a firefly in the night. It is the breath of a buffalo in the winter time. It is the little shadow which runs across the grass and loses itself in the sunset.'

Crowfoot, Spokesman for the Blackfoot Confederacy,
April 1890

BIOGRAPHICAL NOTES

GERARD BEIRNE was born in Tipperary in 1962. He was educated at Trinity College, Dublin and Eastern Washington University, where he completed a Master of Fine Arts degree in Creative Writing. He won the 1996 *Sunday Tribune*/Hennessy New Writer Award.

EMMA DONOGHUE was born in Dublin in 1969 and moved to Cambridge to do her PhD. She has published two novels, *Stir-Fry* and *Hood*, and a book of fairytales, *Kissing the Witch*. She has also written plays for stage, radio and TV, and last year she edited *What Sappho Would Have Said: Four Centuries of Love Poems Between Women*.

NED LENIHAN was born in London but spent much of his childhood in the USA. He has had a wide variety of jobs, and in the 1980s he played bass and sang in a band. He lives in Co. Clare.

MARIE MacSWEENEY was born in Dublin in 1940. She studied Peace Studies in the Irish School of Ecumenics in the 1980s and is now a student of Local History at Maynooth University. Her stories and poetry have been widely published in Ireland and she has had two plays produced on RTE Radio.

BLÁNAID McKINNEY was born in Enniskillen, Co. Fermanagh in 1961. A Political Science graduate of Queen's University, Belfast, she has been an Executive Officer in the Department of Trade and Industry in London, and Economic Development Officer for the Grampian Region of Scotland. She is presently responsible for the administration of various EU initiatives for the Aberdeenshire Council. 'The Outfielder, the Indian-Giver' is her first story to be published.

MICHAEL MEE was born in Ontario, Canada, in 1967 of Irish parents and has lived in Ireland since 1973. A lecturer in law at the University of Limerick, he has been a runner-up in the George A. Birmingham Short Story Competition and the Kilkenny Prize, and had a story in the Irish/Irish-American issue of the University of Illinois journal, *The Crab Orchard Review*. He plans to write comedy scripts for film/television and has performed at the Galway Arts Festival as a stand-up comedian.

ÉILÍS NÍ DHUIBHNE was born in Dublin in 1954. Her first story appeared in *The Irish Press* 'New Irish Writing' page in 1974 when she was a student at UCD. She graduated in 1976 with an M.Phil degree in Medieval English/Folklore. Since then she has become one of Ireland's leading writers with novels, short story collections, children's books, plays and TV scripts for RTE and Telefís na Gaeilge. Her latest story collection is *The Ice Maiden*. She has for many years worked as a curator in the National Library of Ireland.

GILLMAN NOONAN was born in Kanturk, Co. Cork in 1937. He worked in various parts of Germany and Switzerland before his first of many stories appeared in *The Irish Press* 'New Irish Writing' page in 1973. He won the Writers' Week Short Story Award in 1975 and the Maurice Walsh Memorial Competition in 1996 and has had two collections published by Poolbeg. He now lives in Scotland.

KATHERINE O'DONNELL was born on Haulbowline Island, Co. Cork in 1966. She worked in RTE before attending Boston College, where she won the Chancellor's Prize for Prose and graduated with a Master's degree in Literature. She then tutored for four years in UCC while preparing her PhD thesis on Edmund Burke. 'Emotionally Involved' is her first publication.

FRANK O'DONOVAN was born in Cork in 1959 and educated at UCC. He spent a year on scholarship in Rome, studying Italian language and literature. A prizewinner in the 1996 Maurice Walsh Memorial Competition and a runner-up last year in the Fish Short Story Prize, his work has appeared in the *Cork Review* and *Poetry Ireland*. He works as a journalist with the *Southern Star* newspaper.

KAITE O'REILLY was born in Dublin in 1963, but has been so long out of the city that she now considers herself Birmingham-Irish. She is primarily a playwright. Her first play, *Banshees*, won the 1988 Royal Court Young Writer's Festival and in the same year her *Cathleen Ni Houlihan is Dead* was runner-up in the Albany Empire's Women Playwrights Festival. Since then she has had six plays produced in England, Wales and Holland, and others on BBC Radio.

SEÁN RUANE was born in England in 1966. He is a graduate of Trinity College, Dublin, and teaches English at St Peter's College, Dunboyne, Co. Meath. 'Coronach' is his first story to be published.

MARY RUSSELL is an Irish writer with a special interest in travel. Her journeys have taken her to the Sahara, the former Soviet Union, Africa and the Eastern Caribbean. Her books include *Please Don't Call It Soviet Georgia*, *The Blessings of a Good Thick Skirt* and, as editor, *Survival South Atlantic*. She has an MA in Peace Studies from the University of Bradford. A devotee of the short story, she has had one published in *The London Magazine*.

DESMOND TRAYNOR was born in Dublin in 1961. A graduate of UCD, he has worked in various guises in the USA, England, Italy, Holland and Spain. He now lives in Dublin and writes reviews and criticism for many Irish publications. He first appeared in print with a poem in *The Irish Press* 'New Irish Writing' page in 1978, and more recently had a story in *Books Ireland.*

WILLIAM WALL was born in Whitegate, Co. Cork in 1955. A graduate of UCC in English and Philosophy, he teaches English. His stories have been published in many Irish periodicals, and he has won the Patrick Kavanagh Poetry Award and the American-Ireland Fund/Writers' Week Poetry Collection Prize. He has also published novels for young people.

MÁIRÍDE WOODS was born in Dublin. A part-time lecturer and researcher, her stories have been widely anthologised and broadcast. Twice a winner of a Hennessy Award, she has also won RTE's Francis MacManus Short Story Award and its P.J. O'Connor Radio Play Award. Her story, 'The Time of Poplars', was a prizewinner in the 1996 Maurice Walsh Memorial Competition.

Short stories, which must not have been previously published, are invited for consideration for future volumes of *Phoenix: Irish Short Stories*. Unsuitable MSS will not be returned unless a stamped, addressed envelope is enclosed. Writers outside the Republic of Ireland are reminded that, in the absence of Irish stamps, return postage must be covered by International Reply Coupons: two coupons for packages up to 100g, three for packages 101g to 250g. All communications regarding MSS which require a reply must also be accompanied by a self-addressed envelope and return postage. MSS and letters should be addressed to David Marcus, PO Box 4937, Rathmines, Dublin 6.